Advance praise for 7

"Smart writing, clever plotting, and an origina ...st. Charming."

—Graeme Simsion, bestselling author of *The Rosie Project*

"I enjoyed every page of this gorgeous debut. Ally Zetterberg writes with warmth, wit and insight and I was immediately swept up in the lives of her endearing characters. A fantastic read."

—Hazel Prior, author of *Away with the Penguins*

"A truly fantastic rom-com that had me laughing out loud. You'll want to immediately clear your calendar to read this clever and funny book! Five stars!"

—James Bailey, author of *The Flip Side*

"A rich and rewarding take on romance, relationships, family, grief and finding your place in the world. This is a funny, moving, satisfying read with characters that captivated me."

—Jennie Godfrey, author of *The List of Suspicious Things*

"A hopeful, honest debut novel... *The Happiness Blueprint* is the best kind of romcom, one that embraces not only the search for connection, but also neurodiversity, loneliness, grief and the complexities of life... A great read—I couldn't recommend it enough!"

—Sarah Jost, author of *Five First Chances*

"I loved this warm, funny but unconventional love story about two people searching for their place in a world full of seemingly insurmountable challenges—and finding [that their] place might just be with each other."

—Claire Frost, author of *Married at First Swipe*

"A whip-smart, compassionate and funny book that sweeps you away."

—Jo Leevers, author of *Tell Me How This Ends*

"*The Happiness Blueprint* is a wonderful book, full of love and hope, empathy and insight. Ally has crafted two of the most distinctive voices I have ever read. It is hard to believe this is a debut!"

—Laura Carter, author of *The Kitchen*

"A witty, unique and heartwarming tale of two lost souls and their bumpy journey to self-knowledge. *The Happiness Blueprint* leaves you full of joy—I loved it."

—Emily Howes, author of *The Painter's Daughter*

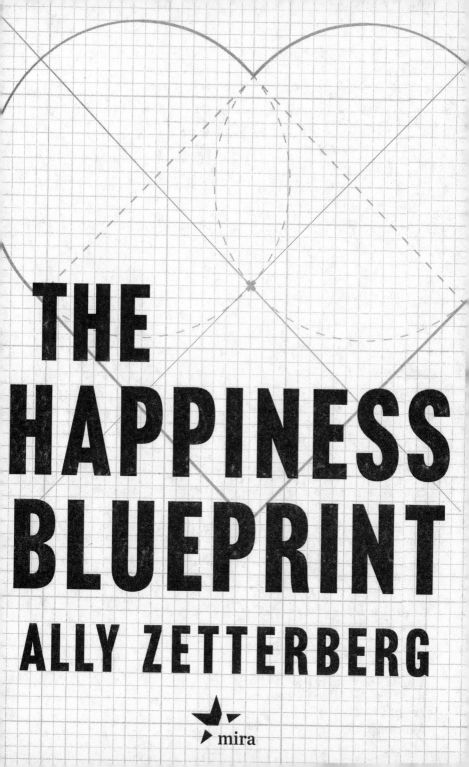

THE HAPPINESS BLUEPRINT

ALLY ZETTERBERG

mira

mira™

ISBN-13: 978-0-7783-6971-4

The Happiness Blueprint

Copyright © 2024 by Ally Zetterberg Literary Ltd

Mira
22 Adelaide St. West, 41st Floor
Toronto, Ontario M5H 4E3, Canada
BookClubbish.com

Printed in U.S.A.

For my grandmothers:

Bodil, the librarian,
and
Gunvor, the reader.

PART ONE

The average minimum temperature in Malmö, Sweden, in February is 28.4°F. The amount of rain and snow in February is normal with an average of 1.4 in. It rains, on average, a total of thirteen days. Most people don't tend to visit Malmö during this period since it's known as a chilly month. You will hardly see any sun, with sixty-six hours of sunshine total during the month.

KLARA

How do I run a construction company?

Google Search   I'm Feeling Lucky

Sibling pairs are a bit like shoes from a lost and found. You put your hand in and can only hope to get two that match, knowing that two shoes are still better than one—at least you don't have to walk around with one foot bare. In my parents' case they won themselves a dust-covered Converse, perfectly functional and sturdy, and matched it with a glossy kitten heel that likes to look down at the flat sneaker.

I, the sneaker, speak.

"I have commitments, too!" I say, trying my best to sound as important as my sister, pretty sure I'm failing. I've said this exact sentence several times in the past twenty minutes, trying hard to be the winner of the Zoom tug-of-war, the holder of prime position and the central big square overshadowing the small ones. The current leader board has my sister, Saga, at the top followed by our mum as a close second.

"I have plans," I say again, for a brief moment flitting on to the screen. Well, it *is* true. At least if Tuesday drinks and defrosting the freezer count. I can feel my blood pressure—actually, it's more likely my blood sugar—rising. *Stay focused, Klara.*

"It's a family emergency," Mum chips in yet again. Thanks for stating the obvious. As if we didn't know that already.

I decide to revert to the technique when you go back to the beginning of the conversation, repeating it all, hoping you have magically missed the solution and that it will make itself known—loud and clear—the second time around.

"How long would his treatment be, again?" I ask, even though I know full well the details, having joined the oncology team at Dad's appointment via FaceTime earlier that day. Three months. Dad is lucky. Just one surgery and then a course of innovative localized radiation to beat what is considered stage 1 of prostate cancer. They caught it early and he will most likely be okay. I'm not too worried about Dad. Cancer is a poignant, scary word, but *1* is a harmless number, thin and unassuming. At the end of the call, we were asked if we had any questions, and I would have had plenty, but now I had a *1* and didn't need any other explanation. I haven't even googled it.

Saga doesn't bother to repeat why she can't do the job, which surprises me. She usually misses no chance to talk about her important academic career at a highly esteemed international university and just generally, you know, her *full and perfect* life. *Got to have that work-life balance, Klara!*

Right now, I'd settle for just having a life. Never mind a balanced one.

"I'm really sorry I can't be there to support Dad myself. There's just so much going on." My sister's face is filling the Zoom square to the point where it has no background. Now if that's not a telling picture of Saga, Queen of Filling Up Every Room She Enters. *Me, me, me.*

"It's only a few months. Think of it as a long holiday—you will even get paid! Really, it's an opportunity." I ponder this. Sweden is in no way my preferred holiday location. But a salary from my dad's company would be an increase compared to what I currently earn—nothing.

"Say I agree, I'm not saying I do, but *if*, how would I even do it? You need qualifications and skills to do that type of job," I say.

At first, we had been so relieved to learn Dad's good prognosis that we had forgotten everything else. Then Saga had pointed out the company. This tiny little inconvenience in rural Sweden with three employees that somehow needed to stay afloat while Dad was focusing on his health.

"Darling, you already work in property!" Mum says, before turning to loudly sip a lurid green smoothie. I can't help but think that if this had happened five years ago, before The Divorce, we wouldn't be having this discussion as she would still be there. Not in a Marbella condo with a widower named Inge whom she'd met at her church choir. I push the thought away. It's not Mum's fault. If Dad doesn't resent her, then neither should I.

"I work for a website that sells them. I don't demolish, construct, or tile their bathrooms!" I mean, what does Dad even *do*? Definitely not something I have expertise in. Which is technical-support chatting ("No, you can't place the properties in your online basket, Susan. You must call the listed agent for a viewing."). Mostly I do nothing that remotely touches on property. Think of me as a helpful bot.

"Please, Klara. Someone has to do it. We need your answer soon," Saga says. Oh no, not that line. Translation: you've got to do it, you are the younger one, and I may have some shared responsibility, but in the end it's on you, little sister. Like when we were kids and messed up the living room building a fort or a shop and the time came for tidying up. *Someone has to do it,*

Klara. If my sister ever happened to commit murder, I bet you it would be my job to dispose of the body, due solely to my genetic link to her and our birth order.

"Let me see if I can make some arrangements," I mutter.

"I didn't want to say this, but... I thought you were on *a break* from work right now?" I can hear my sister's smug smile even though her blurry screen prevents me from actually seeing it. She is well aware that people have breaks from relationships—not jobs. If it's the latter, then it's simply called unemployment. Or disciplinary suspension. *Let's not get into that, shall we.*

"Wouldn't it be nice to connect with old friends?" Mum attempts.

What friends? I think. The ones I had a decade ago have inevitably moved on and away. If I were an old lady, we would now have the sort of relationship that is marked only by the exchange of Christmas cards. Except I'm not, so there aren't even the holiday greetings. If I were braver and funnier, even a faint shadow of my sister, I would have seen this coming and averted it by recruiting new friends. But this would have required actually socializing, going places with a frequency I'm not adapted to (I need rest days from socializing the way others do from the gym) and the ability to keep a conversation going without the help of alcohol.

I currently have a grand total of one friend: Alice, who is my housemate and who says hilarious things like "Yay, I got booked for a hand job!" (She has a side gig as a hand-and-foot model.) Mum and Saga both know this.

"Listen, I know it's not what you want, although I'm not entirely sure what you actually *do* want. But quite frankly, it's time that you pulled your weight."

I look down at my waist before I realize that she is not talking about my BMI.

Then my nephew, Harry—Saga's primary excuse for dodging the Sweden bullet—starts howling like a wolf in the background, hitting a key only a toddler can master. *The noise!* Quickly, I make up my mind. "Okay, then." The Harry siren goes off again.

"Right, that's my cue to leave the call!" my sister shouts in a key only a mum can master. I swear parents teach their children to become a distraction at exactly the right time. It's not fair that they all have an excuse to leave a boring Zoom call while the rest of us have to stay put and listen to the end.

"Fine. But you help out with what you can from over *there*. That's the deal." I insist on calling my sister's new homeland by anything but its proper name. I'm well aware that it is child-ish behavior coming from an adult, however much she misses her sibling.

"Of course. Bye, then. Lifesaver!" Saga leaves the call.

The doctors will be saving Dad's life, not me, I want to argue. But then I think of the convention to liken unpleasantness with death and consider the fact that it is perhaps *Saga* I have saved from *Sweden*.

"Mum?" No reply. She must have hit a button or lost con-nection. Her screen is empty. I'm left staring at just myself in the Zoom square, a sad sight of disheveled dark locks and eyebrows in a discontented frown. Finally occupying the prime position.

I toy with the idea of calling them both back up and demand-ing their attention. *You and I need a word*, I would say with au-thority. *Well, literally just one word. No.* But I do just that: *think it*, and nothing more.

"*Scheibe*," I say to screen me. One of the few words I've picked up from my sister and kept handy in my vocabulary. Unfortunately, I feel like I've had to use it almost daily during my twenty-six years in this world.

I guess I'm heading home to run my dad's company. Great.

ALEX

Move between neighborhoods like I'm haunting them. Left too early for my appointment, and when I realized, I just kept walking. Possibly in circles, as I seem to be seeing a lot of very similar hip coffee shops. Notice after a while that I'm avoiding the bustling Möllevångstorget and its bronze monument named *The Glory of Work*. Lately, I've taken its presence as a personal insult.

It's fucking freezing, and I curl my fingers into my hand, shielding them within my fist. The coat sleeves just about reach down and stop any icy wind from getting to them. Don't mind being cold: reminds me I'm still capable of feeling things.

It's 4:00 p.m. when I finally walk into the Malmö Psychotherapy Center. Dr. Hadid is wearing a bright blue headscarf with a flower pattern when I enter her room. It does brighten my mood ever so slightly; I much prefer medical professionals who are relaxed and colorful as opposed to the GP uniform of shirt, smart trousers and loafers in shades of beige. Find myself counting the small delicate flowers on her head. Math is a good distraction and one of the things I still enjoy. Aware it may not be the coolest hobby for a twenty-nine-year-old. I get to sixteen before she interrupts me.

"How have you been doing, Alex?" she asks.

"Okay, I guess."

"Did you do anything this weekend? Do you want to tell me a bit about your past week?"

Not really, but it's a rhetorical question. They all are, and the whole purpose of me being here is to answer them, so obviously I speak. There seem to be a lot of rhetorical questions to answer when your brother dies.

"I went to my uncle's funeral. What else? Had pizza five times. Capricciosa with added jalapeños. Aren't jalapeños just the best spice ever? A little bit naughty, like telling-a-dirty-joke naughty, but not so full-on that you have to cover your ears. They challenge you, but don't tip you over the edge. I like that in them."

The corners of Dr. Hadid's mouth move upward.

"The bin collection on our street seems to have moved to 5:00 a.m. I'm thinking about giving the company a call to complain."

"Have you tried the earplugs we talked about?"

"I find that then my thoughts get louder, if that makes sense? I prefer to listen to the garbage truck than to my mind." There is a flower on the windowsill; I wonder who waters it on weekends and am just about to ask when Dr. Hadid addresses me.

"I think it's time to start making some plans. It's been six months since Calle died and four since I started seeing you. You're ready. It would give you structure and take the focus off the unhelpful thoughts."

Notice that she's using my brother's nickname. Maybe she thinks she can get through to me, appear more familiar, if she doesn't call him Carl.

"Plans? Like coffee with a friend?" That may be hard since my friends have taken a back seat recently. Somehow, me in sweatpants better suited for the laundry basket and holding a pizza box and a bag of chips isn't their ideal Friday night. Or any other night of the week, for that matter. We talk around that for a while, and a possible route out of the idle existence of Netflix and Nil (the latter referring to my current account balance).

"Let's start by entering to-dos into your calendar. I've seen success with this approach before. Do you have an iPhone?"

I shrug and nod simultaneously.

"Great. So you set yourself a challenge of entering three tasks per day. They can be simple, such as doing the dishes, going for a walk, or updating your CV. The important thing is that you set the intention—*add it to the calendar*—and then complete the task. How does that sound?"

"That's fine, I guess." Brush your teeth, do some reading, make the bed. Sounds like a to-do list for children. Next, she'll be handing me a star-sticker reward chart. Got to take recovery seriously, though, so tell myself off for trivializing the very qualified professional's advice.

Dr. Hadid is unaware of my thoughts and proceeds to write up notes on her screen.

"Good. We will move appointments from weekly to monthly, but please call me if you feel you need one sooner. My door is always open." This makes me smile. If there is one thing a therapist's door always is, it's firmly closed. To guard the consultation room from the waiting room. I have one last question. An important one.

"What about the car and the ring?" I fiddle with the ill-fitting metal around my finger, sliding it up and down, my thoughts turning to something else through the motion, embarrassing, completely involuntary.

"I suggest keep them for now. One step at a time. I don't see any harm in those two tokens if they give you comfort."

We finish up with small talk about her daughter who is backpacking in Asia and how it gets dark already at 5:00 p.m. in Malmö this month, and then I enter the same way I came.

There are twenty-seven flowers on her headscarf.

KLARA

Where is home?

Google Search   I'm Feeling Lucky

Exactly five days after the phone call with my crazy family, I'm strolling through Gatwick Airport, waiting for my one-way flight to Copenhagen. I don't like *one-ways*. A return would be a circle, which is a shape where the distance to the given point is constant. A one-way can only be a line, and lines are one-dimensional and extend infinitely.

I would have liked to know my return flight so that my trip would have form and not be infinite.

My phone pings with a message from Alice.

You will nail it (pun intended!). I'll keep following your blood sugar and tell you to shove some sugar in your face if I see a low alert x.

I buy a tuna baguette at the airport Pret. It always has tuna mayonnaise and four slices of cucumber on a white baguette.

I know that it contains 45 grams of carbohydrates and this is the number I enter into my pump. Nutritional information is very important for diabetics, but you must look at the back—the front information excludes the carbohydrates and is therefore incomplete. The pack has everything displayed in neat rows. I would like to bring a scale with me to weigh out the exact weight so that I can know exactly what I'm eating and can dose my insulin with extreme precision. But Mum put a stop to it in childhood as she wanted to *prepare me for life*. She argued that it is the person *without* a kitchen scale in their handbag that is considered more prepared.

I squeeze the baguette as I stand in the queue. One time it was sold out, and I instead bought a baguette with egg and sun-dried tomatoes, but the filling smelled a bit like the air in the Underground. It must have been a different sort of bread as the insulin didn't work as expected—my blood sugar was high for an hour afterward. Also, the egg spilled out onto the tray, and I had to pick the small pieces up with my thumb and index fingers as if they were chopsticks. I shudder at the mere thought.

I used to be a vegetarian, but I started eating fish recently. Sometimes food items will be sold out, and a more flexible diet means I can prepare for this. It also means I can eat some of Alice's dishes, which inevitably saves me time and effort. I don't particularly like eating living things but found a compromise I can live with morally. I eat species that have a life span of less than five years. I did briefly consider not eating anything with a backbone. But the more I thought about it, it seemed like discrimination toward creatures with a different neurological disposition to us. Life span, on the other hand, is more fair, really; that's how medical doctors decide who to save in the emergency room. You save the one with the biggest chance of survival or, in other words, the *longest predicted life span*. Following my new principles, I can enjoy a varied diet without feeling guilty. I can eat prawns (two years), salmon (five years) and certain other types of fish.

However, sea bass is out of the question (twenty-five years), as is cod (twenty years).

I have time to kill so I sit down on a seat opposite the gate and type into Google *how to tile a bathroom*. Obviously, I won't actually be putting any tiles down—you need training and qualifications for that—but if I am soon to become Tile Boss Lady, then a grasp, even a DIY one off YouTube, seems necessary. I could tell you the differences between British and Scandinavian architecture in a heartbeat, but my knowledge of nitty-gritty building work is limited to watching *Bob the Builder* at age three. I now wish growing up I had taken better notice and shown a bigger interest in my dad's activities, instead of choosing to wait in the car with a book or a Nintendo DS when I had to accompany him on his appointments. *People don't bite, Klara. I'll leave the car open, so you can come inside the house if you change your mind.* Working in Dalby, Skåne, Sweden, would involve some form of large vehicle and multiple locations and attending daily and social interaction with a high number of unknown individuals. Customers. Real, live people with questions, ideas and elaborate yet ineffective designs scribbled on pieces of paper that they hand me across a kitchen table. I'm used to interacting with people via my keyboard. You can only demand so much in a chat box; however loud you shout there, the letters go no bigger than capitals, font size 14.

Next, I log on to the company website, which I discover is a simple, standard design. Dad was never one to splurge on luxuries, and it's obvious he has asked for the most affordable package. I read.

Let us create your perfect space! Established in 1992, Bygg-Nilsson is a well-known firm covering a large part of Skåne, specializing in tiling work but ready to manage every aspect

of your construction project. We pride ourselves on being a
small, select team who take each project seriously and aim
to offer a personalized touch. 100% satisfaction guarantee.

I sigh. It's not exactly going to stand out on my LinkedIn or
look good to my sixty-one Instagram followers.

I click on the before-and-after images, most of them dark
and shot either too close or too far away. Dad's photography
skills are appalling; he can't be trusted to take even a family
photo as he cuts heads off as ruthlessly as Louis XVI. I decide
the first action should be to scrub up the website, and that this
is the perfect remote job for Saga.

Around me crowds have gathered, and a general sense of
stress has manifested. I will do what I always do: stay seated
until every last person has gotten on board and the ground staff
announce *Final boarding call* and look directly at me. I pull up
the family WhatsApp group, which I rather fittingly named
Nonstop Notifications, the only thing holding us four together
across countries and past indifferences. Technology: the glue
of the modern family.

Me: Boarding.

Saga: Yay amazing you will be great K! Just think what it means for
all of us xxxx

Mum: Typing...

Dad: 👍

What is it with older men and their love of the thumbs-up
emoji? Dad should really be using the whitest one but insists
on choosing the second one from the left, as if he thinks he
has a summer tan or a deeper pigment rather than the one his
Swedish lineage has handed him. The thumbs-up is his go-to,
to the point where I often feel as if I'm communicating with

a body part rather than an actual person. *Shall I order a birthday present for Nan?* Thumbs-up. *I just got a promotion.* Thumbs-up. *My house is on fire.* Thumbs-up. There is no way of telling from this ever so slightly tanned thumb if Dad is happy I'm coming or not, so his reaction will be a *surprise*. People say I don't like surprises, but this is in no way accurate. I like good surprises, just like everyone else. What I don't like are the bad ones. Others can shrug them off with a *shit happens*, but I can't: they throw me. Having to go to Sweden after seven years in London feels like a bad surprise, and I can't help but think that if my plan had worked out all those years ago, I wouldn't have been so easily movable now.

My glucose monitor beeps with a lost-connection alert, and I look down at it with sympathy, saying, "It's okay. I, too, am rather lost."

I spot Dad immediately. He looks uncomfortable, nervous even, as he gazes toward the stream of passengers I'm part of. As soon as he sees me, he breaks into a large smile and comes toward me. He's lost weight but looks healthy. I recall the unassuming *1*, and he pulls me in for a big hug, pressing my whole head onto his chest. I let it go on for longer than I'm comfortable with. His jacket smells of Dad, which I guess means fresh air, olive soap and cheap aftershave.

"You're here. How was your flight?"

"It did its job in getting me here. I'm happy to be here, Dad." And in this moment, it's true. Dad *needs* me. A strange feeling hits me that our roles have reversed. I'm not quite ready for my dad to need me more than I need him. I had imagined this moment when I was a lot older. And wiser.

"Coffee?" He gestures to the airport Starbucks.

"No thanks. I'm fine, Dad. I had one on the plane." He looks relieved. It's one thing offering me an 80-kronor coffee but a very different thing to actually buy it. Plus, we both want to get out of this crowded place. He smiles and ruffles my hair. Acceptable when I was a child, not now that I'm an adult dealing with volume, frizz and all the other things that come with, well, adult female hair. I suppose I could tell him to stop, but then I half like the ritual of hair-messing and half know he'd continue it anyway. Dad does what Dad wants to. Part of me can't believe how Mum and Saga got away with this and convinced him to hand over the reins to someone else. Everything has to be Dad's way. Even Saga's wedding was micromanaged by him. A gift. If she hadn't put her foot down, they'd have gotten married in a Swedish barn lined with straw bales as if they were cowboys. Too stubborn to even let his daughter plan her own wedding.

I follow him out of the airport building and toward what looks like the back end of the cargo hangar. I look at him as we walk, not having seen him in several months. He is tall and statuesque with long legs and arms that swing when he walks as if aiding his balance. His back is bent slightly, perhaps from spending his whole life doing physical work, and his blond hair has been replaced with a shade of speckled white that would look quite stylish on a young girl working in the fashion industry. I look nothing like him, having inherited every trace of DNA from my mum, seemingly. In contrast, my sister is a tall and blue-eyed copy of our dad. When Saga and I shared our first flat in London, people—usually men—would ask if I was switched at birth. I know I wasn't because they put those wristbands on you, though mine was around my ankle because I was so small. It said *Nilsson 26 June 1996* and an *F* for *female*. I keep it in a box with memories, next to the Happy Birthday cards from all my birthdays.

We're almost at the end of the parking lot, and I start wondering where his car is.

"Another few minutes," he says, nodding toward the hangar.

I sigh and thank myself for choosing a hooded sweater this morning, pulling it up to cover my hair from the rain which isn't proper British rain but more like the dust they spray in beach bars to cool your sweat down as you sip a margarita. Except here the spitting raindrops are freezing, and I have no drink in hand. There was a reason I left this country.

Well, actually, there were several.

The landscape stretches out in front of us: flat, sparse terrain made up of rock with greenery like tufts of hair. Land breaks into small islands as we approach the shore, my forehead pressed against the van's window like when I was a little girl. I think how funny it is how our bodies never forget and all it takes is a parent within a few yards for us to fall back into old patterns.

The bridge connecting Denmark to Sweden appears, and I feel like I've been cut-and-pasted into a Scandi noir novel or an episode of *The Bridge*. My part of Sweden is known for its crime dramas. Mind you, I may murder someone myself if this colorless landscape and its never-ending fog is what I wake up to every morning. I don't mind my wardrobe being monochrome, but the landscape? I make a mental note. *Try not to become a serial killer. Area seems to inspire it.*

I hold my breath as we enter the tunnel creeping underneath the Baltic Sea and count the seconds until we are out of it and I can take a breath. I hold my breath often. Every time there is a tunnel of manageable length, pedestrian crossings, between lampposts, the length of fields, for the duration of a hug.

When we pass the city of Malmö, I start clocking the journey, to get a rough idea of just how far from civilization I will be. My dad's firm has a good reputation and serves a wide area ranging from Malmö all the way to Ystad on the south coast. His fleet of four customized vans spend hours on the road each day. If the sky is gray, then the rest of Skåne is definitely brown, I conclude. Brown as mud. It's not a golden mud, but rather with dusky, grayish undertones, like iron and strength.

"Well, you know where to go. I will bring the rest of the bags in after I park," Dad says as the van comes to a stop outside the white wooden fence that surrounds the garden. The white house looks exactly as it always does when I return to it, except for perhaps a new coat of paint. It used to be a farm on several acres of land, but my parents bought it freestanding, leaving the farmer the fields. They had a dream of a countryside idyll. Looking now at the simple square house, with a stable converted to a garage and home office surrounded by plowed brown fields, I'm unsure if they found it. I glance at the black door to that office now, a short walk across a lawn and graveled parking area from Dad's house, half expecting it to wave a welcome.

The house is empty, a strange experience. Dad is obviously living there, but he is not the type of person that fills a house with his presence. The inside, especially the kitchen drawers that I randomly pull out, is a museum of my childhood. Which would be great, if my parents had expensive antiques rather than odd serving spoons and suspicious-looking liquor bottles brought back from Spain or Portugal tagged *A gift from Auntie Lynn*. I recognize the waffle maker, the oven gloves, even the kitchen spatulas. Dad has kept whatever Mum didn't take with her when she left, an old-school mentality of *why replace something that works fine?* Updating something for a new style or refreshing the interior are foreign concepts to him. What he and Mum had in common remains a mystery to us all, including the two of them.

My room is full of boxes and items in storage, so I settle in Saga's old bedroom. The lighting follows the season, so when there is light outside, this room is bright, two windows lavishing the sun on wood floorboards, but when it's dark, well…

Saga used to come into my room because of the shadows on the wall and lie next to me, close but not touching, without saying a word. I knew she was afraid of those shadows. I tried to make her feel better with facts. "A ghost is only a vague evanescent form of a person and can cause no harm. Don't fear the dead, fear the living." I was never sure if this had the desired effect or not.

I shuffle items around on the upper two shelves of a fitted unit. I open the cover of the first Harry Potter book. On the yellowed page it says *To Saga on Christmas Day 2002*. Next, I pick up an old Barbie doll. Complete with jeans and crop top, she lies there as if she's Sleeping Beauty, having waited for us to return to her after all these years. I loved Barbies. Decorating their houses, dressing them, setting them out in various positions and groups as if they were busy living life. The children playing, the adults in a group talking like all adults do. *Don't touch!* I would say to Saga. *What's the point if we can't touch them?* she moaned. *I just have to finish setting the game up. Is it ready now?* Saga would reply. More impatient moaning. *Now? Come on, Klara!* But it had to be perfect. I didn't even care about playing: it was the preparation I loved. Organizing them.

I smooth out Barbie's long blond hair and put her back to resume her sleep. The Harry Potter books, some CDs and a figurine of a horse are removed and deposited in a drawer to make space for the items I've brought with me. They are, in order of importance, a picture of my family on holiday ten years ago, a notebook, my favorite scented candle (Musky Vanilla), and my purse of loyalty cards. I only have loyalty cards for the UK, none for Sweden, which gives me a funny, floating feeling. When I get to the bottom of my suitcase I hesitate, then turn the contents—two books on Scandinavian architecture—upside down and close the bag. *I won't be needing them. I've never needed them. Who am I kidding?*

The room should feel familiar because this is the house I

spent my childhood in. Arriving home from a holiday or after
a sleepover always filled me with relief. I didn't care that my
room didn't have a TV, pink walls, or a double bed. It smelled
of home. It smells the same, but it's not home. It's confusing.
Now, home is my bedroom in Alice's flat, an almost-perfect
square of white walls with a queen-size bed, built-in wardrobes
and a large window where I don't have a view (it's a basement
apartment, and all I see is a gray cement and moss-covered wall)
but do have lots of light.

Moving was an easy way to recruit a friend, according to
Google.

I went to view rooms, taking time to inspect the shower
curtain and wardrobe space in each, when in reality it was the
potential flatmate I was assessing. Alice had few facial expressions, in fact, only three. They are, in order of most used: huge
laugh, friendly smile and neutral-resting face. When I'm around
she uses the first two: this is how I know we are friends. I asked
about whether she walked around the house in shoes, socks, or
barefoot and she answered, *Barefoot because the skin has to breathe,
doesn't it?* and that socks worn all day made her think of older
men with athlete's foot. That was promising. I paid my deposit
there and then. The good thing about living at 243A Munster
Road SW6 is that I can get my coffee from La Bottega if I feel
like chatting, and from Starbucks if I feel like only uttering my
name for cup identification and nothing more.

I don't want to move somewhere bigger. Large houses are
full of spaces that have to be filled, and all I can think about is
how much time it must take to clean everything. My boss gave
me a warning once, when I told a YourMove customer who
was looking at eight-bedroom mansions (*not* a *country house*:
that is something rich people say to seem humble) that it was
a bad idea. "You may want to reconsider investing in a large
property," I told the customer. "It's a lot of extra upkeep and
cleaning and maintenance, all added distractions."

"You may want to reconsider trying to talk customers out of buying homes through our site," my boss said. Then he suspended me for two days.

I lie down on the single bed now and stare at the white ceiling, unsure of what to do next, until I hear Dad at the front door.

ALEX

Personal Calendar ▾

○ **NEW TASK:** Test. Who even uses these calendars? Guess it works...guess people who work use them...

○ **NEW TASK:** Meet Dan (let's pretend it's a "meeting" and not just a beer-fueled moan)

○ **NEW TASK:** Read (and throw out) 4 job openings proposed by Jobcenter

Bin truck wakes me at 5:14 a.m. from bizarre dream which I instantly forget. Apart from that, slept well last night. Of course, people never say things like that: we only talk about sleep if it's been bad; we are not interested in the good or the neutral. Sleep is as skewed as Google business reviews.

The outside world makes its way into the flat through my single-pane windows. My apartment is small, with one bedroom and an open-plan living area in the bustling Möllevången with its mango-and-plantain filled market, coffee shops and vegan hotspots. I'm never alone, thankfully; the bustling mix of languages and faces wraps me up in a bubble of belonging. I just have to venture out to be reminded of the world around me.

Decide to get up and have an espresso as a start. Thought about entering *have espresso* in my calendar so I only have two things left to do today but refrained. Need to take first day of recovery program seriously, if it can even be called that.

The pile of bills on the breakfast bar, the only table I have and use when eating on the sofa is not appropriate, needs addressing so I start sifting through them. I prefer paperless; less in your face, easier to ignore if it's somewhere in the cloud or a cluttered inbox. But these aren't mine. The first one is a reminder that the lease agreement on the car is in default. It's getting harder to ignore them. Old Alex would just get on with it, get a job and hustle. But I am not Old Alex anymore. Proof: Old Alex would be off playing paddleball on a Saturday morning. And Old Alex would definitely not find himself wearing a ring that doesn't belong to him. Can still hear Dan's reply when I asked to keep it.

"I've got one on, haven't I? This one is mine, the one Calle gave to me. He was your brother. If you want something that was his, it's yours."

New Alex is a fucker, don't like him and his ways. Wouldn't offer this New Alex a job if he were the last person on the planet, and so I save the employer the trouble of even interviewing him. Save my friends the trouble of seeing him too and also regularly save the shower the pleasure of seeing him. A thought hits me, and I don't like it at all. What would my brother think of New Alex?

Phone buzzes with a reminder from my calendar as I leave the parking lot. Bizarrely satisfying to beat the schedule and already be here. The area is empty apart from some dog walkers and cyclists: icy winds from the Baltic Sea are something you only brave if you have to, not by choice. The white-and-gray building that is Turning Torso towers over me, a twisted, tall turret of fifty-four floors with the open sea as backdrop. It reminds me of a Twister ice cream that's lost its colors. It's on the outskirts of the city but a short walk from the center, one of Malmö's few buildings that offer a luxurious, ultramodern living standard.

The male concierge nods at me in greeting. I always feel awkward doing the same, unsure how big my smile ought to be. Not used to staff and fancy marble floors. Mamma and Pappa thank him and make small talk when they visit. They can't wrap their heads around the fact his presence is paid for and act as if it's his house that he graciously lets them visit.

Feel a sense of being watched as I walk over to the elevator and press the button for the thirty-second floor. My fingertip leaves a mark on the shiny steel that must be polished several times a day to achieve that shine. I wipe it off with my sleeve as if I've done something bad and want no trace left behind. I don't knock or ring the buzzer as I step out of it, I just slide my—*his*—key in the heavy steel door and push it open. It's almost as if I've become him.

Dan is on the sofa with a beer and his smooth-looking, pedicured feet stretched out on the upholstery. A beer is best drunk with either a laugh or with a thoughtful look, and Dan and I are kings of the latter. What is there to laugh about?

Dump the pile of letters that I've brought with me on the round marble coffee table, keeping one envelope as a coaster for my beer bottle, which I walk over to the kitchen to get. Dan has been helping me with life admin for months now, paying bills and filing letters. He's too nice to me; don't deserve it. Sometimes I wish he'd shout at me rather than double as my secretary.

The fridge is odorless when I open it. Ketchup, pickles, mustard and Heineken. A teriyaki marinade and fresh yeast which must have gone off by now. I close the door. Is there anything more depressing than a fridge without food? Without people to feed?

Dan moves his legs to make space for me.

"I have to sell this place at some point. We can't use a 10-million kronor property as our man cave forever," he says. We both have our ways to survive—coming here has been his.

"I know." I didn't ask Dr. Hadid whether this, my third token, was also harmless to keep. I feel guilty for being the one to struggle. Dan is coping better than me when he has every right, even more right, to be broken too. Two weeks' leave taken, ten pounds lost, and a lot of tears and he came out the other end functioning. No anger, no bitterness. Just a constant current of sadness that you see in his eyes. Like a bleak stretch mark on a body. But then, he's not the one who refused to give Calle a lift home that night. Appears healing is a lot easier without guilt.

"I'm thinking of making some changes beforehand. Most people want more than one bedroom and less living area. It would bring the price up and make for a faster sale. I feel like Calle would hate it if I sold our place cheaply, just for it to be developed by someone and all this wiped out." I love the massive, open space that is sparsely furnished. There is a couch in a gray hue, the same as the sea in winter. A large rug across the wooden tiles and a dining table by the breakfast bar. Everything is hidden—drawers, cupboards and the bowl with keys and random bits that every home has, normally on display by the front door. It's a space that could make it into any interior design magazine. Calle had talent.

Memories of trading labor surface.

"I cleaned, aired and organized your bedroom while you were out. Now, finish my CD rack," Calle would say, serious negotiating face on.

"Why does it smell like custard?" Sniffed suspiciously.

"Because I crushed some vanilla pods and mixed them with cinnamon. Your room smelled like unchanged bedsheets before my intervention, Alex."

"Dude. I'm thirteen. What do I care what it smells like?"

"Doesn't mean your room can't smell nice."

I built him wooden cars, then CD racks, then smooth wooden boxes to store his watches in. In return he organized my room and made it smell like vanilla.

Take in the open sky and the wild waters now, Copenhagen visible across the sound where some cargo ships and a passenger ferry are crossing in the distance. I'm at the top of the world, with air to breathe in abundance. If the tall building sways in the wind, it does it so gently we don't notice. Would probably fall asleep here on the sofa if this was my home.

"Any news?" I ask. The amount of shitty stuff I'm waiting for at the moment has no end. When you are young you think waiting for something good is torture. School to finish: every minute creeps along as if it's got a puncture. Adult dinners: how can there still be *one more* course until dessert? And Christmas—well, why do you think those chocolate calendars were invented? When you become an adult and have to wait for something fucking catastrophic, you rethink your whole childhood, and it seems idyllic.

We've been through the police investigation, the witness statement and the forensic report (fifth edit) and have been dealt a prosecutor and listened to the verdict. All legal professionals speak the same. *It is impossible to predict. We cannot be sure. I do recommend adding this document to increase the chance.* For people who need to deal with facts, assimilate them, analyze them and present them, they are an incredibly vague breed of professionals.

"I was just about to tell you, Alex. I spoke to the prosecutor this morning. There is a date set for the trial. April 22." Months later but finally a date. This means I need to hurry the fuck up and be ready for it. My spine tingles with a weird sensation. Bad weird, I think.

"So, seventy-seven days," I say instantly.

"I forget how good you are at math."

My eyes are sore, and I can feel Dan's gaze on my face.

"Have you been driving lately?" he asks. He's the only one that knows what I do at night. What I can't stop.

"Maybe." He doesn't tell me I'm a moron because deep down he understands why I do it, where it comes from, this urgent need. If you do something out of love, it doesn't matter what it is, right? Even if it's crazy.

There is someone we need to find, who has information we need, and no one else is looking.

April 22. I've just been given a deadline.

KLARA

How do I drive a van with manual transmission?

Google Search   I'm Feeling Lucky

The smell of coffee reaches me as I walk down the stairs, each step creaking in a different tone, reminding me of an out-of-tune piano. I pour a cup for myself and fill up a bowl on the floor with cat food I find under the sink. I'm trying to remember how many cats my dad currently has and what their names are. When we adopted four kittens from a neighbor when I was a teenager, we struggled to think of things that came in fours. The seasons, the elements, the directions. I remember suggesting the four physical states, but for some reason *solid*, *liquid*, *gas*, and *plasma* were voted down.

I'm pretty sure the ginger one that now struts into the kitchen is Björn and the black one following him discreetly is Benny. I saw a shy third one in the garden yesterday. Which would be either Agnetha or Frida: the last of the quartet ran into the woods some years ago. Benny arrives and attempts to push Björn out of the way, but the latter hisses and shows pointy yellow teeth. Benny settles a yard away, sadly watching his meal disappear.

"The winner takes it all," I tell him sympathetically, before getting another bowl and pushing it across the floor toward him.

It's like being seventeen again and practicing for my upcoming driving test. My dad's hand hovers anxiously above mine, which is firmly gripping the gearshift, knuckles white and trembling. Considering it took me three attempts to pass my test, I can understand his unease.

"I've got this."

"You almost hit the garbage can!"

"It's moved since yesterday. How am I supposed to know where it is if it keeps moving?"

"So it's the can's fault you reversed into it? I don't think that would hold up in court."

"It's like driving a tractor."

"At least if it were a tractor, you would be on a field driving slowly, not out on the roads with—God help us—other vehicles."

I am a good driver, I really am. I can even drive in London, and Alice and I sometimes pick up a car from the car-share program where you just find the location close to you and drive off. She is in charge of snack provision (road trips are all about the snacks and cheesy tunes at top volume), and I am usually the designated driver. I map the trip in advance and drive it in my head as I shower: *visualization*, they call it. Left on North End Road, I would think to myself. The problem with my dad's home is that the roads are not normal, and they are not marked by signs. They extend and end at what feels random, and I cannot say to myself, Turn right on Kensington High Street, which leaves me lost.

Also, this is not a car, this is a monster. It looks a lot like the cars I drew as a child. A tall and wide box-shaped monster of a van that I somehow need to learn to maneuver before my first working day shadowing Dad—tomorrow.

We have been driving up and down the gravel road outside for half an hour now, attempting parking and reversing at angles. Like yesterday, a discreet rain falls, and the sky looks hormonal, unpredictably dark with clouds fleeting past.

"Just try to relax. Stay calm," Dad says, getting ready for a new attempt. Has there ever been anyone in the history of mankind that calmed down when asked to? I would guess no.

I make another go at it, this time narrowly escaping a flowerpot when I try to parallel park.

"I need a break."

"God, me too."

We sit at the kitchen table, polished pale wood and floral coasters for our coffee cups and cakes. Coffee is in Sweden what tea is in England: we drink it morning, midmorning, afternoon, midafternoon and, if not suffering from insomnia, after dinner. I take a large sip from the dark, watery brew that fills my whole cup and inevitably will cool by the time I get to the bottom.

We have just a couple of days until I have promised to fully take over from Dad, the first day of treatment looming. His hospital bag is packed and his music downloaded, and I have snuck in a pack of juice boxes with straws, the kind I got in my lunch box whenever we had a school outing. Saga has read that sipping fruit juice can reduce nausea from the chemotherapy. She is keeping her promise of helping out so far, sharing useful information and links, but has yet to look at the website. Dad is as ready as he can be for his first day. Me less so. I try to assume the expression of a responsible adult.

"What's the schedule like?" I ask.

"This week you'll shadow me, and then starting next week, I will have my treatments Monday through Wednesday, then the rest of the week I will be at home. *Resting.*" He says it as if it's a filthy word. Like me, he is antsy and dislikes sitting still for too long.

"I will drive you in and pick you up afterward," I tell him, giving myself a small dose of insulin at the same time, pushing the clumsy buttons of my pump. The stress seems to be getting to me. I've been running high sugars since I arrived.

"Thank you, but I will manage. Klara, you'll have things to do. You don't realize it yet, but you will be busy, and you may not have time to be my driver. I much prefer to know things are under control with the business than to have you worry about my logistics. I can order taxis—they do exist, you know, even here." Yes, at insane rates and arriving half an hour late after having gotten lost among the fields that surround us out here.

"I get it. I'll try my best, I really will. How about I do the driving when I can, and the other times, I'll accept you organizing it." I know not to push help on my dad. Having to rely on his child is more mentally taxing than the disease itself, I can see that from the tension in his shoulders. He is the rock, the one we call when we mess up. Who bails us out when we lose our wallet at a Shoreditch gig and can't get home unless someone links their credit card to an Uber account (Saga), or when our dishwasher is broken and we need FaceTime assistance to troubleshoot it (me).

I'm also starting to sense that my job will involve more than just a brushup of the website, which I had initially told myself. Speaking of the website...

"I emailed the web guy to add my email address, but he still hasn't replied," I say.

"Why not give him a call?" Dad asks me.

"I've emailed twice now." I pick at the crumbs of a biscuit, pressing down on them with my index finger to see how many stick to my skin when I lift it up.

"Just call, then. Do you have his number?" Dad persists.

"I'll send him another email in the morning." Dad shakes his head as if I'm a particularly difficult example of a human being. Which, to be fair, I may well be.

"You will need to get used to calling people. You can't run a company by email."

"Now, there's a thought," I say. "Maybe I'm onto something. My big idea, my big break. The email-only company."

"People around here are old-school. They like a good chat," Dad says, then changes the subject. "If I check in with you on Thursdays, is that good? I can't give up control altogether. It should be the day I feel the best during treatment. We can sit in the office and go through schedules and any problems you have had during the week. Check that the guys' mileage trackers add up and things like that."

Oh, yes. All the vans had trackers installed about a year ago since it came to light that an employee had been using it to run a side food-delivery business, I remember now.

"Dad, Thursday is in just three days' time."

"So it's perfect, then." He gives me a nod as if he's about to leave this conversation, and I realize it's nonnegotiable.

I sigh but accept that I will have him watching over my shoulder every given opportunity.

"Sure. Quoting is probably the thing I need the most help with. I thought I could take a video of the space and we look at it together, and you tell me what the company needs to quote." I notice that I use the third person for the company, I don't say what *we* need. I don't want either of us to get too used to the me being here. If Dad is nervous to hand the reins over, he isn't showing it. He stretches out a long arm, like an elephant trunk, to take a biscuit; he must be on his fifth. It amazes me how much he can eat. When he is invited for dinner, he makes a stop at the service station to pick up a bag of crisps in case the portion sizes aren't big enough.

"I did make one of those media accounts for the company

some time ago, the log-in details will be in the Passwords folder." Of course. As opposed to me who scribbles PIN codes on random receipts, Post-its or my wrist (hoping it won't get chopped off by a knife-wielding street criminal), my Dad has a filing system worthy of an accountancy graduate.

"You mean *social media*?"

"Yes. Strange name, isn't it? Staring at a phone is the opposite of *social*."

I can't agree with this one. I am feeling incredibly lonely since entering an involuntarily imposed social-media break. I mean, what would I post about? My sixty-one followers would start to wonder when the usual posts were replaced by me in gray builders' pants, lifting a sack of even grayer joint mixture, in a gray and brown Sweden. I stop myself picking at the edges of my insulin pump's adhesive: biting my nails is a better habit. My dad pushes a paper over the table to me.

"Here. PIN codes and passwords for pretty much everything. Company card, loyalty cards, desktop and loads more." I look at them and pull my eyebrows together.

"It's all Saga's birth date."

"Easy to remember."

"When is my birthday?"

"June…3rd?"

"That's Mum's. Oh my God, Dad, how can you not know my birthday? Was my birth so trivial that my own dad hasn't committed it to memory? I can accept that world fame never happened to me as my ten-year-old self thought it would, but to be anonymous in my own family?"

"Klara, that's not how it is. I only remember Saga's date off the top of my head because it's my password. The first child gets the password perk, if that's even a perk. Ask your friends' families. I'd say firstborn digits dominate the world of passwords. There's a hacker tip for you."

I'm not convinced but let it pass.

"So let me go through this again. There is Gunnar and Ram who do the tiling. Then Mateusz, the carpenter. The plumbing and electric work you outsource, they send us the invoice, and then we add the cost onto the customer's quote."

"Correct. But Gunnar, Ram and Mateusz are all trained in different areas and can move around to where they are needed. Small teams have to be flexible." *Great.* I am a small team of one, I think, and I am not flexible.

"How do they feel about me rocking up?" I ask. I prefer *rocking* to *turning*. *Turning* implies that I will turn away, whereas *rocking* sounds more of a forward motion. The thought of three unknown men taking orders from me is scary. The question has been at the top of my mind for a while now, though not brave enough to roll off it, as if hovering over a cliff. Dad lifts his shoulders in a shrug.

"It's the twenty-first century, and you're my daughter and very capable. They will adore you." He squeezes my hand. "And, Klara, I do know when your birthday is. It's the twenty-sixth of June. Feel free to change the passwords. Maybe it's time I get a new one."

ALEX

Personal Calendar ▾

○ **NEW EVENT:** Jobcenter appointment

○ **NEW TASK:** Dig for money to cover car repayments (don't ask Dan to bail out)

○ **NEW TASK:** Exercise (walk around the block)

Jobcenter has me gripped as always. Doors are heavy and squeak, get stuck midway on the built-in doormat. It's like they have designed the door to make us work at entering, an extra obstacle in order to get that check. Which I desperately need. The waiting area is full, and I nod at them all as I lean against the wall. Like to see them as my peers, not my competition. I imagine the house burning down and us all pulling off some sort of rescue attempt of bored staff and thick files. In it together.

Susanne talks to me today. She is blonde and permed and reminds me of an '80s pop star. Probably was one: this is exactly the type of place they end up. Behind a worn wooden desk on a nylon-clad chair ticking boxes with Bic pens. No neon in sight.

"What did a handsome guy like you get up to this weekend?" she says to me as if I'm some sort of pet or first grader. The fuck? Usually play along with flirtatious middle-aged women but, you know, *depression*.

"I was job-searching."

"Oh." She looks in utter disbelief. As if it's the one thing she wouldn't expect a job-seeking individual to do. Maybe she sees through me? Maybe I should give Susanne more credit. I mean, I *could* get a job. If I really wanted to. It felt like the right step to take. After four months of sick leave—essentially being unable to cope after the untimely death of my brother, my best friend, my favorite person in the world—signing up for employment felt better than extending the leave into eternity. Had every good intention. It's just that when the emails come in and I scan them, the job descriptions give me a big fucking ball of stress in my abdomen and it's just easier to delete them and spend my time with the Susannes of the world.

Home an hour later, and it's so fucking dark and cold I'm curling up on the sofa with an actual throw. Didn't even realize I had one, but someone, at some point, must have gifted me the light blue knitted blanket. My feet stick out at the end.

It's okay to struggle, Alex, Dr. Hadid had told me earlier. I can't hold it off any longer, today is not going to be the first day, is it? I go to my Inbox and then Drafts, pulling up what is already a forty-four-page email. Been writing for close to six months now. The draft is wedged between two other email procrastinations: a request to defreeze my gym membership and an inquiry regarding a cheaper monthly broadband provider. Who writes an email knowing they will never get an answer? Know I'm a loser, but I still don't stop. Can't stop.

Saved to Drafts

Dear You,

Sorry if these emails are starting to bore you to death (double sorry for the pun—you and I always did have the weirdest, darkest of humor). I can't say your name. You aren't here so I'm not sure what your name should be. If cheese ceased to exist on planet Earth, surely we wouldn't all still run around putting *cheese* in our sentences? Saying your name reminds me of the fact that it's just a name now. Your person doesn't belong to it anymore.

Am now triple sorry: I don't have anything cheery to tell you.

The ring is tight on my finger. The ring I shouldn't even be wearing because it's not mine, is it? It's getting warmer now, and it doesn't fit as well any longer. I'm not even sure it will come off now. When I push it up, there is a trace, like a road map, blood rushing to its place. I can't help but feel ever so slightly free when that happens, as if life rushes back into my finger. And me. Then I slide it down again, and I'm trapped in this grief. But I wonder, if I take it off, will you be gone? If the pain isn't there, then what is? Nothing?

No name, no pain.

I'm not ready to accept that.

Hours later I'm still thinking about the email. Grab the car keys off the table. I throw my sweater on, zip it closed and pull the hood up over my head.

Time for a midnight drive.

In the car. Fucking angry. Wish I weren't, but it hits me sometimes. The anger. Perhaps if I knew who to hate, it would be easier. If I didn't just hate *someone*. But somehow *someone* managed to get a protected status, despite this being Sweden and not America. No idea how it happened unless they are an actual judge. Have already checked all judges in Lund. Obviously. Someone is not my issue right now, though; he'll be there on the twenty-second of April. The problem is who will *not* be there.

There was an appeal for witnesses. One came forward and said that there was a second witness on a street corner. In a red jacket with a dog on a leash.

"I'm sorry, Dan. Alex, Mr. and Mrs. Berg. Without the second witness, there is no prospect of a conviction. No deciding evidence. I suggest you get your heads around the fact that there'll be damages, but the more serious charges will be dropped." Fuck all. As if I could let the charges drop like keys falling on the floor. I don't drop things.

Someone in a red fleece jacket saw what happened that night, and I've spent months trying to find them.

My Nikon is on the seat next to me, my last 100 kronor in the gas tank.

The rain blurs the world until the wipers start up. It's 12:53 a.m., and exactly six months ago someone with a red fleece was here. Realize how sick that sounds, looking for a person in fleece. But there is a chance they'll be back. They may live close by, may have walked home from work at that particular time. That was my first hope: that they would appear with their red coat and perhaps a backpack or a dog in tow that needed an evening pee, so I could pull up and, well, *find them*. As the weeks and months passed, I changed my theory. It could be a relative of an elderly resident. The old people don't often get visits, everyone knows that. Swedes aren't like the Mediterranean or Middle Eastern families who open their homes to their parents and grandparents when they arrive at the end of independence. The state is our parent, and it looks after senior citizens while we get on with life. All this is speculation. Truth is I have no idea who this woman is. No lead. Hate to admit it.

There is a large dog in a harness coming around the corner.

Its owner loud on the phone. Hand gestures. *Listen up, Phil, the price is already down...Yeah, yeah, I know...I KNOW.* I wonder if the dog minds. Do dogs mind? Like I do when someone is texting at the dinner table. It's his one highlight of the day, out with an owner who's been at work all day, and he doesn't get his full attention. This man looks like he's not the type to own a red fleece, not the sporty type, so I drive slowly on and find a parking spot next to a loading bay.

It wasn't an accident. Everyone knows that, but only one person *knows* it. My eyes are stinging: it's like I can feel the small red veiny threads appearing by the minute. The city is starting to wake up, and those in charge of its morning routine are starting to appear. Street cleaners, newspaper-delivery guys, along with a family with luggage, obviously heading for a painfully early flight. The two small boys yawn and hold on to tablets as they walk down the street. More dogs walking their sleepy owners. The next lot of people will come at six, the runners in bright, windproof gear, bankers and doctors and CEOs in suits heading in early to work. Even before I started driving I knew the city well, haven't really lived anywhere else. My friend Paul went to Stockholm for his studies, but I stayed around. Always happy and content. Who needs challenges when you have a fine life?

Somehow it's already 5:02 a.m. I pass the cathedral, nine-hundred years old and majestic, towering over the university where half this city seems to either study or work. The windows are dark and sleepy. I wonder for a second if the doors are open. Churches are supposed to always be open, aren't they? And then I wonder what it would feel like to sit alone in the space of a fourteenth century structure.

It will take me ten minutes to drive home, onto the highway and into Malmö's industrial area with its IKEA and soft-play center. Apart from a few trucks, I won't have any traffic. The world starting to wake up is my cue to return home. I think about the fact that no one seems to have recognized me during all these months. I see the same people on the same streets, yet no one has ever seen the blond guy in a new BMW hovering on street corners staring at jackets. No one has knocked at my window and said *Hey, man. All good? Been seeing you around.* It's easy to be invisible at night: it's the time when people prefer to ignore who and what is right in front of them. I'm like a shadow, moving around the city.

Shadow Man is going home for the day.

KLARA

What is my theme song?

Google Search   I'm Feeling Lucky

It's 6:30 a.m., my new wake-up time. If I were in London right now, I would be lying lazily in my room and rereading archived messages to the soundtrack of a noisy kettle and Alice rummaging around. I happily glance at the time, thinking that for once I will be up and ready before Saga when my phone pings. Sometimes (actually, *often*) I pretend that my blood-sugar notifications are messages. That someone special is thinking of me, until I remember that the number of boyfriends I have is zero. There used to be a Mark, who also worked for YourMove, and who Alice calls *bad news*, although this doesn't make sense since I rarely had any news from him during our time together and he did kindly take me out for two-and-a-half course dinners (we'd share dessert).

I have been single for six months and fourteen days. Length of celibacy is one of the things that society likes to count. There is an unspoken rule as to what requires careful precision and what doesn't. Baby age: twenty-four months rather than two years. *Do you come here often?* on the other hand does not require you to say *Sixteen times averaging a stay of two point one four hours each visit.* The same fluidity applies at the bus stop. *Have you been waiting long?* I usually think *Three minutes and forty-six seconds, and whether it's long or short depends on your own definitions,* but I choose to say *Not really.*

Deep down, of course, I want to find love. Doesn't everybody? I said to Alice, "I don't want to become an old lady who has no one to open lids of jars." Alice responded, "Taking lids off jars is literally the only benefit you can think of when it comes to having a man? Ain't that the truth, K!"

It turns out my messenger is Saga this time, who's beaten me to even waking up. In fact, my whole family is alert and under the impression that this is a great time to kick off the chat.

Nonstop Notifications:

Saga: Harry woke up two whole minutes later than usual because we let him stay up two hours past bedtime. Send help. Or coffee. Or both.

Mum: Oh honey, it's a difficult age. Have you tried the aromatherapy drops I sent you? Or sleep music? My yoga teacher swears her twins sleep through the night since she started them on a guided meditation half an hour before bedtime. She is thinking about patenting it the "med to bed" method.

Dad: Whiskey used to work fine in my days 👍

Saga: The only time Harry is in a meditative state is when he's watching random unboxing clips on YouTube or there is a digger on the construction site next door. Enough about me—how are you doing, Daddy?

Dad: I feel great, thanks. Klara holding up ok.

Massive exaggeration right there, as I'm still only shadowing Dad, but I'll take it. Maybe he's manifesting success. Considering my only professional success amounts to managing an average response time of eighteen seconds in the YourMove chat, disappointment feels imminent.

Mum: Make sure to rest plenty and eat enough greens. Stay off crisps and cheese. Got to dash, farmers market. Love you, girls x

Yes, Mum loves us. In a hugging and feeding sort of way. Our relationship growing up consisted of tight hugs, gentle strokes and our favorite dinners prepared on a rotating basis— one weekday each. Mine was Monday and macaroni, that way I could make the start of a new school week slightly better. Saga's was Tuesday and meatballs. The remaining three nights were set: taco night, pizza night and soup night. Now physically removed, she instead mothers via pictures of sunsets, advice on well-being and by sharing her own pink-filtered life. I don't miss her warm, motherly bosom that would swallow up her resisting children, who'd squeak *can't breathe, Mum.* Dad's hugs are tolerable, a quick lean-in so torsos touch and a clap on the back as if I'm his dude.

The WhatsApp group generally serves me well as it's kind of like a group support chat that covers everything from domestic and technical issues to love-life trouble. But I miss the sense of *being loved.* If only Mum could figure out how to love me remotely, the way that I need it.

I like declarations of love in writing. A date once sent me an emoji of a contented-looking smiley with hearts floating around. When I asked if I could please have the written version, "I'm content and lovestruck with you," there was a lot of *Typing…* and then nothing. I would like the smoothness of *I love you* in a message, so it's there for me to pull up and look at whenever I want. Spoken words ultimately exist only in my head, and God knows I think a lot of silly things. Emojis can be interpreted a million ways. Writing is evidence.

When Mum left Dad for choir singer Inge, the worst thing were the jokes from ill-meaning relatives and acquaintances. "I guess he made her heart sing" and "He played the right tune."

My parents sat us down while we were back home visiting, a rare occurrence as Saga and I got older, as if we were still small and dependent (which we may well be; does emotional dependency on parents ever stop? Asking for a friend. Obviously.).

Dad cleared his throat.

"We have some news for you."

"Oh God, don't tell me you are having a baby. I don't want a sibling. Heinrich and I are planning kids. This would be—what?—our baby's aunt or uncle?" Saga burst out.

"What she said. One sister is enough to handle. Can't handle another one of those." I rolled my eyes in Saga's direction.

"I'm fifty-five, girls, and hot-flashing like a toilet on fire!" My mother has an original use of metaphors. To her they make complete sense, and so she will never learn, despite our best efforts.

"Well, you were clearly not too old to hook up with someone," Dad said, spitting droplets of bitterness into the room.

"Wait, what's going on?" I asked, perplexed. *Hook up* wasn't a phrase I realized my dad even knew.

"Girls," Dad said, doing his best to look us in the eyes, switching between us as if watching a tennis game. "Your Mum and I are getting a divorce. Your mother has been *seeing* someone else."

I looked at my parents in disbelief. Divorces happen when you're young, not when you are adults and, in Saga's case, hopefully soon-to-be-pregnant. Saga burst out laughing. She has disputable timing, and while I share her dark humor, I can't force myself to physically laugh at tragedy. Any attempt to do so simply sounds like a polite cough: *Huh-huh.*

"How? I mean, *please* don't answer that. Wrong question. Why and when?" I said. Mum gathered her hands in her lap, innocently leaning forward as if she were in a therapist's office and attempting to put all the blame on her partner.

"We met at church. My evening choir. It was friendship to start with, and then, it just became something else. In fact, it became the love of my life." I looked over at Dad now, who was admirably composed and neutral. *God, I love you, Dad.*

"I'm sorry to have put everyone in this position, but when you reach my age, life has already become short. I hope once you come to terms with it, you will be happy for me, and I guess it can show you that it's never too late to find love." Mum looked at me as if wanting to instill some hope. *You, too, can find love—even if it's at my age.* Absolutely thrilled at the prospect of waiting until my late fifties to find love in a church choir. *Thrilled.*

"Who is he?" Saga asked, looking over at me to see how I was reacting. *All okay*, I smile. *Sensible adult reaction over here.*

"His name is Inge. He is five years older than me, widowed and kind. He has a house in Spain. We… *I'm* joining him there to live full-time. It will be so great for you girls, free holidays in the sun. You're going to love it." Mum desperately wanted our approval, and we tend not to be stingy. Sometimes you have to give something you don't want to, out of kindness for someone you love.

"I will stay in the house, of course, continue my work," Dad said. "Nothing will change around here, girls."

"This is what's best for us," Mum said. I looked at her to see if she was also reassuring herself.

"We understand," Saga told her. At times like this we become siblings in the word's true meaning, and *I* blend into a *we*: something is said that either of us could have spoken. Dad stood up and rubbed his hands together as if attempting a physical outlet of the tension in the living room.

"Right, then. Now that that's out of the way, who would like some coffee? I have cardamom buns."

You are never too old to mourn when your family home as you knew it is shattered, the point which kept you coming back is moved, split in half between two locations instead of one. So I've learned.

I manage to get ready in twenty-seven minutes, and when I open the front door, I find that it's snowing. When it snows in London, people call in to work pretending their street hasn't been gritted or their car won't start. That doesn't fly in this part of the world. There is a white veil on everything from cars to trees, making the morning appear brighter than it is. The sun is still an hour away from rising, but I can see the path to the car without a light.

Frost is like the clingier, less welcome version of snow. I work at it aggressively with the car window scraper that keeps slipping from my hand. The stiff grass creaks under my feet as I shift my weight from one foot to another, stretching to reach across the windscreen. So far, I have managed to clear some sort of shape resembling a penis. I'm not looking out of a micropenis the whole way to work, so I continue scraping. Fingers numb and catching up with my toes now, which are already starting to feel like they left my body ten minutes into the morning. *Great.*

I think of the number of times I've stood like this. We would drag ourselves to the car in the morning, Saga and I. *First one scrapes the window! Not me! Definitely not me.* Yet, somehow it was always me. Saga demanded a square be made on her back-seat window so that she could see out. That and the driver's side was all I had time for before Mum rushed through the door, forgotten water bottles and a collection of keys in hand. *Get in!* I would peer at the white cover on my window, waiting for it to melt slowly as the heat spread throughout the car. About half-way into the school run, my window was clear and my limbs warmed up enough for my toes to wiggle again.

"Put the car on. It's quicker," Dad says now as he walks up behind me, admiring my perfect square. *Of course.*

We huddle inside the car, and cold and tiredness start to ease as it rolls onto the road and away.

"What did you do before the seat-warming function?" I ask.

"Froze our asses off," Dad replies.

Our first property is easy to find. I wasn't sure what to make of it when Dad told me to look out for the gnomes, but as we circle the suburban neighborhood with identical front yards with rhododendron bushes and flagpoles with yellow and blue flags, I see them. The rust-colored brick house with a generous garden and terrace at the back is nestled in between other identical brick houses, but there is a huge difference between this one and its neighbors.

"Wow, what an advantage! They never have to give directions. Can just say look out for the villa with twenty gnomes in the front yard." The small ceramic men cover the lawn, and we can only just follow the footpath to the doorsteps.

At the doorstep Dad pushes the buzzer. I'm happy he did as they also have a brass semicircle on the door, and I wouldn't have known which one to go for. I'm standing on the last step while he towers on the second, and I think about the expression *putting your best foot forward* and decide that's something I should be doing. I take a large step forward with my right, because it's my dominant one and the one I'd score with in football. This seems to annoy Dad, and he moves to cover half of me so I feel like a small child, a tagalong.

"Dad, I'm meant to be doing the work."

"Right." He scoots to the side reluctantly just as the door opens.

"What are you selling? I already bought muffins from the football team."

"Bathrooms. I'll be selling you a bathroom today," I manage at the same time the owner sees my dad clad in gray work clothes. My own set had to be specially ordered and hasn't arrived yet: a ladies' size 12 wasn't in stock.

"Good morning, I'm Peter with Bygg-Nilsson. We're here to give a quote. Klara here is new and shadowing me today."

Inside the small, cubicle-like guest bathroom, Dad shows me how to measure, check that the ground is level and determine the condition of the supporting walls. If I had any hope that this might be an exciting job, in line with any interest I may have, the conversation with the man kills it.

"Cheapest possible. It's just for guests. White tiles will do the job."

It seems the books on Scandinavian architecture that I brought can stay unpacked in my suitcase for more reasons than one.

Outside, as Dad packs up the measuring equipment, the man walks around inspecting the porcelain figures in his garden with discontent.

"We may have to move some of your…gnomes…before we start work. Some of the boxes and equipment going in need space," Dad says gently.

"Be my guest. These bloody Santas, can't get a proper mowing round them," the man moans.

A lady appears behind him and looks at us with terror.

"I don't want them lined up as if they are soldiers guarding a driveway! What will the delivery people think?" I take it these gnomes are the main men in her life.

"I'm sure the delivery guys think we are *totally* normal," our customer grumbles, then turns to his wife. "Can you at least put their hats away, now that it's almost spring?"

Almost spring? Yesterday we had a whole hour of direct sunshine. The Scandinavian bar is low.

I stop in front of a gnome, a half-yard-tall, bearded porcelain man with his head held high and an eccentric suit to match his pointy hat. I nod my head in greeting.

"I like this one. He looks like he knows what he is about. Works a job that doesn't make him hate Mondays. Possibly into winter swimming."

The man doesn't smile.

"When will I meet everyone?" I ask as we drive back to the home office after another two appointments and a quick sandwich lunch eaten in the van. I realize it's getting close to 4:00 p.m., and so far I haven't seen any of the guys. They're just names in Times New Roman in an email Dad sent me last week.

Dad stretches his neck from side to side and takes his time answering.

"They're all on the same project today. I thought it might be calmer with a day's introduction, just you and me. They'll be at the office tomorrow morning. I'll come with you."

Later that evening, as Dad prepares written instructions for my first day alone, I type up the quote from today's site visit into an email. I stall at the very beginning. At YourMove we had templates, and customer interaction was never harder than choosing a sentence from a drop-down box. I've unsuccessfully googled to see if there's a book on professional language, a sort of guide. Once in Oxfam I found a book called *Emojis and Chat Language: The Complete Guide*, and something similar would be highly useful. I message Saga.

Me: Would I be writing "Hope you're well." Or "Hope you're well!" to a customer?

Saga: Seriously, Klara. They mean the same thing?

Me: Well, "hope you're well" sounds like you don't really mean it. And "hope you're well!" sounds like you mean it a bit too much, wouldn't you say?

Saga: Honestly... I have work.

Me: Well, so do I.

Work that I'm not sure I can handle.

ALEX

Personal Calendar ▾

○ **NEW TASK:** Go to parents' house

○ **NEW TASK:** Remember they love you and mean well

○ **NEW TASK:** Get out alive

Arrive at Mamma's and Pappa's with baked goods; was brought up to never arrive empty-handed, even at my family home. *Fika* is the name for a Swedish coffee break, and it can occur anytime of day. There is the morning fika, the afternoon fika and my family's favorite, the ever so popular torture-Alex fika.

They know about the trial date, obviously, but refrain from bringing it up. Too innocent to doubt the outcome of the day, my makers, too convinced there is a law and order in this country and that truth will always win. Because when the worst has already happened to them things must get better, right? I'm suspecting they also think bringing it up will worsen my condition, and emotions are not for conversation over coffee and cake. They are for taking it to the grave.

Conversation accompanying the cinnamon apple cake goes something like this.

"In my day, there was no such thing as depression. We plowed through it." (Pappa)

"Alex is more like me. You know that, Pappa, a sensitive and romantic soul." (Mamma)

My parents are the type of alien people who call each other Mum and Dad, even after their kids have left the nest. Might be acceptable if they had a pet, but they don't.

"Maybe if he would start eating meat again, he would get enough vitamins and iron to kick it." (Pappa)

"Vegetarianism saves me money, and it's good for the planet. Kidney beans have as much iron as meat." (Me)

"Lots of women are not eating red meat these days. I'm sure they would love a man that knows how to cook as well as Alex." (Mamma, in the voice of a long-suffering mother)

In my circle, relationships are valued higher than professional achievements. Proof: qualifying as a carpenter got me 57 likes on Facebook, moving in with my ex-girlfriend amassed 321. Would think in a family where only a handful have a higher education, it would be different. But the focus is consistently on companionship. Mamma has reminded me time after time that Jesus didn't have a diploma, a fact I've responded to by informing her that he also wasn't married. What he had was a partner who was possibly a prostitute, according to some sources— would she like me to follow in his footsteps? *Oh, Alex* (insert typical motherly voice with undertones of exhausted torment yet never-wavering hope).

Guess we just don't enjoy being alone very much.

Sometimes I think, when we were small, Mamma set herself a goal of marrying off her sons much in the same manner that I'm goal-setting now. New event: marry sons off wearing floral dress and hat, task status half-completed.

Whatever makes a good son I'm not sure I'm it. Feel I should be doing more. Treat them to what they deserve. A weekend trip. A dinner at the Triangle with views across the sound, similar to the ones in the apartment that's now empty and hollow. Think perhaps my parents can hold on because they have me, they have one reason to go on, and if I could be my best self, their reason would be stronger.

Shove a whole piece of cake into my mouth. *Manners, Alex*, Mamma says with her eyes. I think she regrets not giving me a long full name, the type you use sternly only when a child is misbehaving, but all she can do now is add an *Oh*: *Oh, Alex*. In our guest bathroom there is a picture of His Majesty the King Carl Gustaf of Sweden and Her Royal Highness the Queen Silvia of Sweden. My parents are royalists so when they had children, the theme was a given. Wish I could say I was named after Alexander the Great but it's Princess Alexandra of Denmark, most famous for her stylish hats and matching coats.

Mamma talks again.

"I wanted your thoughts on this." The torment over my life choices seems to end, at least momentarily. My mother produces a clip from the local newspaper. "They are putting up a giant pink unicorn statue on Gustav Adolf Square ahead of this year's Pride, and there is an opportunity to sponsor it and add a name inscription. I thought we could do it in Calle's memory…"

I laugh out loud at the thought of Calle's face at the mere mention of a larger-than-life pink unicorn. Calle was a successful marketing professional, very good at adult stuff as opposed to yours truly, not a six-year-old girl. The thing about my parents is that they are good people. In fact, they are so full of love and goodness that there isn't always space left for insight, reflection or common sense.

"I will discuss it with Dan." At least it will put a rare smile on his face. And Mamma seems to be doing better.

Fucking throbbing headache when I'm finally about to leave an hour later. But here's the thing: a headache is a low price to pay for family, folks that love you. Consistent people in your life you cut some slack. No problem. Just having people is a privilege. I try hard to remember that as my dad says in the doorway, "Never thought a child of mine would be *unemployed*."

"Job-searching. After sick leave," I offer as clarification. Knowing very well nothing in that statement is clear to him. Pappa lost a son on a Friday and went to work on a Monday. Because that's what you do. You work and work and tell yourself you have a purpose. The funeral was on a Tuesday and on the Wednesday he had built a new garden shed. Calle's personal belongings arrived on a Thursday, and on the Friday a new recycling waste station had appeared at the end of the road, to the delight of the neighborhood. While Pappa built shit, Mamma baked. Buns and rolls and shortbread cookies until her hands were rough and worked like an early-century laundry woman's. When the freezer couldn't hold any more, she started donating to local charities. What else was there to do? Baking still made sense, building things still made sense, even when life no longer did.

Pappa grips onto the railings he built for them to hold on to as they walk out of the house and into the world and peers at me.

"Your legs working? Your arms? Then, you're fit enough to work."

"Not that fucking easy, Pappa. Can't you just leave it for once? Go hammer some more planks instead of *me*. Shit."

"Hey," Mamma steps in.

"Sorry. Shish kebab." Mamma never allowed us to say *shit* so we covered up by saying *shish kebab*. Shit kebab. In the same manner *fuck* becomes *falafel*. Neighbors must have thought we had a thing for Lebanese food with all the shish and falafel shouts coming from our house.

"That's my boy." (Mamma)

Get to the gate when I her hear voice again.

"Wait, take some cinnamon rolls home. I have bags of them!"

At least I can tick off a calendar entry.

KLARA

🔍 How do I survive the first day of work?

Google Search   I'm Feeling Lucky

The next morning Dad insists on taking the bus to the hospital but agrees to let me pick him up in the afternoon. He gets out of the car at the bus stop, leaving a trail of faint aftershave behind. He only wears it when he is going out to an important destination, kind of like me and my lace going-out underwear or black work socks (black means *business*). For every day and work he wears no fragrance other than the scent he picks up from wood, ceramic and nature.

In the side mirror I watch the yellow regional bus approach and stop to collect him, its lights like eyes peering through the dawn, then I drive off. I stay at a speed of ten percent below the limit because ten percent is a permissible number. Accepted above word count on university essays and also the rate of tips for service staff which makes it *decent*. I creep at

29.8 mph, then 17 mph, until I'm back where I started and ready to open up the home office.

I told Dad I would be fine without his introduction, but standing at the office entry, I feel less than sure. I have spent the past half an hour reorganizing and decluttering the space and adding my own touch. I don't mind items that are known to me, but a room full of new items is a recipe for disaster. I end up staring at them and memorizing them to the point where I forget what I was supposed to work on. In primary school the teacher swiveled my chair around so that I faced the wall. *The seasons-of-the-year poster is too interesting. I'm still distracted*, I piped up when my worksheet was once again handed in half-completed. *Klara, if you looked at the desk rather than at the walls, you would be fine. We cannot strip the walls for you. One poster you can deal with.*

I take one last look at myself in the hallway mirror, most likely an unwanted item from a demolition job. What other reason would there be to put a mirror up for employees in worn work wear and boots other than that it was free?

I tie my hair into an even tighter bun; its endless occupation is trying to break free from the constraint of elastic, as if it's allergic. If it had a voice, my hair would be an anti-elastic campaigner with a car sticker and a Texan accent. I stay standing in front of my reflection. I have a beauty that de-escalates. It starts off well with a symmetrical, well-proportioned face, large eyes and full lips, moving on to arms, perfectly useful ones, freckled and slim, a large but firm bust that stays where it's asked to, a soft tummy full of lines and red dots, the ones that would make a medical examiner conclude *type 1 diabetes*. I am definitely in the so-called pear-shape category. Not that I care; comparing women to fruit is just rude. My legs are in working order but nothing to look at, short in relation to my torso. Then it ends with a low: my feet, large and bony, remind me of odd, bumpy root vegetables brought in from the harvest. I would like to hope people eye me up from top to bottom, like that they get my good bits first because first impressions are what last.

Once I saw someone write the theme song to their life in their Tinder profile and wanted to do the same, but the only thing I could think of was *Head, shoulders, knees and toes*. Alice says the song has to sum up our *experience*, not our physical *appearance*, and that the theme song to *her* life is the shitty flute version of "My Heart Will Go On," because it's an emotional train wreck that just gets progressively more frantic as it goes on.

The look I get from Mateusz when he enters the lot is many things, but not what my dad said it would be—*adoring*. Unless perhaps you mean *adoring* as in a steak you're just about to sink your teeth into.

"Good morning!" I say in a voice resembling a cheery primary teacher welcoming her class to a day of endless mental math practice. I'm wearing my large hoop earrings. When they hit my cheeks regularly, I know that I'm smiling and nodding enough. I often wear earrings to help me remember to smile. Today I am going for every forty-five seconds, since this is a *semiformal* meeting.

"Morning," he grunts. I get no hand stretched out in response to mine. Mateusz is a strawberry blond man in his late forties who would benefit from walking more, eating less and washing better. Orthodontics would also be advisable. He must be a very good carpenter, I conclude, watching him walk into the office with a reusable cup in hand.

"Usually there is coffee brewing when we arrive," he grumbles, appearing in the doorway again. "Now I'll be late for my first appointment."

There was no question there to answer so I simply smile, the earrings dangle, and I remain in position as welcome committee to anyone who arrives in the parking lot.

The next person to arrive is Ram, who appears quieter, not particularly smiley but nevertheless polite enough to greet me.

"Nice to meet you. Do you need anything?" he says as he pulls his ash-colored hair back into a ponytail. He is the youngest of the employees, but he is probably still ten years older than me.

"Thanks, I'm all right at the moment. I was going to ask you the same thing. Let me know what I can do to make your work easier. That's why I'm here." My earrings dangle.

Mateusz cuts in, exiting with his coffee in hand, pushing his chin forward when he speaks. He has obviously forgotten that only minutes ago he was complaining about having to do a very simple thing himself as he remarks, "We are used to running things ourselves."

"Right, great, that's good to hear. I will just be back-office support."

"Like our secretary? Great. Do you mind making a good cup of coffee next time?" Mateusz says. I ignore the insult for the sake of peace and the good of the company.

"I'm hoping to learn a lot as well," I reply.

"There are schools for that. This is a workplace, hon."

Thankfully, Gunnar rushes in, saving me from answering. He is the oldest in the team, about my dad's age, a slim and muscly man.

"Good morning, Klara. Let's go inside, shall we?"

When Mateusz has left, I pluck up the courage to speak again.

"So there will be just one small change while I'm here. You can use the fridge for your lunches and other foods, but please keep the fridge's penthouse free," I say. Blank stares meet me from two sets of eyes.

"That would be the top right compartment in the fridge

door, to you nondiabetics. Perhaps where you would keep your butter. It's where my insulin lives. Lastly, please refrain from bothering my father while he's out. He needs rest. You can bring up any problems or other issues with me, and I'll deal with them." More blank stares. I force a smile again, making sure I can feel my earrings as they gently brush my cheeks, and decide this is good enough for now. "So I guess that's it, then. Thank you all."

Gunnar and Ram fill their thermoses, and they all leave in their vans, a line of white vehicles splattering dust on one another as they drive just that little bit too fast. I walk back inside the office and pick up a sponge. I wipe the area around the coffee machine. I can only hope these men have greater precision in their craft than they do when filling travel mugs.

The first half of the morning went smoothly. I responded to emails and fixed appointments. I've made a template email to make this process quicker, much like I had standard responses at YourMove. I only had two near brushes with death while driving (or rather, the van had one brush with a lamppost and one with a box of tiles), which, keeping in mind the size of the van and the fact the only vehicle I've driven recently is a supermarket shopping trolley, has to be considered a success.

At midday I packed a bag and waited to be picked up by Mateusz, who was meant to show me our biggest ongoing project.

"Let's go," I tell my pump, glancing down at my tummy where it's currently placed, as his van comes into sight. I open the front passenger door to find his backpack and leftover McDonald's lunch on the seat.

"Is this seat taken?" I ask politely. He laughs but doesn't stretch out a hand to move it for me. Usually people move their bags when I ask them this on the Tube. I begin to close the door to get in the back.

"Chuck it in the back, will you, and hop in."

"Sure. Thank you." I clench my knees together until my inner thighs are sore, trying to take up as little space as possible. The van has an unfamiliar smell, and it's very much in need of a wash. I wish there was some soothing music playing, but Mateusz appears a fan of *Best of Eurovision 2005*.

"You don't look Swedish." His teeth are even bigger close-up, and he seems to have used whitening only on the front ones. Maybe he ran out. "Where is your mum from?"

Well, surprise, we can't all be blonde Viking goddesses. Some of us are dark-haired, short and plump.

"My mum is from Gothenburg, Sweden," I share.

I can conclude that Mateusz does not follow my rule of ten percent below the speed limit. I try to calculate which percentage he hovers at, but my math skills fail me. In this instance I'm grateful as it shortens the journey significantly. We've stopped outside a large, leafy nursery playground, and I unbuckle my seat belt before the engine is turned off.

"There's a litter bin on your side," he says as I open my door to get out.

"Yes, there is." I'm unsure what's so special about this bin, but I study it carefully when I wait for him to take his things and catch up with me. It's green, which seems a good color choice for blending in with the trees around us. When I peek inside, I see that it's not even half-full, which indicates that it has been recently emptied. There is no time to google *small talk about litter bins*. I'm wondering if I should say something intelligent, and what that thing might be, when Mateusz appears and dumps the brown bag with leftovers into it.

"Well, thanks. You were closer to it than me," he says.

I follow him as he steps onto the cobbled street and then immediately swerves when a cyclist speeds past.

"Bloody cyclists think they own this city!" he spits out in some kind of harsh font Microsoft must have dropped in the developmental trial stages. I look down at my feet.

"We *were* walking in the bike lane," I explain.

"Bike lane? Shouldn't even exist. They don't pay any road tax or contribute to the upkeep of the roads in any way. Plus they just chain their bikes up to the railings and don't even have to pay a parking fee."

I don't understand Mateusz's anger. The only time bicycles annoy me is when their owners wear those ridiculously tight, distracting pants.

I send a message to Saga when I'm finally released from the grip of Mateusz's van an hour later, my feet back on my dad's land to pick up my own van.

Me: If I tell you about my day, can you tell me if I messed up or not?

I check my phone several times. No reply. I would like Saga to tell me *well done*. That I did okay. But lately she hasn't done that. It's almost as if she treats me like a child who no longer believes in Santa Claus. Why bother pretending? Because I don't believe in myself, she's stopped trying to make me.

After work, at 5:03 p.m., I head back to Lund, this time to the hospital. The side roads are full of bikes carrying students swaying tipsily, as they make their way from their flats out for the night. They are a trademark of Lund, a student must-have, if you will, that the city that has more bicycles than cars. The town center looks smaller than I remember as I pass it. But then, doesn't everything when you're an adult?

I once considered this a great scene for a weekend night: the tapas bar, the outside terrace on the square, followed by the only club there was, La Fiesta, Spanish by name but not by nature. Every good night finished off with a half-hour bus ride home, alighting by the side of a country lane and walking the last half mile in chilly darkness using the flashlight app on my phone when my calls to rouse Dad from his sleep and drive to pick me up had failed.

The hospital is on the outskirts of town and is a large complex with several buildings. It's the workplace and main attraction for many foreign residents in the area. I haven't been here since I was a child, but I still know it by heart.

I am under strict instruction not to enter the oncology ward. "There is no emergency that justifies you barging in. I'm telling you now before you come up with one," Dad told me before waving me off this morning, leaving me no choice but to disapprovingly grunt a goodbye and accept his order. The roles are reversed. Dad used to be the one waiting in the car outside a party venue, under no circumstances allowed in to collect my teenage driving-licenseless self. I didn't go because I particularly enjoyed parties, but I enjoyed being *invited*. I used to save the messages on my secondhand Nokia 3310 and would pull them up to reread them when I needed a bit of a boost. To keep being invited I had to sometimes attend. When I would finally stumble out with a mint gum between my teeth to cover up any suspicious alcohol-like odor, I would find Dad reclined in his seat, chin tilted up and mouth slightly open as if he were a bird waiting to have a grain dropped into his mouth. Dad never questioned me when I got into the passenger seat; instead he pulled up at the village's only fast-food joint, a small shack with a hole in the wall where frozen burgers and sausages with minimal meat content were prepared and served up on paper plates with chips and an additive-filled sauce. I ate the fries, scooping sauce up and trying to avoid dripping it in the car as we drove home. "When she starts drinking alcohol, a carbohydrate snack before bed can help counter the effects on her blood sugar," the nurse had told us at a checkup. I'm not sure greasy fries was what she had in mind (snacks, according to medical personnel, tend to equal carrot sticks, flat bread with hummus or low-fat yogurt) but I loved Dad for his interpretation.

"Don't tell Mum," he said as I, knowing the drill, disposed of the evidence in the garbage can before coming inside the house.

I eat a cheese roll in the cafeteria while I wait for Dad. It's served Swedish-style, open with each half buttered and with a slice of cheese and cucumber on it, rather than filled and assembled like its English counterpart. I lift the slice of cheese up and see that the butter is spread unevenly: it leans like a ski slope to the left. I wish I had gotten a knife with it so I could fix the asymmetry. I pick up one cucumber slice and use it to shovel the butter off the slope like snow and spread it with the green tip of the cucumber wheel.

The chair is uncomfortable. I wonder who orders the hospital furnishings? The one I'm sitting on is a faded black, as if the paint ran out and the remaining drops were stretched out to cover the chair anyway. It's pure metal or a cheaper aluminum alternative, and I can feel my seat bones against the hard surface despite the natural padding of my buttocks. I shift on it, and it makes screeching noises against the floor.

The only appealing aspect of the cafeteria is the view of the patient courtyard and an art exhibition on the walls: colorful flower shapes from a humid rainforest on canvas. The artist must have been dreaming themselves away to Brazil or the Philippines.

I wonder if the chairs were the same when my parents used them and what was on the walls then, when I was here, in 2002.

ALEX

Personal Calendar ▾

○ **NEW TASK:** Abstain from writing to Calle

○ **EDITED TASK:** Only write to Calle in the evening

○ **EDITED TASK:** Don't write to Calle unless there is a full moon

There's a fucking full moon.

Saved to Drafts

Hi Calle,

Just realized as I write this that I've started saying your name again. My tongue missed it. I've been thinking about grief. Some people get tattoos. I could get a C or a date perhaps, which would move further and further away as each day passed until people looked at it and would think, What happened a decade ago that made its way onto this man's skin, the barrier that sits where the human ends and the world begins?

I have no need to wear my grief, it's already weeping through my pores like alcohol would during a hangover, its distinct odor over my body like a mist. Active grief needs no reminder. It's when people start moving forward, or rather away, that they want an anchor, an etching on their physical self. At least, this is what I imagine.

Practicalities: you have a sock subscription, you never mentioned it. Happy Socks, it's called. I also learned that Tele2 Sweden wants to upgrade your phone, as apparently you are a valued customer. *Yes!* I want to write them in reply. Valued customer, valued human. But strangers don't want to listen to who you were to me. They want to close accounts and finish their workdays on time, as they surely have family time, cooking and *Strictly Come Dancing* waiting for them at home.

Life goes on, as they say, until it doesn't.

KLARA

Q What is type 1 diabetes?

Google Search   I'm Feeling Lucky

I was six years old and slumped across my mum's lap like a restaurant napkin, her legs shaking under the weight of me.

"Oh God, Peter," she cried.

"Just stay calm. She will be fine." My dad's voice sounded
anything but sure.

"She's not fine, can't you see? This is not sleeping, this is
unconsciousness!"

"Where the fuck is this driver going? Why are the sirens not
on? My girl is in here dying, and they're cruising along in silence." Dad was the one shouting now.

"Don't start. The ambulance staff are doing their job, they
know what to do." Mum attempted to calm him down—and
herself. They took turns being the panicked one and the reassuring one. I wished with a six-year-old's perspective that they

would share the load and cooperate this well in day-to-day life, not just in emergencies.

I didn't feel sick. Tired, yes. And pukey. The vomit sitting there like foul orange juice, asking me to bring it up but hiding when I tried to, leaving my stomach muscles cramped and fooled. I felt thirsty, as if I had run a mile on a hot beach and forgotten my drink. But I didn't feel like I was dying. Was I dying? *Really?* I wished I could open my eyes and look around. I was sure that if I could look into Mum and Dad's eyes, I would know the truth. Now I was left with just the soundtrack of the emergency, my eyelids too heavy to move.

"I didn't understand what they were saying, what is wrong? Is she in a coma?" My mum was crying, that much I could tell. My head bounced on her legs as they shook.

It had started a few weeks earlier. I was suddenly finishing my water bottle in school, to Mum's joy. *I was finally staying hydrated!* Then I started wetting the bed and continued to do so despite the promise of a present (God, I wanted that Barbie camper van so much I tried to hide my drenched sheets in the morning and pretend it never happened) if I went three nights without an accident. I got tired and moody and ran a temperature. My parents took me back and forth to the doctor's, but all they got were different antibiotics for suspected strep throat.

Then one day I wouldn't wake up, and they called the ambulance. They—a man and a woman—leaned over me on the sofa, and the female voice commented on my breath. "She smells fruity," she said. "Let's check her blood sugar," the male voice replied. After they had squeezed a small drop of blood from my middle finger and the number had shown up on the screen of the device, they said, "You were right. Okay, let's go." Then everyone started to rush about. My mum's voice was the loudest: "Where is her teddy? Get me my wallet! You stay with Saga! No, the neighbor is here already, thank God!

Hurry up, Peter, get her a change of clothes. Some pajamas. I have her water bottle, yes! Love you, Saga. Byyye!"

My dad's voice broke the tense silence inside the ambulance, attempting to explain what he himself didn't quite understand.

"Maria, they said that her blood sugar was dangerously high. It's basically turned her blood into syrup, and she is busy burning it all off. She is dehydrated, and if she doesn't get fluid and insulin soon, her organs will start to shut down and then she will be in a coma. She needs insulin and fluid, and she needs it now." His voice was different, without the usual strength; he sounded like a little boy, no more than my age. He collected himself and added, "Maria, love, I think Klara might have diabetes."

The hospital stay was a blur of coloring books, reward stickers and lucky dips into the fantastic-surprise bravery box. There was reheated food on chunky tableware that smelled of school cafeteria and metal cans. I remember the loud click of the finger pricker when it pressed a tiny needle into my soft fingertip, giving me an opening big enough to squeeze a drop of blood out of.

I had Coco Pops for breakfast. We never got sugary cereal at home, only wholesome toasted bread and yogurt with granola muesli or a boiled egg. At least you could eat everything when you were diabetic. And it wasn't my fault, or my parents'. And it is definitely not caused by too much sugar. It's just something that happens in the body: the pancreas, a tiny, useful little gland, starts to shut down until it's as useless as an appendix, and we have to inject insulin to compensate.

The thought occurred to me that this was a punishment for not doing my math homework: now I was stuck with numbers for life. Everything edible had a number: a slice of toast, 12 grams of carbohydrates; an ice cream bar, 18 grams; a banana, 20 grams.

Saga came to visit me. When the doctor did the rounds and asked if *she* had any questions, her first one was *Will my sister be okay?* and the second one was *Will I also get diabetes?* The doctor replied with a *no* and, guiltily, I felt my heart sink. I was alone now. Different. We were not the same after the hospital stay, the first time we had been separated for more than a night's sleepover. When I was discharged, I had a burden that she didn't and an experience that was only mine.

I hated the strain I put on my mum. The first seven days was just Mum and me learning how to deal with our new life, of her reading me books from the hospital library, of having my grandparents visit but not bringing sweets like they used to, when we were still afraid of me not being able to eat them. (Fact: diabetics *can* eat sugar.)

"Do you want to try yourself?" The nurse asked on the third day at injection time. This was a relief. When the nurses bent over to inject my stomach, their hair was level with my chin, and when they looked up, their breath traveled toward me, forcing me to turn my head sideways. I had to hold my breath for the whole duration of the injection. Seventeen seconds on average. The nurse placed the insulin pen in my hand. "Pinch some skin between your index finger and thumb, then angle the needle and put it in slowly and steady. Keep it still and count to ten while you press the top of the injection pen. That's it. Then pull it out. Good job!" I pulled the thin needle out and wiped a drop of fluid from the site, a hole so small it was barely visible. I hadn't needed to hold my breath this time.

I looked over at Mum and the nurse. They were beaming like I was a superstar. The smell of insulin lingered, a chemical but sweet, soft, almost pleasant odor. It smells a bit like Band-Aids and a bit like new plastic shower curtains, or, when I got older and found new comparisons, the office printer ink.

I found that it hurt less when I did things myself. Finally, I was in control, as at least I knew where and when the pain would hit. The nurses all complimented me when I started to inject myself, and Mum's pride was obvious. So this is what I had to do now? I learned that I got the most attention when I was tough. Kids wanted to see me press that drop of blood out, amazed at my bravery. Adults wanted to marvel at my ability to correctly guess the carbohydrate content on food items so they could pat me on the head and say *Isn't she a little dictionary of nutritional information!* So I gave them what they wanted.

I became tough and fearless. Or at least, I tried.

ALEX

Personal Calendar ▾

O **NEW TASK:** Text a friend (Paul)

O **NEW TASK:** Return Mamma's call(s)...

O **NEW TASK:** Add extra veggies to dinner (jalapeño not considered a veggie)

Mamma has sent a voice note. These were an initiative on my behalf to decrease the number of messages she was bombarding us with, especially memes. Inspirational quotes and animal babies—if they have been made, trust Mamma to forward them. Except, Mamma treats each sentence as a new voice note. Am now inundated with her stories of neighbors and local council gossip in chopped-up, two-second clips. Listen to the first and last out of the seven she has just sent, hoping that will give me the summary version, like reading the introduction and conclusion of a leaflet. Make out that she wants me to check my emails.

It's in—the draft witness statement. Open the attachment.

Witness A, of Djaknegatan 2b 21 11 Malmö, to say as follows:

I was reversing out of a parking space after finishing my shift at work (I work as a carer a block away from where the accident happened). I heard a big crash and turned back toward the noise. I couldn't really see anything, but I heard a scream so I stopped my car and jumped out. A man was lying on the ground a few yards away from a bicycle, and a white van was driving away. It was quiet and it was the only vehicle there, so I thought I should note down the registration number. I guess watching so many crime series kept me switched on.

A woman was right next to the cyclist. She had a red fleece jacket and was holding a dog on a leash. I assumed she would help him so I called 112 and asked for an ambulance. I told them something like "A cyclist has been hit and they are bleeding from the skull and abdomen. They are unconscious." And then the address. I stayed on the phone. They kept talking to me.

I suddenly noticed that the woman with the dog was gone, there was no one else around. I ran over to the guy, and I put the phone on the ground while I pressed my jacket at the place where the blood was coming from, which was the stomach.

The ambulance arrived along with a medical car, and I stepped away. I stayed until they had finished on the ground and were making their way to the hospital. There were other pedestrians and a black Clio had stopped by the side. The police were there, and I told them what I have said here. I told them that I didn't see the driver, or the actual crash. I just saw the van drive off.

A white van.

Feel jealous this was the last person to see Calle alive. Does he know what a privilege that is? What I would have done to be in that position? In a position to *do something*.

Am painfully aware that this doesn't contain what we were

hoping for and that we need a Witness B. I have exhausted my options. Looked everywhere. I plead with the prosecutor in an email, perhaps something can still be done. *Please.* I write back.

The witness saw the van drive off; he testifies that the driver didn't stop at the scene. It's got to be good for something?

The reply comes quickly.

Hi Alex,

I do hope you are well. As we have discussed previously, in anticipation of this statement, the driver is not contesting the fact that he drove off but rather his defense argues that he did not realize the cyclist had been hit. He was convinced that he had simply brushed the side of the bicycle. As mentioned before, he drove a new vehicle and argues that he was too unaccustomed to the vehicle to feel accurately the impact of the collision. He denies fleeing the scene as he was unaware of the cyclist being injured.

As discussed, we will push the point that his alcohol level was above the limit (based on the positive test taken when he was tracked down the following morning) and go for a reckless-driving sentence. We do not recommend pursuing the more serious vehicular-manslaughter sentence due to the above-mentioned points and the lack of witnesses at the scene.

Kind regards,

No witness. Unless I can find one. I put my phone away and kick at the wall like a child, then hop around on one leg swearing at my aching toes.
Real mature, Alex.

KLARA

🔍 What is the life span of an egg?

Google Search   I'm Feeling Lucky

I've sent out a handful of quotes. I've taken videos for my dad to assess. Now I listen as a man I met yesterday tells me in a voice mail that he is not going ahead with us and the quote was way above the other one he received. My stomach clenches. I can't help but feel that this rejection is aimed directly at my person. I avoid rejections as much as possible, I never ask for discounts, upgrades or anything that has a high potential of receiving a *no*. *No*s sting like the leaves on nettles.

I have no time to dwell on the cancellation as the phone keeps ringing. My iPhone is always on highest volume because people who keep their phones on Silent mode unnerve me. They are the kind of people who say nothing in favor of using body language, assuming it is obvious what they're trying to express with their hunched shoulders, smiles that don't involve their eyes and hair-flicking.

"Hello, you have reached Bygg-Nilsson." I have practiced this greeting in my bedroom with the cats as audience.

"Hi, I believe you missed my calls a few times." A male voice fitting into an age range of forty to fifty says. Southern accent, slow and thick, like driving through mud with each word.

"I didn't miss them, I looked at my phone as it missed them," I clarify. "I happened to be busy." There is a silence followed by a clearing of the man's throat.

"Could I speak to Peter?"

"Peter is unavailable. However, *I* am both available and eager to deal with your query," I say, again using a phrase I practiced last night. The cats seemed to approve. The man also seems to be impressed because he proceeds with his query.

"The company was supposed to come and give me a quote; no one has been in touch regarding logistics yet."

"I apologize. There has been an administrative handover. However, I can fit you in this afternoon." It will take some reshuffling, but I'm keen to appear flexible.

I send a message to Mateusz to pick up the keys for the job site himself so that I can attend the last-minute appointment. Mateusz is off sick, apparently.

Mateusz: Sorry, Klara, think I've got food poisoning so not coming in today.

Get well soon, I reply.

I feel sorry for Mateusz. He seems incredibly unlucky with food poisoning on Mondays, our busiest day of week.

I try Ram next. Because I dislike telling people what to do, my technique is to simply declare what needs to be done. It resembles talking to oneself; however, I switch *I* for *we*. This usually encourages the other person to reply *I can do that* or *leave it to me*. But I'm finding that this technique doesn't work as intended on Dad's employees.

"*We* need to deliver joint mixture to the villa in Södra Sandby," I hint loudly as Ram walks past me on his way to the parking lot.

"Do you have the address?"

Of course I have the address. My main responsibility is knowing who needs to be where at what time, including material and tools, and this inevitably requires knowing the addresses of all our projects.

"I know the address."

"Cool. All okay, then. Have a good one, Klara." He puts his AirPods in and walks off with his ponytail swaying. It's only then that I realize he has left me with the task. This makes me want to say a bad word, and it's not *scheibe* or *fiddlesticks*.

The balding man on the other end of a pinewood kitchen table speaks in a size 20 font, Copperplate Gothic. This suits him because it's on the Google list of worst fonts, and it lacks class.

"I have done a fair bit of DIY in my days, just need a professional to take over now. Don't have the time." He raises his eyebrows. "I thought, best to get someone in so the wife doesn't file for divorce soon." At this he laughs. Having seen divorce firsthand, I disagree that it's a laughing matter. I stay quiet.

"Follow me and I'll show you the Haven."

I am no tiler or carpenter, and my only claim to the trade is being the daughter of one, but what meets my eye in the basement of the 1950s house looks like it is an amateur installation of an electrocution chamber, with electrical cords and suspicious-looking openings in the walls.

"Well, here it is, the start of the spa. Sauna and shower room with a relaxation corner."

"Wonderful," I say. This is what I usually say when I enter someone's home and they show me their humble abode.

"Right, yes. I did all the heavy work, didn't I? Will be a

quick job for you guys to finish up." The man kicks at an empty pack of nails, and it goes flying a bit farther than I think he intended. "I thought, why don't I give Bygg-Nilsson a call and see if they can squeeze this in somewhere between projects, eh? It would be grand to have it done by spring. Got a couple of mates coming for the weekend, and they are all looking forward to seeing it."

"Currently there is a two-month wait for any project start," I tell him.

"Two months? I've practically finished the hard bit here. I just need a professional because I ran out of time." I can't imagine the electrocution chamber being finished on our lunch breaks and odd hours. It would perhaps even require complete reinstallations. I say this to the man. He is now talking in font size 24.

"You could try speaking to our office," I say as I scribble the general-inquiry email address on a piece of paper. "They may be able to help you get in sooner."

Needless to say, *I* am currently *the office*, and the general inquiries end up in my inbox. I exit the house as fast as I can.

An hour later, I'm in Södra Sandby, a small village surrounded by equestrian farms ten minutes' drive from Lund. An elderly couple are having a new kitchen put in, and Ram and Gunnar are there working, but Dad has requested a video update. It wouldn't surprise me if it will be used as his entertainment during chemo sessions. "You may want to bring a book," the nurse had said. Well, I'll keep him in steady supply of construction clips instead.

As I turn onto the main street—the *only* street here with any shops—and find parking, I work out my estimated time of arrival at the house and then type into Google *Is 4 minutes and 57 seconds considered late?*

Fast steps, neck bent, icy wind hitting the naked gap between my hat and coat. I always walk on the side with odd numbers because I feel sorry for them, being odd and all. The frozen ground of the front garden creaks as my weight lands on it with each step. On the front door there is a painted horse-shoe, which I use to knock.

"Sorry, I'm borderline late," I announce, taking a moment to compose myself. The hallway is neat, and I wipe my feet thoroughly on the doormat.

The old lady with white fluffy curls introduces herself as Greta. I can't hide my delight.

"I like your name because the letters also make the word *great*." It's the type of mistake you would do when typing, write *great* instead of *Greta* and autocorrect wouldn't even correct it. If my name were Greta, I would have accidental positive affirmations on a routine basis.

"And I like your accent. Where is it from?" she replies with a smile.

"I'm from here, actually, just five miles away. But I've lived in London for many years, and now I'm stuck in that place where I have an accent when I speak Swedish and an accent when I speak English." It's true: when you move abroad, slowly the new country tightens its grip on you until your identity is some gray area in between cultures and languages.

"Well, the accent is charming. I couldn't believe when I heard we had a girl coming. You don't look like your dad. Such a nice man." I get this a lot, both that I look different and that he is a lovely person. I think many customers choose his company because of him. It's certainly not because of the fantastic website or Mateusz.

I glance over at the small square kitchen table and see that she has prepared a big fika, complete with homemade cinnamon rolls and biscuits. A pot of coffee is placed in the middle, which she is gesturing to.

"Thank you. You're officially my favorite customer," I say. "Now, shall we go through the samples I brought over?"

I take a sip from my second cup of coffee of the day. Greta leans in.

"Between us, though, could you chat with the builders about bathroom manners? Toilet seat down and no drops on the floor—that sort of thing. I know this is a job site now, but it's still our home, and it certainly makes for additional work on our end."

I turn the discreet color of a beet.

"I'm ever so sorry," I say. "I will have a word with them, and this won't be a problem going forward."

I come home and find that Dad's made dinner again, if fried eggs on toast counts as dinner. The ketchup and sweet chili sauce are in their usual place in the middle of the table. I recognize most of the tableware from when I was a child. I check my step-counting app and am pleased to see that I have not only achieved over six thousand steps, I have also ended on an odd number, so I reward myself with a glass of wine. Dad declines my offer to pour him one.

"What about the egg?" Dad asks as I sit down and straighten up my cutlery so that the knife and fork are placed completely vertically. "I know you eat them, but what's the actual life span? Do you go by the life span of the egg or of the chicken it could turn into?"

I've already googled this, which presents a valid dilemma to my diet.

"Ah. Interesting. For the egg to change into a chicken many things would need to occur, first it would need to be fertilized. Most eggs sold commercially are from poultry farms and have not been fertilized. In fact, laying hens at farms have not even seen a rooster. For an egg to become fertilized, a hen and rooster must mate prior to the formation and laying of the egg. I'm quoting Google here. This egg here," I say and poke at the yellow with the tip of my fork and some yolk spills out onto the bread and plate, "this egg would have a life span of whatever time is left until it reaches the use-by date on its packaging."

"I will keep a lookout for the shorter use-by dates if that helps, Klara, honey," Dad promises warmly.

"Maybe we should get takeout tomorrow? My treat," I say. I love takeout. And online shopping. It's opening a lid and getting a surprise while knowing exactly what's inside. Which basically means there can't be any bad surprises.

"Be my guest, but it would be cold by the time you arrive home with it. Fred's Grill and Pizzeria is the closest one." *Of course*, I've been driving the van all day, and when I finally arrive home, if I want a decent meal, it involves a half-hour drive. Delivery service nonexistent. Escape to the country at its finest.

After dinner, I try to organize my life. I have never had a calendar this full. The lines form against the page in varying distances, and I can't help thinking of how long it would take to hold my breath between each one as if they were pedestrian crossings. It would be many short, shallow breaths, as if hyperventilating. When there are too many notes, they blur together, and I can't see where one ends and another starts.

Today's notes are:

7:30 Key drop-off to Gunnar. Bring pastry at the same time.

8:00 Tile wholesaler to collect samples.

9:00 Office time and invoices.

10:00 Customer meeting in office to discuss new project. Name: Hans, presumed age: 40 plus. Only other information: he's a Mac user ("sent from my iPhone").

11:00 34 Smålandsgatan. Woman called Hilda. Favorite color (assumed) red. Cat named Sot. Likes when we take shoes off.

Then I ran out of space in the margin. I turn the page to look at the afternoon.

"Only write what's important for the job. Like what material and equipment needs to be brought, where the client has left the key for you, if it's under the doormat or next to a flowerpot, that sort of thing," Dad tells me when he reads over my shoulder.

"I see. But how does one know what is important? The cat's name could be important. What if he walks into a newly cemented area for example? He may need to be called back."

"We don't usually have to herd cats."

"I felt like I was herding cats on my first day."

Dad shakes his head and walks off. I notice that he is holding on to the wall as he does so. He seems to have become more and more like a small child lately. He is recently a fussy eater and goes to bed early, and I have to force him to get dressed in the morning. I decide to prepare his clothes for the following day, folding them neatly on a chair outside his bedroom door. Jeans, T-shirt, sweater and thick white socks at the very top of the pile. I rearrange them to resemble a smile, stretched and curved, though I'm not smiling as I do.

It's Thursday which means it's time for Wine and Whine. Our sisterly, weekly catch-up session. Saga's name is on my screen, and I press green. Her blond hair is in a messy bun, and she has her reading glasses on.

"Hey," she says.

"Hey." I have this habit of mirroring Saga, sometimes intentionally, sometimes not.

Why do you always have to copy me, Klara? Get your own vocabulary!

"Trying to sort out Dad's website, but it's impossible. Harry is like a cat. Whenever I open up the laptop, he comes running." She sighs.

"Some help is better than none. Seriously, Saga, I need you to do something. Anything. You did promise to help with whatever you can remotely."

"I know, and I will. Soon."

Saga is getting on my nerves big-time. She keeps promising help and then not showing up. She was supposed to contribute too. Social media is something she could do remotely, but so far there has been reason after reason as to why she hasn't gotten around to it. Last night, she was up late baking sweet-potato brownies for Harry's school party, for example. I get that toddlers are hard, but he is at nursery. And she has her lunch break. And he goes to bed at seven. I could go on. I'm all alone here, and she continues her life like usual.

"Can you be more specific?"

"Next week."

"Okay. No problem." *Read: big problem.* There's a change of subject, which means she knows this.

"Do you want to sync your step counter with mine? Trying to do six thousand a day as I realized the walk to the coffee machine and cookie table in the staff room plus bathroom trips only average nine hundred a day."

"Just drink more coffee. It'll also make you pee more. Problem solved."

"Heart health? Heard of it?"

"I walk 6K-plus steps a day, and my heart is in no way healthy, it keeps breaking. Doubt six thousand steps is the solution. Also, sex as cardio is overrated. It starts well but ends in heartache."

"At least the sex you've been having this past year *is* still cardio. After four years of marriage, mine doesn't even feel like a brisk walk."

"That is way too much information. You know that I'm more comfortable with oversharing myself than being at the receiving end of intimate-information overload."

The truth is that since starting this new job, my steps are up. Between the car, the worksites and the office, there are a whole lot of steps happening.

"My biceps hurt for the first time in years. You should try carrying bags of joint compound between the trunk and the warehouse shelf."

Harry interrupts us now with a *Mamma!* Heinrich is following after.

"He's asking for you," her husband says, then adds "Hello" to me.

"A kid asking Dad for his mum is basically demanding to speak to the supervisor," I tell him.

"Apparently his mother is better at putting pajamas on. Unless she does it backward, I'm interested to hear the difference in experience."

"He is such a good one," I say to Saga once he's retreated out of camera focus with Harry for another pajama attempt. She doesn't realize how lucky she has been. Unless she has hidden it well, she has never been dumped. Literally. Her success rate of being asked to stay in a relationship is one hundred percent. *Obviously, I must be doing something wrong.*

"I guess so. Although I do most of it. It's not like he does bedtime *every* night." Saga *has* to complain. Terrified I may think that she doesn't actually do it all.

"Maybe if everything didn't have to be perfect, he would have more time to help with bedtime." Saga needs everyone to be on top of everything. *All the time.* Like she is. Insurances have to be renewed, fridge stocked to the point where she could host a spontaneous banquet, child's clothes name-tagged and a full tank of petrol in the car at all times. Even though she commutes by bus.

We end the call and I go to bed. The quiet is very quiet so I take a clock from the living room to add some background noise. I check my app and I'm at 6,452 steps. An even number.

I swivel out of bed and my feet flinch as they meet the coldness of the floor. I walk to the window and back, and then do an extra step to finish on 6,461.

ALEX

Personal Calendar ▾

○ **NEW TASK:** Buy more acetaminophen

○ **NEW TASK:** Buy ibuprofen

○ **NEW TASK:** Go for a drive. Only thing that helps headache in the end

Saved to Drafts

Dear Calle,

I don't think you need to worry about Dan anymore. I know you would—always did—and old habits can be hard to break. Do they break in death, old habits I mean?

I saw him today. He is sad but healthily sad. You know how you check to see if a child or an animal is doing okay? I did this with Dan. He is eating well, sleeping well (at least from what he reports), and I have no reason not to believe him. Went to the Indian place on Stortorget, and he had about three naans, so that should reassure you. Tells me he doesn't need the ring back so it's still on my finger. "Alex, it would just go in a drawer to be kept safe. I know you won't want it forever," he said. And he's right: it was your wedding ring after all, not mine, but for now it helps, and I need all the help I can get. Keeps saying, "Stop saying thank you and stop apologizing. What happened wasn't your fault." Still don't believe him.

Mamma and Pappa are good, as good as they can be when they lost half of what they had. Building less, baking less. Avoiding them as much as possible, as my current emotional fragility remains not understood. It's different from theirs, so Pappa in particular doesn't get it. Feel guilty for it, emotional fragility increases, avoiding continues, and so the cycle keeps repeating itself.

I have this nagging feeling that things would be better if it were me. They have had me for an extra three years. Got more of me than you. Their time with you was cut short, but their time with me keeps ticking. Ticking like a clock or a bomb, though? That's the question.

Sometimes my life feels more like a bomb than a clock.

Yours, A

KLARA

Google Search   I'm Feeling Lucky

I have to attend a wet-room conference. *Wet room.* It sounds like some kinky environment used for orgies or those fancy, private dress-up parties named something utterly unsexy, like Killing Kittens, that Alice's ex-boyfriend was trying to drag her along to once. It turns out it's just a term for bathrooms and a certification for tiling that needs renewal every fifth year. It requires an employee to be present at a half-day workshop with lectures and speakers. (I mean, who will they be? The suspense is killing me. *Distinguished professor of tiling and wet rooms?*). Since I'm the only one that isn't useful in the actual construction work (Dad's words followed by quick apology), I am the chosen one.

I walk into the Radisson Blu in central Malmö at 8:03 a.m., safely within the not-late allowance. There is a blue synthetic carpet with red dots covering the aisles and a palm tree next to reception. I soon find out the dress code for construction worker workshops is Levi's jeans (or similar, cheaper versions purchased at Dressmann), shirt tucked into said jeans and a shoe that is either a boot or a sneaker. I spot two ties in happy colors.

The speaker is one of the men with the happy-colored ties, and he seems moderately passionate about the topic but highly passionate about the fact that he is speaking. After seventy-five minutes of PowerPoint slides and him repeating what they say as if providing voice-over, he opens the floor to questions.

I feel like I *should* ask a question. Something about the EU regulations for joints, or perhaps about whether drying time of joint compound is affected by the humidity level in bathrooms. But as I raise my hand, index finger pointing up as if I'm attempting to pop a balloon, the room goes silent and forty or so men stare at me. *Pop.*

"Will we receive our new certification by email?" The speaker looks at me, as does the sea of heads around me, and tells me that, yes, it will be issued within twenty-four hours. Then I put my hand up again for no other reason than the first question went so well. These are the intelligent words that escape my mouth: "When is breakfast?" There is a muffled laugh. And a distant snort. I feel myself turn pink. I only tried to ask the question on everyone's mind. Dad had said everyone was there for the buffet. Turns out we were meant to keep that to ourselves.

"Since the young lady here is hungry, why don't we break up the first session ten minutes early? That is, if there are no more questions."

I don't have any more questions.

Standing in a corner of the room, I nibble at a croissant. I tried the fruit salad, but the chef must have used the same knife to cut onion with not so long ago, so I left it on the counter half-eaten. There are chairs free, but I don't know which one to choose, the one next to an older man with a colorful tie or the one next to a couple of younger men in sneakers. I wouldn't like to hurt any of the chairs' feelings, and I haven't had enough time to figure out a classification system for fair choice so decide to remain standing.

A voice makes me turn.

"Are you enjoying breakfast?" The speaker is next to me, a coffee cup in his hand. I glance at him quickly. Age around forty, boots and blue jacket. Some of the hairs on his chin are white, but I'm guessing he assumes they blend in with the blond.

"Croissants alone are a reason to stay in the EU, am I right?" He nods to my left hand. The way he pronounces the word makes me think of a *cross ant* and wonder if he's ever even been to Europe. His eyes are on my cleavage. I don't understand why women complain about this: it's much less intense and more pleasant than eye contact. I can't think of anything to say so he continues.

"Are you free this lunchtime? I have the afternoon off before heading back up to Gothenburg. You seem to be a keen learner." This is a lie. I only asked about the breakfast. I was simply keen to learn when the buffet was served. "I have substantial knowledge and would love to share it." Now I get it. It takes a while. "You are *so* not street-smart, Klara!" Alice would howl at me regularly. "You would hop into a car with any guy offering you sweets." It's true. It's only when my heart starts pounding in my chest and I find my eyes look for the nearest emergency-exit sign I realize that someone is chatting me up. Luckily, he has asked me a *yes* or *no* question; those I can answer in about two seconds as opposed to the other ones that require careful analysis beforehand.

"No, I'm not free."

"Well, that's a shame."

"Not for me." He stares at me. I wave with the croissant,

and this has me thinking back to his pronunciation of it—not *croissant* but rather *cross-ant*, a butchering of the beloved pastry. I want him to get lost so I try to imitate the look of a cross ant, although this is tricky since I've never actually seen one.

He steps aside, muted, and I dash off to the bathroom and then on to the safety of my lavender-scented van. The van is not bad. I have wiped it down with a nice-smelling cleaner and put some snacks in the side of the door, and the heating settings are perfectly tuned so that it's a small oasis of calm and recuperation. Like one of those cocoons you can rent at a large airport to rest and sleep in.

I put on my R and B playlist. When I was a child, Saga used to calm me down. When the stress was building up, she found the one thing that could divert my attention and relax me.

"What happens in the second chapter of *The BFG*?" she would ask me, and I would recite to her how Sophie sees the giant, which turns out to be the BFG, and he has a suitcase and a cloak, and she hides under the covers in her bed. I would then stop for a breath, and Saga would say, "Good. Now the third chapter?" When I got older, she did this with Eminem songs. I preferred them to pop. The rhythm. I had to recite them quietly so that others didn't hear because they contained a lot of bad words, and if I were loud, it might offend those within earshot. Saga was brilliant at comforting me until we passed teenage years; then I seemed to acquire an unknown quality or perhaps it was a habit that made her tolerance for my company dwindle. Any longer than an hour and it felt like one big sigh.

On my Apple music playlist all my favorite calming songs are marked with an *E* for *explicit content*. It helps you know what to expect.

I glance at the screen now, starting to regain composure.

I don't mind *going out of my comfort zone*. I mean, I *wouldn't*, if only my comfort zone were larger than a van.

★ ★ ★

That afternoon I was called back to the big property the team finished two bathrooms in last week. The team tiled and fitted a large en suite bathroom with a his and hers sink in a loft. They opted for an off-white mosaic and black details, very trendy, the type of room that has an exclamation mark tied to it. At least, that's how I see the word. *Trendy!*

My boots clink against the fine gravel of the driveway. I stop to stroke the soft nose of a pony that is in a field next to the road. Horses have the relaxing smell of forest and childhood to me. In London I would never be able to afford riding lessons, but in Sweden it's the second-largest sport after soccer and something that has extended through to the working class.

"Thanks for coming," the lady, *Nina* according to my notes, says when she opens the door.

"Sure. One hundred percent customer satisfaction," I say quoting the website Saga still hasn't done any bloody work on.

"We seem to have a problem with one of the toilets."

"What sort of problem would that be?" I ask.

She is silent for a moment before saying with a lowered voice, "This is slightly embarrassing. Is there a way to make the water level decrease in the toilet? It seems to reach up quite high."

"No," I reply. Because I don't know. "It does not use up more water because the level is higher," I explain, concluding that she has called me back because of electricity-cost worries.

"I'm just going to say this. God, I'm happy you're a woman!" She looks at me as if I'm supposed to know what she means. I don't. But I'm pleased about what she said: I was under the impression that there was sexism in the industry and that customers expected and rather *hoped* for male handymen. "When my husband sits down...on the toilet...his...well his...*penis* seems to touch the water." She says *penis* with as much fear as I would say the word *bomb* in an airport.

"That sounds quite uncomfortable," I reply agreeably.

"God, I'm so happy you're not laughing at me. I can't tell you!" She laughs loudly.

I don't tend to laugh at my customers, as that would be bad for business. I pull out my phone to take notes in order to reach a solution. The page says her name, address, project dates and materials ordered and used. It also states that she drinks her tea black and wears slippers inside.

"How many inches would you say it is?" I ask. A glass of sparkling water has appeared at the kitchen island next to me as if by magic. This is the type of house where everyone who sets foot inside is provided with refreshments. I take a sip and look at the lady whose face is now strangely pink.

"How many inches?" I repeat. Patience with customers is a talent of mine, crafted during my time at YourMove. People would often not understand my question and need a repeat, completely to be expected considering the number of foreign-language speakers in England.

I smile and repeat, adding for clarity, "How many inches would you say that your partner's penis is? I know that the toilet bowl has a depth of 20.5 inches, and once I have the other numbers, I can figure out a solution."

She touches her left earlobe where a small pearl sits. The skin has gone a deep shade of red, and I imagine the heat it must radiate. I wish she would stop twirling it. Or do the same to the other so they would be less distracting. They are very different colors now. White and red. Like the red apple against Snow White's skin. She coughs.

"I...I wouldn't know."

"Would you be able to measure it tonight and send me the details? I can leave a measuring tape if you haven't got one."

"You would...leave your measuring tape?"

"It's no trouble."

I drain my water glass and move toward the sink to deposit it.

"Please leave it. Don't worry about the glass."

"Thank you."

"I'm not sure my partner would be too happy with any measuring. I was hoping you'd be able to simply adjust the water level."

"Ah, good thinking, but it does not in fact adjust." This was an example of a customer who expected us to do it all: even a small thing like measuring a body part is too much to ask.

"The only solution would be to switch the toilet for a special, taller bowl. I could have it ordered and replaced. But it would be a costly option. Think it over."

"Thank you for trying," she tells me in the doorway, the earlobe recovering some of its freedom finally, and the red subsiding.

"My pleasure," I say, then turn back, wanting to put the customer at ease with a subtle joke.

"Or should I say, *your pleasure*. That is a considerable size."

Nonstop Notifications are dying from laughter, and I have realized what is so funny. I should have known—preschool children laugh at toilet jokes, then follows a gap in which they are frowned upon, then once mature adult age has been reached it is once again the case that any mention of a private part is met with delight.

Saga: At least she will always know he's clean...

Mum: Klara's workday is better than reality TV.

Dad: How about a net solution? Something that holds it up above water?

Me: Do you want to put the patent application in or shall I?

I laugh. But somewhere deep down I also know that Nina will be laughing at me once her own embarrassment subsides, and I feel I've somehow messed up again.

ALEX

Personal Calendar ▼

○ **NEW TASK:** Think of excuse to cancel meeting Paul

○ **EDITED TASK:** Think of excuse other than having to drive at night

○ **EDITED TASK:** Fuck it. Just meet up with Paul, you loser

"It's on me," Paul says after we hug, hands slapping one another's back. Great, that means I can have an actual drink and not just go for whatever is the cheapest on the menu, which disappointingly happens to be a Polish alcohol-free beer.

"How have you actually been, man?" Paul asks. He's wearing a hoodie and sweatpants despite the fact it's seven o'clock and we are in a bar. His hair has changed into cornrows since we last met. I'm trying to remember how long it's been.

"Better." When the guys ask me how I am, I've understood they actually want to know—*they care*—but my answer needs to be the short version and delivered in an upbeat voice. The recap rather than the full twist-and-turn, digging-into-my-emotions story.

"You look it. Did you enter this into your to-dos to score a point? First time I'd be wholesome enough to be included in a recovery program, if that's the case."

"Everything goes in the to-dos. Kind of starting to like it." Almost obsessed with filling those three entries with, quite often, nonsense.

"What's new with you?" I ask.

"Met this girl on Tinder," Paul says. "Not sure why I even bother. I've read somewhere that a decent-looking guy has a 5 percent success rate of getting a match on Tinder. Basically, it's torture. We knowingly put ourselves out there knowing 95 percent will reject us. Most of the time when I flip through the faces, I don't even want to date anyone anyway, it's just become a habit," he says.

"That's not right, man. Like browsing the online store for new trainers you can't afford. Window-shopping girls," I say.

"Since when are you the Love Coach?"

"If you want a love coach, go and see my mum. Marrying off sons is her favorite thing. You know I couldn't care less about finding love."

"Well, some of us have hearts. And dicks," he says, smirking. "Don't worry, you'll get there. It hasn't even been that long."

"Long enough for the car repayments to be piling up. Not sure what to do about it. I'd like to keep it, but it's a lot of money for a car. Any suggestions?"

"The car is okay. The ring is just weird. It'd make more sense if Dan wore it. That being said, have you had more girls after you, though? I heard from a friend at work that girls were all over him once there was a ring on it, as if they saw him as wholesome and loyal suddenly."

"I haven't been out enough to try your friend's theory."

"I know, Alex. It was a joke."

"I will need to take over the lease of the car if I want to keep it. It's only half-paid, and the monthly installments are high," I share with him.

"If I could keep the car, I would. It's awesome."

The car is Calle's shiny new BMW that Dan has kindly let me keep for the time being. We haven't agreed on a date where I need to return it or if it's *actually* mine. It's a gray area. It's the one thing we are robbed of when someone dies suddenly, their last words, last wishes. I wouldn't even care what Calle would say—buy a pet fish and name it after me, give the car to that phenomenal Uber driver who prays for his grandma's varicose veins in Arabic every time we drive somewhere, throw my bad underwear out before Dan can see them. *I don't even care.* Some instruction would have been nice. Now Dan and I are stuck with all his belongings, and I at least don't have a clue what to do with them.

Don't tell Paul that another reason I can't give up the car is it would stop me being able to haunt the streets of Lund at night to find someone I can blame more than I do myself.

Notice a group of girls looking at us from the other side of the bar. Is it because of the ring, like Paul said? There was a time when I would have shot a smile and invited them over. When I thrived on the attention I got. No one noticed me until I turned seventeen. I was just Alex, the dorky kid who refused hanging out to spend his time playing video games or skateboarding in the park. Had started high school and got through the first year. Then my shoulders grew broader, I shot past Pappa in height, and the fat padding on my face seemed to have shed to reveal cheekbones and a jawline I never knew I had. I was good-looking, and it became my commodity. Always had a girlfriend, not really sure I loved any of them, but I certainly didn't *mind* them. Then I guess I was approaching thirty, looking at Calle and Dan, and started to think love was possible.

Paul nudges my arm.

"Earth to Alex."

"Sorry. Listening."

"Why don't you get a job again? I mean you have the easiest

profession to get a job in. It could help you get back on track with life."

"I'm not sure I want to go back to being a project manager. Just the thought of all the people it involves gives me a fucking headache." I used to be in charge of a small team for a large local carpentry firm, a move to further my career and keep up with my friends who all seemed to get fancier and fancier job titles and more professional LinkedIn headshots done. One friend went from banker's assistant to head of risk investment opportunities. No idea what that even means. Turned out a manager role wasn't for me. All my time was spent in an office making spreadsheets and phone calls, and my hands were itching to work so badly I offered friends my services on weekends. I was very popular for a while.

"So get a different job. Just a regular one. Do some carpentry work. I'm sure you can start part-time or even freelance. And if you don't like it, quit. What have you got to lose?" *My peace and quiet and mornings playing* FIFA. I don't say this out loud.

The drinks are finished, but neither Paul nor I get up to get another round.

"I know you're worried. Trust me. I know. I picked you up that day, I drove you there." *There.* Fucking *there.* The place where my parents almost didn't show up. Only to the cafeteria to meet me for a lift home, lattes in hand and best clothes on. They were nervous, didn't know what to do or why this had happened and were still so focused on losing Calle they couldn't deal with another crisis. I could swear I saw them look over their shoulders scared to run into someone they knew and have to explain that their son wasn't there for a broken bone or a fever. No, his buddy had picked him up from work because he had suddenly been found sitting on the floor, shaking like a drug user who's gone cold turkey. Except it was a panic attack. When I realized Paul had brought me to the ER I knew I'd never set foot at my workplace again. Or any workplace, it seems.

"It would solve the car dilemma," I say instead of going into that dark territory. I am getting by okay, mainly because I've been a squirrel all my life, saving for a rainy day, which came last August finally. But I can't afford luxuries such as a posh car, or even a beer, without something coming into my account again, which has been subject to one-way traffic the past few months. May not have luxury of ignoring Jobcenter's emails much longer.

"There you go, then."

As I step outside and say goodbye to Paul, the rain soaks me in seconds. Life in Sweden is predictable in the best of ways: no war, no earthquakes, no political coups, and so it's only fair that the weather does not follow suit. I look at myself from the outside for minute. What has become of me? Is that you, Calle? Did you just open the sky and spit cold water on me to say *wake up*? I shelter by the edge of a house and take my phone out of my pocket to kill time. What the fuck? How did this get here? I didn't put that entry there. I shoot a text to Paul.

Me: Did you just mess with my phone and tamper with my calendar/plan/life?

Paul: Guilty.

For fuck's sake. I look at the to-do notes for tomorrow, blinking hard once, hoping they will disappear. They don't.

O **NEW TASK:** Look for a job (properly)

O **NEW TASK:** Apply for job

O **NEW TASK:** Go to interview/accept job if an option

The rain peters out. The smell of it lingering like in a cool, humid steam room.

Guess I have no choice, then. I am going to break the status quo: I am going to get a job. It will make Dr. Hadid happy, if nothing else. Text Paul, Thanks, buddy.

KLARA

🔍 Do I need to get laid?

Google Search   **I'm Feeling Lucky**

I've spent the biggest part of the morning out on appointments, and when I finally arrive back at the warehouse, it's three o'clock. I wave hello to Gunnar who is stacking up boxes using the small forklift, doing a neat job fitting them all in at the end of the parking area. I know that they are for the bathroom in Veberöd and the guest apartment in a basement of a villa in Lund. The guys pick up what they need for each day's work here instead of storing it in the customer's limited living space. It's a much more pleasant system. Appointments are not the only thing I have to manage. There are the keys to each customer's home, I have to plan the schedule of three other people and organize the material, which has to turn up to the right property at the right time. My dad handed over his black leather-bound calendar as if it were the holy grail, his handwriting neat and precise, line after line all the way up until the autumn. After just a few days it was riddled with my illegible writing so that even I am now struggling to understand my own instructions.

I clutch my reusable metal mug and push open the office door and am just about to say a loud and cheery hello when I freeze, realizing I should be the only person here. The voices of two men, Mateusz and Ram, reach me. Why aren't they in Lund? I could swear that's what their schedule says. For sure they have no business in the home office at this time of day. What they say next startles me.

"She's on her period, that's for sure." Who? His wife? *Me?*

"She needs to get laid, probably hasn't been shagged in years. So stiff, walking around here like she actually serves a purpose." They both break into laughter. *They are making fun of me.*

Do I need to get laid? I know this comment is bad because once I was pointing out to the supermarket staff that some red apples had gotten in with the green apples, and the young boy with an acne-scar-dimpled face said, "Chill. You need to get fucking laid." Alice took a step forward and said, "Are you offering?" like it was a threat, and the man apologized. *Men think that dick is the answer and medicine for everything. Depression? Sore throat? Prescribe some glorious dick*, Alice said on the bus home.

I googled it anyway, just to be sure, and the first thing that came up was *Cosmopolitan* saying that if your bed was taken over by books, magazines, a laptop, hadn't seen fresh sheets in an eternity and was full of crumbs, then yes, you may need to get laid. I would never tolerate crumbs in my bed: they are worse than the pea that princess had to endure under her mattresses. Hard and crispy and small enough to accidentally get into your knickers.

Now I'm standing frozen. My stomach clenching like a fist. Then I dig deep and get that fist out, ready to fight, hauling it out from where it's punching me. I walk around the corner.

"Excuse me, gentlemen. Can I have a word, please?" They

stare at me and the ground alternatively, as if expecting something to pop out of it. A mole perhaps.

"It was just harmless jokes," Mateusz says finally.

"Those type of comments are not acceptable." I feel a mix of anger and sadness boil up inside me. All this time I've felt like a failure, like I'm doing things wrong. And here in front of me are two people who clearly don't even try. Who dodge work and use their time for mocking me.

"No bad feelings, eh? We were just joking around," Ram says.

"Those types of comments are unacceptable at work. I'm sure my dad wouldn't tolerate that either."

"Oh, what's the big deal? Maybe I was right, maybe you do need to get laid." Mateusz snorts to himself.

"I see. Well, guess what, I do need something laid. You two. Laid *off* with immediate effect."

The disbelief on their faces is priceless.

"Peter is going to hear about this. You think you can come for three months and do what you want to this company?" Mateusz barks at me. But he does pick up his bag and heads toward his van, Ram following after like a puppy.

In real life, there is no choir of sisters cheering you on saying *Whoa, you stood up for yourself, you feminist, you!* There is just a pounding heart, sweaty palms and the sound of men's laughter as they walk off pretending not to care. I would have liked a choir or a round of applause. How else am I to know it was the right decision? I can't believe I just did that. It's all a mess now. I have a calendar so full I need to hold my breath to look at it, and now my workforce has just decreased to one (a thin, unassuming number not ideal as total staff count). In this particular circumstance, *one* is a scary number. Lonely and easy to knock over.

I call my dad as soon as I'm alone.

"What happened?" He knows my upset voice better than anyone else.

"We—*I*—just lost two employees. As in I fired them. They are lost because I told them to get lost. They…they said some things about me… I haven't had a good feeling about Mateusz since I arrived." My voice breaks. "I'm sorry, Dad."

He pauses.

"If you fired them, then you must have had a good reason. I don't question that you are doing the right thing." I'm grateful because it all happened so fast. Too fast for me to know if my reaction was, in fact, an overreaction.

"Thanks, Dad." He is trying to be supportive, but I can hear the panic in his voice. He must feel as if he's watching the house burn down and he's not allowed to run in and help stop the disaster or reach for the hose. I look down at my feet. My toes tap the floor nervously. I should never have come here, should never have allowed myself to be persuaded. *What Klara touches turns into a mess.* Why didn't anyone listen?

Dad makes a shushing sound, which has the same effect as his large hand on my knee. It stops the tapping.

"We will sort this out tonight, petal. But, Klara, one thing. We need three men on the ground. You have to put together an ad and fill the positions immediately. No time to lose. A carpenter is the most urgent."

PART TWO

The month of March in Malmö experiences essentially constant cloud cover, with the percentage of time that the sky is overcast or mostly cloudy remaining about 62 percent throughout the month. The clearest day of the month is March 31, with clear, mostly clear or partly cloudy conditions 40 percent of the time.

KLARA

Q Where can I find female construction staff?

Google Search   I'm Feeling Lucky

We're heading toward March, which means that it gets dark at 5:30 instead of 4:30. What a treat. I wrap my coat even tighter around my body, cursing the sun for only being decorative. Like the pointless gas fireplaces in London.

Mateusz and Ram reluctantly handed in their van keys and tools once they realized my dad was behind me, and I would feel relieved if it weren't for the warning I got in the tile warehouse this morning.

"I would watch it, if I were you. They won't go calmly or without trouble. There will be talk and all sorts of things," Lennart says. He is the owner and a kind man I remember from childhood for placing lollies, stickers and other treasures in my hand whenever we met.

We have too much work. If I felt useless before, it's nothing compared to now. All I can do is look on as Gunnar stresses and works overtime to finish. It doesn't take long to find out that Lennart was right.

"We had a call this morning," Gunnar says when I meet him back at Dad's house. "The client in Veberöd wants to cancel his booking with us. He is going ahead with Ram."

Great, so the guys who I am replacing are luring our clients away. I watch his concerned face.

"Have we had any others canceling?"

"I looked into it after the call. In August, a small project, same reason obviously. If they are willing to do the job for twenty percent less, why wouldn't the customer choose them? How are they to know they're getting lower quality?"

The hard-earned wet-room certificate, I think. They don't have one when they should.

"Damn it. We can't afford to lose projects like that."

"I'm more worried about what they might say... I overheard a group of guys in the hardware store say how the firm won't survive the three months without leadership. I'm sorry, Klara. You know I'm on your side."

"It's okay. I prefer to know."

I can't give Dad back a company that has no cash flow and nothing to do. I may have overshared with Gunnar, but he is faithfully behind me, and it is his job and livelihood that are concerned. God, I never understood the responsibility that employing someone is. They rely on you to feed their family. I have to keep this going for his sake. And Dad's. And mine. I didn't want this responsibility, and perhaps a week ago I could have shrugged it off. But when I made the decision to let people go, I took on a role. I can't give it up now. I curl my toes inside the steel-toe shoes I finally managed to track down in my size.

"All our partners are still supportive," Gunnar says. "The tile supplier, the hardware store, we are everyone's top recommendation. Couldn't get better ratings."

"What about social media?" I ask myself out loud. "Are we

doing enough?" Gunnar shakes his head, and I answer my own question.

"No. Unless a before-and-after of a bathroom tiled three years ago is considered persuasive advertising, then no."

"I would keep this quiet. No need to get Peter worked up and worried. Not yet," Gunnar says, and I think, the only thing I brought with me from London was a history of failures. How on earth can I fix this?

I asked Dad for a template to use for the advertising of new staff, but it turns out he hasn't hired since 2010, and even then he used a poster in the tile shop with little paper strips you could pull off. I doubt who I'm searching for would find me that way. But I'm pleased to say I have a plan. I've figured out what is missing. What I need is some female energy. In London there are pink taxis when a woman is driving. A whole fleet of girls! Obviously, Dad won't approve of a paint job on the vans, but I *am* free to hire who I want. Dad's tiredness was rated an 8 last night so he won't be joining interviews. *As long as the cancer is a 1 we can handle an 8 on this other scale, Klara*, he reassured me.

I start composing an ad to place on a recruitment website, taking all of my bad experiences in this industry so far into account.

"We are a successful and established business specializing in wet room, tiling and bespoke carpentry seeking a new colleague. Qualifications a must, as is a recent criminal background check. The ideal candidate should:

- Be female

- Reply to messages in a timely manner (no ghosting bosses or clients)

- Have infrequent episodes of food poisoning on Mondays

- Not look at clients' backsides (incurring complaints)

- Have a good track record of putting toilet seats down

Is this you? Then, we'd love to hear from you! Please apply with CV and cover letter to klara@byggnilsson.com

I sit back in my chair, click Post and imagine the fleet of pink vans we are soon to have.

Four days later I have enough emails to spend the morning reading through applications, listing the five that sound interesting in alphabetical order. My first interview, with the A candidate on the list, is arranged already the same afternoon, and I read through her cover email one more time as I pack up and leave the office to join Dad inside the house for a quick lunch.
She writes:

To address your specific points:

Only thing I've been guilty of ghosting is a dentist appointment.

Very good at eye contact (no looking at body parts). Practice the useful tip of focusing between person's eyebrows for best effect.

Feel I may exceed your expectations on the toilet-seat point: am also fully trained in the use of toilet brush.

Practically a cleanfluencer. If influencing my own OCD positively counts?

Available immediately (never happened before, don't miss this chance!)

Kind regards,

Alex

I'm liking this girl. I forgot to ask about personal hygiene and liking pets. Not too strict on the first one as long as requirement of using deodorant daily is met; second one is trickier. Customers like talking about their pets. *A lot.* Stroking a dog as you enter a property is practically part of the job. I communicate this to Alex, and to my delight she seems okay with it.

Love dogs, only ever had a problem with one particular pet but that was a pet badger recovering from surgery (long story) and it was living in (and eating) my living room. Application of deodorant performed twice daily (do you need the brand ahead of decision making?)

I smile. I imagine her as a feisty girl with a short haircut who wears the pants in her relationship. She doesn't like heels but looks amazing when she does wear them. She drinks her coffee strong but with sugar, out-lifts the guys in the weight corner of the gym and never backs away from the challenge of carrying a box of tiles up a flight of stairs. She is an amazing driver and will laugh at my pathetic attempts to parallel park. She has at least one tattoo and reads thrillers and fantasy in her spare time. *Okay, enough already, Klara.*

I send her the address for our interview. I'm finding Swedish professional language a challenge. There is no *Mr.* or *Mrs.* or *Dear* used, just a *hi* or *hello* and a first name. There is no system. I just instinctively have to know what is suitable.

It's a date! Kind regards, Klara Nilsson.

ALEX

Personal Calendar ▾

○ **NEW TASK:** Get to interview

○ **NEW TASK:** Act professional and cool (like the job is already yours)

○ **NEW TASK:** Don't show signs of weakness or depression

Interview lady seems a bit weird. Possibly not Swedish. *It's a date* is not something you say even to your actual date, unless you're stuck in the '80s by means of time travel or denial. Choose to ignore weirdness as also seems funny and easygoing enough, and I have my calendar not to disappoint. Doing well in that sense, have ticked off *water plants* (singular cactus but the calendar doesn't have to know that) on a consistent basis now. I am making my calendar happy, and that is what matters as this will, eventually, make *me* happy, according to Dr. Hadid.

The service station smells of mustardy hot dogs and freshly brewed coffee. I've been coming here for years.

"Any chance you can throw in a coffee with that fuel?" I ask, doing my best smile at the counter, well aware it doesn't have the same effect as when I was a kid. At least not on straight men like Patrik.

"Coffee is 25 kronor. You know that, Alex. It's very reasonable," he says, passing me the receipt for the quarter tank of petrol, which should get me to the interview and back.

"I should have my loyalty card somewhere in here." Dig deep and find some gravel, chewing gum and a coin. *Why have my pocket contents not evolved since I was five?*

"Fine. Only this once." He hands me an empty paper cup, and I gratefully walk over to the self-service area, filling my cup with a filter brew and topping it off with some milk.

"Don't worry, I won't be broke forever! I have a job interview this afternoon."

"Ever considered selling that car of yours? You wouldn't have to beg me for coffee if you released that fifty grand. Still can't believe Dan just gave it to you."

"You know it has sentimental value. I'm not ready to let it go just yet."

"So you keep saying. Good luck today. You deserve it. How long is it since you lost him…?" I hate that. *Lost him.* As if we didn't take enough care and he just got away, like a pet with a garden gate left open. We didn't lose anyone: he was taken from us. I'm sure of it.

"Always missed," Patrik says. It's true. Everyone liked Calle. Usually more than me, if they knew us both.

On my way out I notice that the poster appealing for a witness that I put up and which sat there for months—six to be precise, until the color faded—is now gone.

KLARA

"Yes?"

The knock on the door has me sitting up straight. Three times in a row, as if spelling out a word or a secret code rather than asking to come in. Tap-tap-tap. I had expected Alex to deliver a gentle, questioning sort of a knock before appearing in the doorway and becoming my new construction BFF.

The door swings open before I have a chance to say *come in*. This is *not* a good sign. As a head followed by a torso pops into view, my foot starts tapping and I really *really* wish I had some heavy soothing rap blasting in my ear. Because this is a *surprise*. Whoever I was expecting, I was not expecting *this*. Firstly, it's a him. I study him in detail just to be sure. Yup. Gender is definitely *male*, assumed preferred pronoun *him*, title *Mr.*

My chest feels tight.

"I'm Alex," he says with a southern accent that rolls on each letter, lingering in the doorway, noticing my hesitation. *Alex.* Of course, he's a *male* Alex. *You knobhead, Klara.* I regain my composure and—I'm proud to say—manage some coherent speech.

"Oh, sorry, do come in. Please excuse my surprise, it's just that I specifically asked for female applicants." If my statement embarrasses him, he hides it well, giving me a slight smile as he enters the room, obviously determined to go through with the interview. He has stopped in front of my desk, and I'm ridiculously aware of just how tall and broad he is. He practically blocks the sunlight from entering the room, and I'm about to ask him to scoot to the side because rays of sun are precious in this country, when he addresses me.

"We have something called discrimination laws in this country." I look at him with disbelief. He has very blue eyes. I quickly bring up the ad on my phone, scrolling through the published version. *Scheibe.* He's right. There are my ever so important requirements all listed in order but without the first important requirement: *gender.* It must have been automatically removed when posting the ad. I guess I should have included that it was in order to balance the female to male ratio, and maybe it would have been allowed. Too late now.

Shit. All I wanted was some female energy and Mr. 10/10 Tradesman turns up, looking like he just stepped out of a Google search for *attractive Swede with tool kit.* Messy blond hair, pale skin—as in vampire-pale, but in an attractive way—and silver-blue eyes the color of a frozen lake. He is wearing a T-shirt, unzipped hoodie and joggers, in a lightweight fabric which has most likely been marketed as *gym to coffee date* attire. But still. Hardly very professional. Despite my disapproval I can't help but look. His disheveled appearance is...*distracting.*

I do *not* like distractions.

"Discrimination laws, you say?" I manage, my voice is so shrill it wouldn't surprise me if it's in a frequency only dolphins can hear. The corners of his eyes wrinkle. The room feels very small suddenly, as if I'm locked in an elevator with a stranger.

Gosh, do I always produce this much saliva? I bite my lip.

"If I can fulfill the criteria, you have no reason not to hire me." Is that a smirk? And a *dimple*? He deposits a thick bunch of documents in front of me, seemingly forgetting that he could have just done a few swipes on an iPad and produced them digitally, thus saving time and paper. And that he sent it with his application already.

I quickly skim the pile in front of me. Then I scan him—there is *a lot* to look at—and only stop when Alice's excellent advice on meeting strangers pops up. *Relax, Klara. Whatever you do, don't stare. Your intensity makes people feel as if you're giving them an X-ray.* I look down at my own feet, tapping the floor, at which point Alex continues talking.

"I also have solid experience in construction in general, not just carpentry, if you go back a few pages." He leans in over the table to point me in the right direction, and I can't help but register his smell. He smells of fresh linen and shampoo, no aftershave or overpowering perfume. I also notice his wedding band and…that makes sense. Gorgeous men are usually married. It's gold-plated and softly rounded, slightly too tight on the finger. *Taken* it says. Like a towel on a Tenerife poolside deck chair. Not up for grabs, darling. *Good*. Because I'm not in Sweden to fall for confident, blond men. I'm here to work and try my best not to mess things up further.

"Right. I see." But I don't really see it. He appears to have left his position at a Malmö firm six months ago, leaving the reference section blank. Blank pages and gaps are particularly annoying: it means we have to fill them in with our own imagination. I have understood that it's rude to ask the person to fill in their intentional gaps. Say they tell you that their boyfriend cheated, and you ask with whom? That was not part of the story, and the gap had been left there on purpose. I decide to ask something other than *What have you been doing for the past six months and seventeen days?*

"Why do you need this job?" I look him in the eye and therefore the words come out slightly slower than they usually do. I speak the fastest when I look at the ground.

"Because life?" He gives me a knowing smile, and I relate to him for a split second. Then I feel annoyed. Vague, I think. Answering with a question.

"Listen, I'm hardworking and punctual, good at what I do. I have managerial experience too. I currently have no job for reasons beyond this interview, and I just need a break. It would be great if you could give it to me despite my Y chromosome."

I flinch. Apparently, he can be straightforward, *arrogant* even. Hiring him would be a huge mistake. *Whatever I do, I must not hire this man.* I don't have a reason, though: he fills the criteria and is available immediately, hasn't tried to negotiate the salary, and appears clean and respecting of basic hygiene. I can't fight sexism with reversed sexism. We need a carpenter and, voilà, here is one.

He looks around the room when I don't immediately speak, and my gaze follows his like he's a potential shoplifter. Am I *sweating?* Can't be. Because tall, arrogant men do *not* make me sweat. This interview has to end because I need fresh air. Air that is not shared with *Alex.*

I hand his documents back. He stretches out his hand to take them, but I drop them onto the table before he can reach the file. I do *not* want to touch that hand. Or the person it belongs to.

"Alex. Thank you so much for coming all the way out here. I know it's a bit of a trek from Malmö. I will let you know the outcome by tomorrow." I look at the floor when I speak, already planning next week's schedule in my head, a schedule which sees me and Alex working in different locations.

I walk him to the door. Have to make sure he's really leaving. I watch him press a fob, and a black BMW in the parking lot lights up twice as if saying *hello, hello*. God, this guy must be full of himself. Probably spends his weekend washing the thing. I bet he spends more on its cleaning products than I do on my hair conditioner.

"Nice car," I say in my best sarcastic tone.

"Thanks, it means a lot to me."

Ha. I was right. Told you, kisses-his-car-good-night guy. Long after he has driven off on the half-frozen road, the consistency of a defrosting steak, I feel stirred and unsettled.

Goose bumps. The interview process has given me actual goose bumps.

ALEX

Several hours later I am still processing what just happened. Which sounds like this: an interview. But that felt like fucking this: nerves, flinching, sweaty palms rubbing on trousers and…*excitement?*

Fuck.

Interview lady looked nothing like expected. She is average height, but that's where average leaves the room. She has the largest, brownest eyes I've seen. She was wearing a baggy black T-shirt with the company's logo in white, and jeans with heavy boots, steel toed. That shirt hung loosely over her body, hiding every area of interest. Not that I'm interested. *Not at all.* Her dark hair was in a bun on top of her head, wavy strands of it breaking loose as if angry at something. Wouldn't want to mess with her hair. Or her.

She is the type of girl guys want to tell to smile more, I

couldn't help but think, as she looked at me like I was some-thing the cat brought in. All the banter and weirdness from last night's email exchange gone. Tried to stay professional, but all I could think about was how I need to get this job—need to pay the car bills, need to reclaim a sense of purpose in life, need to check off items on the calendar—but I now also want this job so that I can see her again.

A few hours later, Interview Lady is changed to Boss Lady in the Alex mental headquarters as she calls and offers me the job. Short, matter-of-fact tone, professional. Notice annoyingly that her voice makes my heart rate go up. And that I can't help but smile. *Smile.* When did that happen last? She seems anything but thrilled, and her *looking forward to seeing you on Monday* con-veys the exact opposite meaning. Don't care. Feel something I haven't felt in months.

Dig out my work clothes and decide I feel happy to see them. Think about taking the ring off. I don't usually wear jewelry when I work. It fights back as I jerk at it forcibly, then move on to rinse it under water with a drop of soap. When I finally place it on the bathroom shelf, my finger has a white imprint where it used to be. Like a ghost ring. Bothers me. My ghosts are what're haunting me.

End up putting the ring back on an hour later.

KLARA

🔍 What is the appropriate distance for personal space?

Google Search   **I'm Feeling Lucky**

Three days into his employment—and much to my amazement—Alex is working out wonderfully. He is on time, a hard worker and naturally polite. Customers like him. Only oddness would be his habit to stare. At me. I'm usually the one doing the staring, a hard one like Paddington Bear, I've been told. Mostly people's eyes firmly avoid mine once they've met them. Like I'm in a constant stranger-on-the-Tube scenario.

His stare is not intruding; I don't exactly *mind* it. I guess this is what it would be like to be famous, or a very beautiful person, the kind that people watch. It's not a stare that says *imagining you naked* or *wish you could finish talking now* or any of those things. He looks genuinely interested, like a child would, perhaps. And telling children to not stare, well, it seems futile: children have a tendency to do exactly what they want. So I've accepted staring as part of the deal.

It's our first staff meeting since he joined. Me, Alex, Gunnar. *Then there were three.*

"Good morning, boss." Alex doesn't say it like a joke, not like people tend to do since I've found myself in this position. He simply walks up and shakes my hand. And—oh.

I'm in proximity to Alex. *Very* close, my built-in sensor is going off alerting of imminent danger, or something. It's clear that I have not yet adjusted to our new team member. Our bodies are an inch away from touching, and I'm painfully aware of it. The small hairs on my arm stand up as if they're trying to break through the confinement of the skin, and it's hard to swallow, like I'm in the dentist's chair and every gulp is a loud awkward event.

And *his smell*. It's overpowering, and somehow I can swear it sticks to the thin hairs in my nostrils like frost on straws of grass, because even after he's passed by it's there. Wildflowers and crisp sea. Is that even a *thing*? Haven't seen it on a fragrance ad. *So he smells like seaweed?* Alice asked me when I told her all about the annoying new employee.

I googled *can you ask employee to wear perfume?* but the verdict was that it's only acceptable if you work in certain professions, building work not included.

I feel like Alex doesn't realize the effect he has on…*people.*

Luckily, before I can think more troubling thoughts, my arm beeps.

"Yes, what is it, Ollie?" I address the arm as if it is about to answer me, staring down at it, then remembering Alex. I pull up my shirtsleeve to reveal the small flat rectangular box that sticks to my arm with an adhesive sticker.

"Please meet Ollie. Ollie this is Alex. He works with me."

Alex acts as if talking to a small gray chip is the most natural thing in the world to do.

"You've named your pump?"

"Ollie Omnipod. My main man, keeping me alive every

single day. Right now, he's telling me he's running out of insulin in six hours."

"Pleased to meet him. Any friend of Klara's is a friend of mine. Why Ollie?"

"I like alliteration. I have Charlie the CGM as well." I show my left arm and its inhabitant. "I like the idea of two people on my team, my bodyguards, if you will. Charlie is a popular guy. He has four followers. Although, three of them are my family."

Alex nods in greeting to Charlie, looking genuinely pleased to meet him.

"Bluetooth?" he asks.

"Yep. No such thing as magic, is there?"

It shouldn't be this easy to get on with Alex. I don't do well around people like him. *Beautiful people.* People with well-defined biceps and smooth skin and who wear confidence like it's a new sweater they'd just found in a shop. *Oh, this old thing? Nothing special.* Well, to me it's special: people who smile like Alex remind me of everything I'm not. Which is a lot of things.

The main problem with Alex is that he disturbs my peace. And I like my peace. A survival kit is in order if I am to handle this, and my first tool in it must be Safe Distance, I conclude. I decide on two yards, give or take. Any more seems too extreme, especially when handing something over such as keys or a note (my arms are not that long). Google says that personal space starts at eighteen inches or an arm's length and ends at forty-eight inches, the height of an average six-year-old. With Alex I need more than that of a primary-school child. A place for everything, and everything in its place. Alex's place is *not* right next to me.

I sit down on the chair farthest from my new employee.

"Any news on a new tiler?" Gunnar asks me now. "Even given the cancellations, we're struggling to keep up."

"Yes." I think I got my girl this time. "I have an interview this afternoon."

A young apprentice named Hanna who has just graduated with a diploma in tiling and for whom we would be her first paid position. She was a recommendation from Lennart, which I happily took, especially since my first attempt to hire a female turned out so disastrously.

"Good, Klara, because have a look at this." Gunnar shows me his screen which I study with concern. Another email saying someone regrettably needs to cancel the job, and even after Gunnar explained that their deposit would be lost, they insisted. I am starting to have a bad feeling in my tummy, like one single moth flying around, but I decide not to worry Dad about it yet. I have Gunnar, Alex and Hanna to put things back on track now. And Saga, if she could ever get her act together with the website she promised to sort out.

"We can't do anything other than keep being the best at what we do. No point in stressing about it," Alex tells me and I can't help but notice that he's already including himself in the team, *we*. I have a sudden idea.

"Will you teach me some carpentry? If there is time. And if it's no trouble." I used to love houses, once upon a time. Before reality hit me in the back of the head and ended my plans and aspirations, limiting me to reading books on architecture. But still, I'd like to be more useful.

"Sure."

"Thanks."

Alex is pulling his sweater off, and in the process it gets tangled with the T-shirt, and his flat, hard stomach shows. I immediately regret suggesting carpentry lessons because I can tell that the work conditions won't be ideal, what with teachers undressing and showing abdomens as they please. *Keep walking.* Turns out I don't follow my own instructions. I stop in the door frame as if it's impossible to leave without looking back. In all fairness he stared at me, so why shouldn't I be able to look at him? For self-preservation I should probably avoid it. There's no other way to describe him than this: he's the Viking font, Mjölnir. Bold, unique and attention-grabbing but in a size 8, which also makes him quiet. And can make it difficult when trying to read between the lines.

"Bye, Viking." The words slip out before I can even process them. Luckily, he seems amused rather than offended.

"Viking? As in killer pirate?"

"Well, *Viking* is actually a verb. You set out *viking*. They were normal tradesmen, blacksmiths and farmers who went raid-ing, so my sister tells me. I didn't mean it as per its definition, I meant it as some sort of compliment. The same way people call you *princess* or *pet*, despite the person being neither. Viking is also a Microsoft font." *Oh my God, stop babbling, you knobhead.*

"I got it. Thanks. I like it," he says, and something very funny happens inside me as I reverse out of the room with small steps.

"You can call me Viking anytime."

Goose bumps *again*. I must turn the heating up despite Dad's grumbling about energy prices. Can't have everyone around here getting goose bumps all the time.

Hanna has energy. Her T-shirt is neon green and reads *stay lit* in block capitals. I could use some of that lit-ness, because every time the buzz of being around Alex wears off, an ex-haustion hits. I feel drained, as if I've used up all my emotions and have nothing left. I guess some fonts just strain your eyes more. I'm sure if I were to google *best fonts for eyesight*, I'd find Mjölnir at the very bottom.

I sigh, pick myself up and focus on the interview.

When I show Hanna the checklist from the ad I posted she laughs and says, "I think I'll like working with you."

Dad has briefed me heavily on not oversharing. *Do not tell them we are losing contracts or what happened with the last two employ-*

ees, K. So I focus on the positives: the pension contribution, the delightful team members and our bean-to-cup coffee machine.

"You have only just graduated. Do you feel ready to work independently?" I say.

"Absolutely." She sticks her chin up as if she worries I won't believe her. But I do. Even though she's only nineteen, she has a confidence that is so effortless I can spot it from this briefest of meetings. I used to think if I surrounded myself with normal, confident people it would rub off on me, and I would absorb some of it and get to call it my own. It was only much later that I realized that confidence, like a gym membership, is personal and nontransferable.

My finger slides across the iPhone screen, and I look down at it. Blood-sugar surveillance is the perfect excuse to take a minute away from the intense conversation and eye contact of an interview. My graph line is perfect, horizontal and centered.

So I'm forced to look up again.

"I'd be happy to employ you on a trial basis," I say. "You'd be working with Gunnar, our resident tiler, until you get the hang of it all."

She lights up. "Amazing! Thank you *so* much."

"One more thing. Are you by any chance adept at website design and social media? My sister, Saga, was meant to take care of it but has turned out to not be helpful at all." I realize I just overshared and cover my mouth with my hand to avoid anything else slipping out. Hanna doesn't seem to mind.

"I'd say I could handle that, yes."

"Splendid."

ALEX

Personal Calendar ▾

○ **NEW TASK:** Sync calendars

Shared Calendar ▾

○ **NEW TASK:** Can you see this, Klara?

Reply (Klara): Received, with many thanks.

Survived a week at work. More than survived. When you are busy working there is no time to think about your dead brother or if you have met all your milestones a year ahead of turning thirty. No clue about that last one. No one has invited me to any milestone checks since I was five, only a full physical at the GP with blood pressure and cholesterol screening when I turned twenty-nine. How would I know if I had failed at life since they stop checking on us in adulthood? No one goes *Do you eat a varied diet, Alex? Can you think of three topics for small talk in a minute? Put these two in order of importance, a working movie-streaming subscription or a pension fund?* We are left hanging, wondering if we are normal.

I stretch the sharp, stiff measuring tape out along the wood. It has a light brown color with patterns that are circular. It would have been cut from a fairly young tree; the outer side of the trunk is my guess. I run my finger over it, it's polished perfectly, smooth and flexible. I mark it with my pencil (which needs sharpening) and go to run it through the cutting machine to take the ends off. There is no need to try it against the wall—I know that the skirting will fit. That's numbers for you. It's not a guessing game. The one thing I excelled at in school was numbers. The noise rings in my ear and through to my brain, the front of my forehead wobbling like jelly from riding the sound waves. Should remember to wear my noise dampeners next time.

My boss has asked me to teach her as long as it's no trouble. Must stop calling her that; she has a name. In fact, it's a nice name. *Klara*. It means *manage* in Swedish and comes from the Latin for *bright* or *clear*. She does seem like someone who can manage a lot of things, the type of person you'd say has a lot on her plate. The clear part, however, not too sure. She seems rather distracted and has a foggy sadness about her that I can't figure out the origins of. I keep wanting to make her smile because when she does, she lives up to her name. Clear, transparent and unclouded. Bright, even.

Have to say, for someone whose name means *clear* and *managing*, she is surprisingly bad at timekeeping and has poor organizational skills. Not sure if I should offer help or if it will be met by her trademark murder stare. Learning how to avoid it as best I can. For example, she prefers messages to calls. The first day I made the mistake of calling, and I swear the murder stare was so strong I could feel it through the phone.

"Who even calls these days? I thought it was an emergency." (Klara)

"Phones are still in use, you know. Acceptable and efficient way of communication." (Me)

"Acceptable in an emergency. Is there one?" (Klara)

"You have a point, I guess. Mostly salespeople and the—" I stop myself from adding *therapy receptionist* "—dental office calls me." Great. Now she'll wonder what big issue I have with my teeth. Only issue in that department is that my mouth is too big for my own good.

Teaching her is no trouble at all. In theory. Practically, it kind of is. It's a shame wood can't stop me being distracted by Klara when it works wonders in the other areas of my life. The trouble is, I'm way too aware of where she is in the room. Felt relief when I figured out that my possessiveness must be because she has a medical condition—it's only right that if I work with her I should be alert. It's practically my *responsibility*, part of my role. As a fellow human. Nothing else. Definitely nothing else. Depressed and not even looking at women.

Ended up in a Google trap last night of researching diabetes (again, my *responsibility* really), and it's fascinating. The math aspect is fascinating. Carbohydrates in versus glucose spent and then the insulin acts as a variable that affects them both.

Earn myself another murder stare this morning.

"I know you have diabetes, and you don't have to tell me everything, but I'd like to know a little, so I can help you if you need it. Since we work together now," I say.

She full body sighs.

"I'm not incapacitated, Alex. I just have unpredictable blood sugar. I know myself and my body well enough by now. That includes my limits. But if you must know—if I'm low, I need sugar. If I'm high, I need insulin. It's all in my bum bag. That's all you need to know. Please don't bring it up again."

"Here I was thinking you were trying to be stylish." I point at the black Nike accessory that clings to her softly contoured waist.

"Have you seen me? Style and Klara don't go together." She

sticks a plank under my nose, arms stretched out. I wonder why she doesn't just take a step forward: she's so far away from me she looks like she's about to fall over. "Is this good?" she asks.

I tell her yes, and then I hesitate because I don't want to overstep some boundary—she loves a *boundary*, it seems. But she did just stick a plank under my nose, and when I stepped toward her, she was so close I could feel her breath against my chest. Not that I was thinking about it. The breath. Or the mouth that it came from. Force myself to focus on something else. Like her clothes. They are a soft blue sweater and black pants that may or may not be leggings.

"Why don't we grab some lunch? Skip the quick sandwich for once," I suggest. "Seeing that we both need to eat, we could just go together."

We head to a small Japanese lunch restaurant close to the train station. There's not a single Japanese person, staff included. I take a poke bowl, Klara goes for sushi. She explains her diet to me, the brief version. Seems incredibly complicated. Can't judge, though, as mine currently exists of pizzas and jalapeños.

"Ants are off-limits then, you know, if you ever go somewhere they serve them dipped in chocolate. A single ant can live until it's twenty-nine," I say, hoping to impress her with this piece of knowledge.

"What about a married one?" I love that she laughs as much as I do at her joke.

She dips her sushi rice first into the sauce, and the sauce travels through it coloring half of the rice brown. You are meant to put the fish in first, I've read it so many times but I don't tell her. Perhaps she has a reason for it—Klara has a lot of reasons for a lot of things. I think hard about what to say, all the questions I want to ask are too personal, even for someone without a murder stare. Do you have a boyfriend? Have you permanently moved in with your dad? How did you get the scar on your chin? How do you like your eggs for breakfast?

I settle for this: "How are you enjoying your time in Sweden?"

"Honest answer? It feels strange. The place has evolved since I left. I keep repeating phrases and expressions that were popular in the 2010s. When I left, we were dancing to Girls Aloud and Abba-Teens. Have you always lived here?"

"Malmö? Yes. I'm happy in the city. I never tried the countryside where you are. I like the fact there is always someone around. I don't have to make an effort to socialize," I say. Hope she doesn't find me boring. Never been anywhere, never done anything, stable Alex always staying in his lane.

"I guess that's the benefit of marriage as well. Even with all its challenges, you have someone around," she remarks, and I think of Calle. And Dan. Because they're the married people I know. I touch my ring. "I wouldn't know, of course. Is that how it is?" she asks, and I look up.

"Yes," I say, thoughts elsewhere. She stares at her phone, then at me. She has moved forward on her chair as if ready to sprint off. "I guess that's what being married gives you. Comfort."

Talk of marriage seems to unsettle Klara. Her large earrings are very still against her cheeks. Then they jump to life again.

"Please tell me that I'm wrong. Are we supposed to be in Dalby in twenty minutes?" she says.

"You tell me. You're the boss."

"How does this keep happening to me? Sorry, Alex, but you have about five minutes to finish your meal. Oh, it feels wrong to have ended the salmon's life span early to only spend five minutes on it!"

Not entirely sure how Klara has managed not to mess up an entire job yet. It's like she doesn't know that there is such a thing as a calendar that comes with your Apple devices. Her scribbles across her dad's leather-bound one do not count as organization. I almost installed a handrail and wheelchair access in the wrong apartment last week because the screenshots she sent me of said calendar are illegible. I feel a sweat coming on just looking at the messy attempt at time-keeping. Numbers, being on time and neatness are my jam. Entering tasks and completing them... I think your tactic is working, Dr. Hadid...

"How have you managed until now? You're an adult living abroad and all, the international hotshot from London gracing the south of Sweden with your presence."

"Hardly an accurate description. I shared a flat with my best friend in London, never lived on my own and spent my days on the computer feeling like I repeated the same conversation over and over but with a different person. I've never been the boss of anyone or anything."

"Still, I feel like you—we—are doomed if we continue the way things are going. This morning I got a reminder saying *buy tampons*." She laughs a big belly laugh.

"Sorry, that was obviously for my eyes only."

"Damn, I wish you had told me before. Already picked up the tampons on my way to work," I say jokingly. "I bet you're the type of person who has five hundred unread messages clinging to your inbox."

She glances at her phone. I stand up, and we start walking. Impressed at the speed at which she finished her meal.

"Three hundred and twelve," she says over her shoulder as she speeds off ahead of me. "Look, in London we had a response coordinator, reference responses and a schedule. I never had a reason to get my shit together. Why are you so ace at notes and diary entries anyway?"

"Let's just say it's my thing lately." *My only thing lately.*

"Well, feel free to take my calendar over. I hate the thing."

"Seriously? I won't pass on that offer. Send me your logins, and I'll slide into your calendar, then." *What did I just say?*

Sounds like a dating technique. But, actually, this works. We will have less confusion, fewer annoyed customers. Win-win.

Just as we reach the van my phone pings with Klara's calendar access information. We're now synced.

KLARA

🔍 What should be on my bucket list?

Google Search   I'm Feeling Lucky

Six weeks into Dad's treatment, and there has been a change. No more eggs on toast. Dad suddenly looks a lot older, as if he's my grandfather instead of my dad.

"I can leave the car at the tile shop around the corner. Saves us the parking," he suggests. I'm joining Dad at his appointment today. We could arrange a taxi transfer now that he is too tired to drive himself, but I prefer to be there. Plus, we used the thirty-five-minute drive to talk through the expenses and what I need to prepare for the accountants.

"Dad, we are certainly not walking four blocks to your chemo appointment to save 150 kronor!"

When I arrived, I thought that Dad had *stage 1* rather than *cancer*. That they could somehow be separated, like numerals and words normally are. But he doesn't look like a 1. He looks more like an 8 on the pain scale. For me a headache is a 4, a stubbed toe a 7 and a broken wrist from falling down a tree a 9.

"How would you rate your nausea?" I ask him. He smiles.

"I would rate it a 2.5 today, Klara."

I decide to google prostate cancer. I hadn't done this before because I had a numeral, a *stage*. But now there is this nagging feeling that disease cannot be categorized as a number, and it is rather soft around the edges instead. It floats out, and we can't contain it. Perhaps there has been a misunderstanding and it is a performance stage we are talking about, where cancer can twirl and hop as much as it wants.

Google tells me that stage 1 cancer is small and hasn't spread. I couldn't imagine aggressive cells spreading through my dad's body, but apparently, I don't have to. It's confined to the prostate gland—I like this word also, *confined*. Clear boundaries. Then it says that the survival rate is nearly one hundred percent for the next five years, and I think, at least I'll have a dad until I'm thirty-one. No need to stress or worry before then.

"Dad, I've made a plan for the next five years," I say. "There are lots of things I'd like to do."

My bucket list includes: averaging typing speed at four seconds in the YourMove chat (have crossed this out as I'm no longer working there), and coming up with a word that rhymes with *orange* or *pint*. It also includes getting married or engaged. Since a relationship is unlikely, I instead think of other wedding-related goals I could have, to revise the list. Google tells me a realistic goal is one that you can reach given your current mindset, motivation level, time frame, skills and abilities. Realistic goals help you identify not only what you want but also what you can achieve.

I decide if I can't get married, I would like to be a bridesmaid. My sister's wedding doesn't count because the only planning she allowed me to do for the event was organize my own travel there. Even the shoes I had to wear along with a piglet-snout-colored dress (my sister called it *rose* pink) arrived in my mailbox one month before, as did my instructions for the day. Saga had drawn a map of the church with arrows marking my position at all times. This was a good move, although I improved it further by drawing small figures on it. A stick-man priest, a Jesus display and guests with triangular dresses and hats. During the service I pulled it out for amendments, something Saga questioned later on.

"What were you writing?" I thought you were only supposed to have eyes for the groom. Apparently Saga had eyes for her little sister as well.

"I corrected the map. The priest had a beard, and I hadn't drawn one."

"Seriously, Klara."

"If you would have made yours more complete, not leaving details like that out it wouldn't have been necessary."

I'd like to be in a WhatsApp group called What Happens in Mallorca Stays in Mallorca or similar for something like a bachelorette party. Alice says she doesn't believe in marriage, and my only cousin hasn't had a girlfriend since 2019 when he got catfished by two sisters from Michigan, so my chances are slim.

I think about what my dad would have on his bucket list, remembering that he always wanted to teach me how to change a tire. *I want my girls to be independent.* I take out my phone to schedule this toward the end of my stay when Dad is presumably more energetic. At first the calendar confuses me with all its events in different colors. I trust that Alex is on top of it, though, so much so that I left the old leather diary at home yesterday.

I frown as I read a new entry from Alex. I must have ignored him lately. Since our lunch that left me shaken. I'm not proud of it, but I feel jealous that someone gets to be his wife and have his company and calm voice as soundtrack to their life.

The new entry in our shared calendar reads:

○ **NEW TASK:** Say an actual good morning to Alex

I swiftly change it:

○ **EDITED TASK:** Stay out of Klara's way before 9am

Then decide to make my point even stronger.

○ **EDITED TASK:** ...before 10am. Thx very much x

Alex is back with another change:

Reply: Unless there are croissants?

Fair point. I could probably handle funny feelings induced by closeness to my very attractive but unavailable employee when a pastry is on the line.

Reply: Deal. A good morning for a croissant.

Then I go and check the heaters, in case Dad has sneakily turned them down, because I'm still getting occasional goose bumps.

ALEX

Shared Calendar ▾

O **NEW TASK:** Add Alex to blood sugar monitoring app

Reply (Klara): Is there a work-related reason?

Reply (Alex): Appoint Alex as company wellness officer (Now there's a reason)

Reply (Klara): Check your emails, Officer

Saved to Drafts

Dear Calle,

Thought writing to you was weird and testament to my poor composition, as someone I know would put it, but then I leave it a few days and guilt hits me. Like you're waiting for me to tell you my news. Guess what? This time I have some. Big fucking news. I got a job and I got a boss (obviously) but she is this little thing that just holds my complete attention, and when I'm with her I feel like calling up Dr. Hadid's office and saying, *Hey there, no need for these notes or further sessions. Nothing but joy in my chest now.* Then she moves away—she does this A LOT. As if she must have physical distance between herself and others at all times. I mean, my boss is fucking unique. But a good unique.

She keeps walking five steps ahead of me, and whenever I move closer, she bolts the other way. What's up with that? I find myself lying awake and wondering what it means. Not used to people being difficult to read like that. And the looks she gives come right out of the blue, like lightning or something. She's intense, but she's also quiet and very steady. But also incredibly unorganized? Can't seem to figure her out, but will continue to try—too much fun not to.

Keep seeing red hikers' jackets everywhere. Are they back in fashion or something? Can't wait in a line or look out the window without my heart jumping up into my throat. Thinking it's guilt playing on my mind because I haven't been driving as much. Only out looking on weekends now, not possible with work at 7am. Are you disappointed? Do you want me to go on?

"What would you do if you found the witness? How would it change anything? It won't bring Calle back," Dr. Hadid said. It would bring justice, that's what it would do. Justice for you, justice for Dan—even for Mamma and Pappa. They need it more than they let on. With no witnesses, you can argue that you didn't see, didn't hear, didn't mean to, didn't know the car wasn't safe to drive. If someone's seen you, it's not so easy. I can't change what happened, I can't go back and say, *Yes, I'll drive you home.* Justice is the only thing I have.

Who knew following someone's blood sugar could be so satisfying? Find myself peeking at the graph more often than I should. Her allowing me that follow is bigger than any Instagram action I've ever had. But not obsessing. Definitely not obsessing.

It's lunchtime, and I should really head off. There are plenty of places I could be—the office, my van, the village. But instead, I sit down on the bench next to Klara outside the office, half expecting her to lash out and shoo me away like a pigeon or shift to the other side of it as if I've got a reeking greasy takeout she needs to get away from. Surprised to see her stay put in silence.

Klara lifts her face toward the sun and pulls her sleeves up, revealing her insulin pump.

"Sun's out, pump's out," she says. I've recently learned that she is only here in Sweden temporarily. Not sure how I feel about that. Haven't had the nerve to ask exactly how long.

"What do you have in London that pulls you in so much? Polluted junctions and inflated rent?"

"That's not all it is. You have to live in London to understand it."

"I know, but seriously. You can go back to a flat share, a nine-to-five job and saving toward a sky-high property deposit. Or you could have fresh air, your own place for almost no money and a job you seem to love." *You could have me. Dream on, Alex.* This is the woman you have to pay in croissants just to get a *Good morning.* If that's not setting the vibe straight…

"You don't just change a plan. I was forced to do that once, and it threw me. I'm still adapting years later. Now I stick to what I know. I'll get another job in customer service chatting, work hard, save enough for a deposit via some scheme property in an up-and-coming area. And then I meet a nice man, preferably tall and into monogamy. Bonus if he cooks and sleeps on the right side of the bed. Not willing to switch sides."

"I sleep on the right side." *Seriously? Of all the intelligent things I can say to a woman to up myself, that's what I go for?*

Notice Klara is sweating. Drops of perspiration are trickling down around her ears. The small hairs curl up into spirals.

"You should take that off," I instruct her.

"I get like this when I'm high. Can't stop drinking and everything is too hot. It's like menopause, I imagine." She pulls at her sleeves and yanks the sweater over her head. She is wearing a black crop top, or is it actually a bra? I settle on it being one of those items of clothing that works two jobs, that hustle. She hands me the sweater, not quite sure why and what I'm supposed to do with it, and her hand touches my wrist. Something flushes through me, and I feel like I've just been pulled from a deep daydream, except all she's done is place her fingers on my skin.

I swallow hard. I fold up her sweater and place it to the side, then go to fetch her a glass of water. As she drinks it, I lose my *fucking mind* and bend down to move her hair off her face. As in—sensually stroking strands of hair off her face and looking into her eyes. No idea why I'm doing this, I must be mental.

"Alex," she says. Klara has said my name a hundred times, but this time there's a heaviness to it.

Aware I overstepped and not sure what happens next.

KLARA

When I come home and my pulse has returned to a normal rate again—I have had a cold shower followed by a gin and tonic outside, hoping the freezing fresh air will shake some sense into me with its northwesterly gusts of wind—I message him.

Me: I think we should go back.

Alex (replying very, very fast): Back where?

Me: The friendship zone.

He doesn't answer fast this time. *Typing*...comes and goes. I time it like you would when taking a pulse. Checking for danger or a problem. Fifteen seconds on average between the *Typing*... I'm not sure what level of disaster that involves. Wish there were charts which explained the length of *Typing*...

I consult Alice, who seems the best one to involve on the subject matter due to the fact that she won't start questioning why an employee has left the friendship zone to the same degree I imagine Saga would. I may have been wrong.

"You said what? You do know that you sound like a meme half the time. Pretty sure there actually *is* a meme like that."

"That can't be a bad thing. Memes are succinct, poignant and straight to the point. They also carry an element of humor, which could be said to act in favor of a perception of friendliness. Which I do want to maintain since we work together. What would the workplace look like if we went around touching each other's hairs?"

"I'd say memes can make you seem cold and distant."

"Are you saying I should be leaving the friend zone hand in hand with the married employee?"

"Klara, all I'm saying is chill." See I wish I could *chill*. I have been trying hard to repress my thoughts about Alex, but in the end it's too hard, and I let them wash over me.

"I've put the thoughts I've had down to one of those random fantasies that everyone has."

"We all share random fantasies?"

"Yes, like randomly inheriting a large sum of money from a wealthy relative who hates people but appreciates you for your veganism."

"Okay..."

"Or how it turns out you had a beautiful voice all along but it's only discovered at a karaoke session when you drunkenly perform a Taylor Swift song, but oh, guess what? There's a talent scout there, and they give you a record deal immediately. Or how you'd give a vulnerable, candid interview to Oprah, telling her all about your struggles growing up and how you've come to be the success you are now despite the odds."

"Yes. Have had that last one. It really is incredible how I can have risen to branch manager despite the trauma of my best friend giving away her half of our friendship necklace to her big brother who had a crush on me." She snorts. "Wait, tell me about your Alex one?"

"Oh, it's nothing special. You know how you dream that you wake up one morning and just function like everyone else, and the person you work with is actually single and available to be dated by people who function like everyone else? It's that sort of fantasy. Which I don't mind. As long as my hair isn't touched and the lines between fantasy and reality aren't blurred."

Alice pauses slightly longer than usual, as if she's at a crossroads and not sure which way to go.

"Maybe you read too much into it? You weren't feeling great. He may just have been helpful," she says eventually.

"Yes. *Maybe.*" It's just that I've never wanted to be touched on my face by my other two friends before. I don't mind hugging Alice: she squeezes tight then releases fast, like a blood-pressure machine.

We're friends. *Friends.* Better start thinking it in capital, font 72 every time the thought of Alex's mouth pops up in my mind. Any smaller and I might just happen to push the tiny word off the page altogether.

I close my eyes, but all I can see is Alex's mouth forming words, *kind* words, directed at me. I need to do some baking. Organize the recycling, pull labels off and wash out containers. Anything. I'm getting silly and way too distracted by this *thing*, whatever it is. I keep catching myself thinking about Alex when I shouldn't be, playing our chats over when I'm in the shower, driving or cooking, and imagining what he was thinking.

There is no message from Alex all day, but when I check our calendar there is a new edit to our next staff meeting. Location: The friendship zone, it reads.

When I next see him, on Tuesday, I struggle to walk straight, as if I'm somehow intoxicated, and say intelligent things like, "Aha! *Great,*" when he speaks to me, having no clue what he was just talking about, and then I retreat to the quiet sanctuary that is the kitchen. I will get caught up in accounting, filing and sending out invoices. That should divert my thoughts nicely.

I make an espresso because coffee is meant to balance you and increase your alertness and cognitive function in the short term. It works. I feel like myself again. Balanced and normal and, most importantly, *in control*. I am proud to say I am no longer in danger of becoming fixated on any part of my employees' physical features. Splendid.

My levelheaded self decides that it would be a good idea for some team-building. I message Gunnar.

"What do you say about a simple drinks evening tomorrow? To celebrate that we're a full team again? Dad would enjoy it." To be fair he'd probably grumble about whether it is strictly necessary, how much of the company's capital will be spent and whether the next day's work will at all be affected. But once it's happening, he will enjoy himself.

Gunnar: Great idea 👍 Will keep evening free.

Learning to mix with my employees (namely, Alex) as friends will be valuable. And Dad could use the cheering up. I pull out my phone to enter it into the calendar.

ALEX

Shared Calendar ▾

○ **NEW EVENT (KLARA):** Company get-together after work. Wife welcome!

Assume this isn't for me. I do get Klara's personal ones every now and then (this week's highlight was *hang hand-washed underwear to dry* that gave me a glorious mental image, which I could definitely have done without) but this one baffles me. Whose wife is she bringing to the company drinks?!

Respond with a new note: Are we welcome without wives as well? Or are plus-ones compulsory?

No reply so I think how I haven't written to Calle yet today and how maybe, just maybe, Klara has something to do with the lessening in frequency. Tonight I feel that familiar void, though. Five weeks away from the trial and no progress made.

Saved to Drafts

Calle,

I have a few voice messages stored on my phone. You were that strange person who preferred a voice note over a message, always the talker. I would write you a novel-length text and you'd send an audiobook-length reply. When I listen to them now, it's like a shadow of who you were, like I'm not listening to the real you but a technical, processed version.

We never sound ourselves in recordings. Makes me sad that when we die there is no trace of our true self, we're mainly gone. Now all I have to remember you from, the only place you exist, is in my patched-together memory of you. Will your face twist like your voice has? Will your hair turn a different color when I think of you in a year's time?

I hold on to the small details that are so sharp in my memory I can't ever forget them. They are your feet, way too small for your height. I see them in flip-flops on a beach, small blond hairs even lighter than your skin growing at the base of the big toes. Your ears look like mine. So all I have to do is go and give them a proper look and I'd be okay. People neglect feet and ears, but they are body parts with less distractions. A face can look a million ways—an ear cannot hide its shape with a frown or an eyebrow shape and tint. They are reliable, and I thank myself for remembering them.

Inevitably this has me thinking about feet and ears. Klara has lovely ears, I have noticed. The type that I could easily remember. Don't tell this to Dan or Paul because I'm aware complimenting women's ears is not the norm. They are petite and point ever so slightly outward; they have flat creases, formed like a perfect half of a heart (I wonder if the two fit together; must find opportunity to inspect both left and right side of face without being noticed as am now intrigued) and usually wear gold or silver jewelry. One time they wore huge hoops and bounced under the weight. They're never naked, but I can imagine it, bright pink like cheeks when they are hot, and a pale brown when it's early morning and the frost hasn't lifted yet. I think I would do a very good witness statement concerning Klara Nilsson's ears if I were ever to give one.

KLARA

How many tasty rocks are there in the world?

Google Search   I'm Feeling Lucky

I have put Hanna on bar duty, something she's taken very seriously, as she arrived with a bag full of flower garlands and mini umbrellas.

"Margaritas don't call for umbrellas," she says, adding, "but they're the only drink I do well."

I watch her line up the glasses on a tray and salt the edges.

"Did you ever think about salt? It can't be the only delicious rock in this world. Somewhere there must be another type of rock waiting to be discovered," I say and make a mental note to google it later.

"Let you know if I ever find it. Go get your dad. We're almost ready here."

The phone rings, and Saga and her good mood fill my screen. I hadn't realized it was Thursday. "Just came back from the grocery store without Harry. Which is basically my happy place because I get to exist as a single entity *and* be around food."

"Great. I'm a bit busy right now." *Busy staring at the door that Alex and the rest will walk through any minute.*

"Oh." She leans forward as if she expects to see my busyness behind me on the screen. "There's music?"

"Yes. We are having some drinks." I allowed Hanna to compile a playlist as my own music is usually no success at parties and more suited to alone time in the van.

I only hear half the next sentence because Alex walks in, and my senses stop working. *Obviously.* Heart thumping so hard it echoes in my eardrums. He's alone. Does he get broader and taller every time I see him? It shouldn't be physically possible, especially considering his starting point of tallness and broadness. Alex is at least six foot. One. Two. Three. Maybe more? He's wearing a formal shirt, which I've never seen before. *Splendid, one more image of Alex to add to my already full cloud of images…*

"I have to go, Saga. Call you later."

"Wait, what?"

I'm aware of her disbelief at this. Her little sister with plans! Hanging up on *her*! *Leaving her to whine to her wine!*

When I look up from my phone, Alex is standing in front of me.

"Hi." The thought occurs that this is a very informal setting and that a greeting hug would be normal. I curse myself for not preparing for this moment mentally. I'm frozen stiff, waiting for a collision, wondering if I should go for it or wait to see what he attempts. *I can do this without dissolving like a sugar cube exposed to heat.*

Turns out I can't. Because when he leans in there is a whole load of stubble action going on, brushing the top of my head. My face is level with his chest for a good four seconds, long enough to inhale all the scent which sends my imagination into overdrive and makes me lose my ability to speak in coherent sentences. Or think them. Which is why all I manage is, "Oh, alone." I am an idiot.

He gives me a very long, very unsettling look, smiles, then leaves me. He walks over to Dad and Hanna. I watch. Dad claps his shoulder, and I think, I've done something good, here, perhaps. Dad likes something I brought to the company—Alex and Hanna. Even if I mess up and we still get cancellations, at least I got that right.

Dad seems to enjoy himself for about an hour, then he walks over to me. I made a conscious effort to hide any business-related papers, and I can see him looking suspiciously around the room and at the bare desk.

"That's about as much fun as I can handle." He comes over and hands me his glass.

"You did well. Numerous chats. Only one of them about tiles, as far as I'm aware." He smiles at me.

"Good night."

Dad goes to leave, and five minutes later I follow him, to retrieve extra ice cubes. Just outside the front door I hear him talking to Gunnar—he hasn't left after all. Dad has a hand on his friend's upper arm as he speaks.

"Can you make sure they get the right mileage tracker? I will email you the details of the police station and the case number." It's a whisper but loud enough for me to hear.

Police? There must be a speeding ticket. It can't be me since I always stay ten percent below the speed limit. I'm grateful that I don't have to handle any correspondence with the local police and decide I need to remember to thank Dad for taking it off my to-do list.

I take the bag of ice and head inside again.

ALEX

Shared Calendar ▾

○ **REMINDER:** 8am project start Dalby

Reply (Alex): Want to sit this one out?

Reply (Klara): Only drank Margaritas at a rate of 1.3 an hour. Fresh as a daisy washed in Lenor. See you there

Have a voice mail from Dr. Hadid. Apparently she'd like to see a next of kin. My support system. I go through my people mentally. Mamma, Pappa, Dan and Paul make the top. The thought of my parents in a closed room talking about feelings sends shivers down my spine. Dan—have tortured the guy enough with my problems. He needs space to heal as well. Which leaves me with Paul. Reluctantly pick up the phone.

"You know how you love me so much and I picked up the slack for you on numerous times, referring to Barcelona trip 2015 and one Saturday night in Gothenburg more recently? Time to repay. I need you to come to therapy with me. My appointment is in two weeks."

"You're kidding. You're bringing me to couple's therapy?"

"Your words, not mine. Listen, it will be an hour of discussing how you can be the good friend you already are and give your versions of events on New Alex and Old Alex. Then we can grab a beer."

"Fine. You had me at beer. And Old Alex. Kind of want that guy back." Enter it in the calendar:

O **NEW EVENT:** Couple's therapy

Have a notification straightaway. The event has a new note.

Reply (Klara): Did you want the afternoon off for this?

Oh, fuck. Have now messed up and accidentally shared private notes.

Reply (Alex): Not in couple's therapy. Can explain.

Reply (Klara): Sure. Nothing wrong with it, don't feel embarrassed.

Reply (Alex): No—really.

Reply (Klara): I've noted you as off those hours. You're welcome.

Reply (Alex): Thanks. Although not in couple's therapy...

KLARA

Shuffling things around so Alex could go to his therapy session was easy; we still don't have enough work. I try to picture it. Would they hold hands? Sit a yard apart on the sofa? Did my parents go to therapy? Is that what happened right before they divorced? I shake the thought away. Clearly he's embarrassed and doesn't want me to bring it up, let alone think about it. I turn up the music. I need a distraction, can't spend all morning thinking about couples and their need for therapy.

The ICA Maxi has a huge parking, which, now that I drive a van, is why I shop there. I can't eat any more eggs on toast or Fred's Grill hybrid cuisine. I tried the next village from us but was met by a similar establishment: Brown's Pizza and Indian Food. If I am to diverge from my mealtime habits, the reason has to be good enough. I feel like opening a takeaway from Brown's would turn into an unpleasant surprise that I can do without.

I dump my groceries on the conveyor belt like a load of dry laundry. *Why is everyone looking at me?* I lick my lip as a first step, although it was ages since I last ate, and there can't really be anything there. I touch my backside, pants in place, no huge, glaring hole. The cashier is also eyeing me up and down now. I haven't *just* bought white pasta and chocolate bars—there is a pack of quinoa and salmon fillets too! It comes to me suddenly. *My food items are piled up as if I'm attempting a re-creation of the Leaning Tower of Pisa.*

If you ever find yourself in a Swedish supermarket, there are two things you need to know. The food is ridiculously expensive, just get over it and buy what you can. Secondly, you *must* order the items on the band with the barcode toward you. This is a staple in Swedish politeness. The Swedes don't go around pardoning and excusing themselves, but they do show respect to the cashier. Fail to do this and the cashier as well as the full line behind you will consider you bad news. In Sweden we love queues, so much so that even the groceries need to form one.

I try to reorder my items as swiftly as possibly, hoping that my eyes convey a look of *I'm sorry, meant no disrespect with the architectural grocery build*. I gather my things into two paper bags, too shy to ask for the plastic ones even if I prefer them. I have to do what I can for the environment. Especially since I am now going around in a big diesel-driven van. Then I wait patiently for a receipt so I can politely refuse it.

I rush back to the car, stuffing the groceries in with paint cans and dusty work shoes. Seat belt, Eminem, heating, hand brake, accelerator.

And—*crash*.

Scheibe. I can hear the sound of metal crunching up like a paper being squeezed and discarded. How am I in Reverse and not Drive? *Bloody gearbox.*

I finally have the clarity to press my foot on the brake and stop whatever damage is happening. I want to cry desperately. This is the type of situation where I call Dad. It's just that I'm here to be a grown-up and step in for him, as he is currently at home resting after being radiated on his groin for an hour. I push my tears back and try to calm down. Not helping. I sit for another moment before summoning the courage to get out of the van and have a look. Please don't let it be bad. Or expensive. At least there are no Ferraris or Porsches in the village supermarket parking lot. It could be worse. I could be in a swanky Range Rover area of London.

It's not a Chelsea tractor but it *is* a Mercedes. White and sparkling clean. Tears well up again. I scramble in my pockets for a piece of paper and end up pulling a sheet out of the now-retired work calendar along with a wrapped candy from my emergency supply. I lean the paper against the window of the van and begin to write my details down.

"Dear Person with Nice Shiny Car, I hope this finds you well, with a spring in your step and a smile on your face. I hope you are feeling zen this Thursday afternoon and that your day has been excellent so far because I've just made it suck a tiny bit. Leaving a chocolate with this note in case you, like me, are a stress eater—" I stop as the car I am about to put the note on lights up twice at the click of a fob.

"*Hej.*" A voice is behind me, then surrounds me until it's wrapped up my whole being in memories. Because it's a voice I know. I haven't laid eyes on him yet, but I know that the man behind me is Tom. I can hear it and feel it. Part of me is scared to look, wondering what kind of man he will have turned into, so I do it quickly. I turn around, and my stomach flips.

"Klara." He doesn't sound surprised. Rather he looks as if he was expecting nothing less than me reversing into his car on a Thursday afternoon in Veberöd village. Why, why, why? It's not women that are mysteries, it's bloody men that are impossible to interpret. My heartbeat is fast, and my palms sweaty. I'm like an onion: give me one poke and I break a sweat. He is as cool as a cucumber (excuse horrendous vegetable puns, brain busy processing Tom stuff). He is older now, *obviously*, but he still looks the same. It's as if eighteen-year-old Tom has simply applied an Instagram filter and stepped into today. His dark blond hair is swept to the side with, I assume, minimal amounts of hair product. He is dressed in a crisp blue shirt and chinos despite the cold. When I knew him, he did his best to keep up a preppy image and would never be seen without his Tod's loafers, snow or no snow. But today he wears blue sneakers, his pants perfectly rolled up to end half an inch above them.

"God, I'm so sorry about the car. I'm still getting to know this beast here." I gesture toward the van, which is looking sad with its back dented. He ignores my apology completely as if it is of no interest to him. Instead, he looks at me intrigued.

"I heard that you were home."

"I guess that means I'm already infamous. Crashing the van won't help my reputation."

"You're wrong. You have no reputation because you've been away the past few years. You're a mystery, Klara. I'd love to find out what's been going on with you." And then he smiles. I feel myself swallowing, and my cheeks heat up. Tom put *love* and *me* in the same sentence, never mind the meaning of his actual words.

A familiar face comes out of the shop and walks up to us before I can read more into what Tom has just said. Seeing Lennart is comforting.

"Don't beat yourself up, Klara girl. I know a guy that will get it fixed for a cheap price. Let me send you his details."

"Thanks," I say, then turn to Tom again. "I guess I should take your number, then. For insurance purposes?" I add. *Oh, stop it, Klara. What other reason could there be? No need to clarify.*

"Right. Brilliant," Tom says now, finally acknowledging the accident.

He digs into his trouser pocket and pulls out a Louis Vuitton wallet. He hands me a business card, and when I take it my hand touches his. It's like a static shock, except there is no static so it's just a shock, really. It's all my muscle memory, *not my fault*, my hand recognizes his skin, somehow. Has he felt it too? I look up at him but his eyes don't give anything away. Getting nothing from his face, I turn to the card in my hand instead.

"Right, then." I glance at the card. "You joined your dad's firm. Congratulations." That had always been Tom's plan, which makes sense if your dad is the area's best criminal defense lawyer: there is no alternative route once you finish law school.

"It's great to see you, Klara." His confidence is even more obvious when standing next to my nervous self. We're a game of opposites.

"Yes, you too, it's so great, really wonderful." It *would* have been wonderful to see him, say, eight years ago. To have him turn up at the coffee-shop table where he dumped me and tell me *Ha-ha! Did you believe that thing I wrote on the cup?* Or even him turning up a week later would have been wonderful. *I'm so sorry, Klara, what a silly boy I've been! I'm back, bigger and better, all in. Here are some flowers, and can I rub your feet, please?*

Instead, there was silence, and he turns up in a parking lot years later, and I tell him with a shaky voice that it's wonderful.

Later that night Dad has gone to bed after having eaten half his dinner, and I'm curled up on the sofa with a knitted throw over my legs, and Benny the cat asleep on one of them. "Would you move, please? My leg is falling asleep." I try, but he ignores me, as cats usually do. "Fine," I say wiggling my toes, too polite to move and wake him up.

I call Saga, because it's 8:00 p.m. and Thursday night which means Wine and Whine time.

"Hey," she says.

"Why are you whispering? Is your throat okay?"

"Harry's sleeping." My nephew can sleep through a street carnival in his buggy (I took him to Notting Hill Carnival last year in an attempt to establish myself as the cool aunt) but not the soft sound of his parents' voices.

"Is Heinrich out?"

"In the kitchen, working. We basically have separate lives now. Marital bliss. But I don't know how else to do it, when I come home after working all day, talking to students and my colleagues, finish dinner and put Harry to bed, all I want is a shower and for no one to touch my body for ten hours. I should really be going to bed now, but the silence and not having anyone yell *Mummy!* is too good to give up." She turns her head away from me and does what is a scream in a whispering octave in the direction of her husband in the other room.

"Heinrich says hi," she says turning back to me.

"I fear we have turned into those attractive flatmates everyone advertises for: professional, work long hours, rarely have friends over. We just pass one another around the house but stay respectfully clear of each other so as not to get on each other's nerves."

"Family life sounds dreamy."

"Well, yeah. And I only have one child."

"Are you not drinking?" I notice her cup and unless she has started a worrying habit of taking her adult beverage in a floral tea mug, that is definitely peppermint tea in front of her laptop.

"I'm trying to stay off it Monday to Friday," she replies.

"So I *wine* and you *whine*. No surprise there," I say quietly, balancing a fine line that is the difference between obvious discontent and polite disapproval. Saga appears not to have heard me.

"How's Dad?"

"He's great, today's a good day. He pulled weeds and mowed the lawn, dripping in sweat when I came home."

"You let him do that?"

"What do you want me to do, tell him off? I'm not his parent, remember. He's actually mine."

"You are meant to help him, look out for him." This is the problem with Saga—making a big fuss over little things and as little fuss as possible over big things.

"Well, you are welcome to come over if I'm doing such a shitty job! It's all *Poor Dad, he needs help* when you sit in another country, but me who's actually here gets no credit."

Saga is quiet, clutching her mug of tea. I usually know her quiet pauses, have become good at analyzing them, but this is not the Change Your Mind one, the Know Your Place one or Don't Say a Word one. She has a new one in her repertoire.

"Why can't we ever speak without you making me feel bad?" she says.

"You feel bad? I wasn't the one criticizing you."

"Okay, whatever. I'm glad you're okay. I have a lecture to prepare now."

"Great, enjoy Christopher Columbus."

"Klara, I specialize in postwar, postcolonial relations between England and India. They don't involve a fifteenth-century murderer."

I am not sure which one of us hangs up first. Benny, my trouper, jumps off my lap and onto the floor, wandering off looking for a more permanent place to spend the night. I should do the same but stay where I am and reach for the bottle of Sancerre to top up my glass. How can it already be empty? I practice a moment of what a Pilates instructor in a class I was brought (read: *dragged*) to taught me: *checking in with myself*. I don't like Pilates. Too many limbs and bums moving outside of mats. I kept mine firmly inside my mat boundaries, pretending the floor was lava, but the teacher came around and put his hand on my lower back, and I kept thinking he was standing in the lava and resisted when he took my ankle and extended it. But the *checking in* I can do. Is my head spinning? Yup. Am I feeling unusually antsy? Check. Okay, time to join Benny in bed, then.

But after just one more scroll. I open up Facebook. I think of Tom. I haven't checked him out in years and type his name into the search engine. *Tom Vidén.* Nothing. Not sure why it's not coming up. Maybe he's one of those people who don't use Facebook. The type that anyone should be suspicious of, the same type that had unpublished phone numbers when I grew up. *Unpublished number!* Mum would hiss at us. Honest, hardworking people hide nothing, not even the ten digits they've been allocated.

I take Tom's absence from social media as a sign to go to bed and trot off upstairs.

Next morning is the usual blur of scalding hot coffee, work pants that are not fully dry despite having hung to air-dry all night and a fast slap of makeup on my face. Last on the list is my blood sugar, which is thankfully cooperating this morning. The graph line is nice and straight on my screen, and I thank myself, my dinner last night, and the diabetes god I often have serious conversations with. Then I stop midmorning rush. *Wait, why do I have Facebook notifications? I never write anything.* I only use it to spy on people I don't care about enough to keep in contact with but still care about enough to see as my competition in life. And to wish relatives a happy birthday so I don't have to send a card or, *horror*, call them. Twelve people liked my post. *Oh God.* I typed the name into the wrong box. Instead of putting Tom's name in the search box I entered it into the status box. My Facebook status for the past eight hours has been *Tom Vidén*. The name of my ex. *Oh. No.*

I want the earth to swallow me, to disappear into thin air and every single cliché you have ever heard. Delete, delete, delete some more. Has he seen it? Too late, I've already deleted it, and I now have no chance to see who (*oh, the horror!*) liked this post. Please let him not have seen it. I consider adding an explanatory status. *Wrong box!* Or *My Facebook got hacked!* Or better yet *My brain got hacked!* But decide that may be even more awkward.

I freeze a second time when I get out to the van. *Speaking of the devil,* as Alice would put it; I'm convinced he's no longer the devil, so let's rephrase: *speaking of Tom.* I have a message.

Tom: Hey, it was nice seeing you yesterday. I'm happy your car decided to bump into mine (sorry for the pun). My Mercedes would have asked that nice big Renault with the large rear out, but since she got hit pretty badly, I was asked to represent. How is dinner tomorrow night? Lund?

Gaaah. "Okay, girl!" I say to myself although I'm alone and probably not young enough to be a girl any longer, just because it's the type of chick-lit thing I imagine a highly successfully dating woman would exclaim. I read the message again. And just one more time. For a moment I think how I'd rather have Alex train me in carpentry. Or, you know, stare at a wall while the paint dries with Alex. But this might be exactly what I need. A distraction. I'm only here for a little while, and I've been so focused on my dad and his company and not crashing that into the ground. Plus, I do love a bad joke and am a sucker for a good chat-up line, so here goes.

Me: Invitation accepted on behalf of Miss Van Renault.

It is my unsworn duty to inform Alice of any developments in the dating area, and hers to me, so I reluctantly inform her from the car.

Predictably, Alice is not impressed.

"Isn't that the guy that broke up with you on a take-out cup?" she asks. "Bad choice, Klara." She reminds me of my sister telling her toddler off. *That's not a good choice, Harry, is it? Pouring milk on the dog?*

"Well, yes, but we were kids. Only eighteen." It had stung. Tom was my first love and proper boyfriend, and I had gone up to the counter to check what was taking so long, and found only my cup there, with a message on it. I had thought the barista had added an inspirational quote perhaps and looked around the room to find Tom to read it to him. Except he wasn't there, and all it said was that he was breaking up with me.

I still feel my stomach clench when I take my cup from a counter, half expecting new nastinesses written on its side. I always ask for my coffee in a to-stay cup, if at all possible.

"And you thought accepting a dinner invitation would be a good idea why?"

"You know how bad I am at saying no. He did a good text."

"If it's just banter you're after, you can just date a clown. Oh wait, that's exactly what you're doing."

"I wouldn't want to date a clown. I was kind of hoping I could find a decent guy that has at least *some* redeeming qualities such as loyalty, intellect and domestic ability with a side dish of humor and banter. But maybe that's too much to ask."

"Possibly, yes. And you think your ex has any of those qualities?"

"Maybe he's changed? It was years ago. Don't you think it means something that, of all the people I could have hit with my car, I hit Tom?"

"How big is the population over there, again?"

"Fine, but still, it must be some sort of sign."

"You are fabricating a meet-cute from reversing your car into your evil ex's. You're not in a romantic comedy, Klara."

"I clearly remember you saying I needed a rebound when Mark broke up with me."

"That happened months ago. And your ex is not a rebound. That's repeating history. What did the text on your cup say again? Please, do remind me."

"Sorry, Klara, I can't do this. xox, Tom."

"And?"

"And a smiley at the end."

"Neat."

"I guess I long for some closure. We never spoke since that time at the coffee shop. I left for London the week after. If he would just admit that he made a mistake, or that he regretted the way he broke up with me or something, I could move on, stop wondering about it and why he did it."

"You need approval from anyone you meet, Klara. I'm not saying it's just you, all us women do it if we don't become aware and stop. This evening I stayed behind and tidied my desk because the cleaners were coming in the morning and I wanted their silent approval of my workplace and of my person being tidy. Be more male. You want to know that he approves of you, but who gives a fuck? How about you don't approve of him? Did that thought ever cross his mind? I bet not."

"But he's here, and I know him, and I've dated him—all huge points in the positive column. I'm never going to be the dating-app type, and I'm certainly not the go-to-a-bar-and-socialize-with-strangers type. I'm much more the revisit-things-with-your-ex-because-he's-right-there-in-front-of-you type."

"Just because he's there doesn't mean he should be," she says, sighing. In fact, she's sighed so much in the past ten minutes I'm worried she'll run out of oxygen.

"Okay, Alice, I need to go. I will consider your points and make an informed decision."

"If you insist on going ahead, let me at least send an outfit for you to wear. Doubt you brought something appropriate for a Dazzling the Ex date." I'm about to reply that my black jeggings and black polo-neck top are perfect. When in doubt, wear black. I have never been particularly interested in fashion. Like food, clothes are intended to meet a basic human need. Provide warmth and protection. I have quite enjoyed wearing work clothes these past two months. I would quite like to *dazzle*, though.

"A good surprise. You're the best," I say. Alice knows what I like and tolerate in terms of fashion.

"Just one more question. You never told me what you did with the coffee and the cup."

"The coffee?"

"I mean, did you throw it in the sink, put it on display in the college hall for everyone to see what a douche he was…?" she says.

"I drank the coffee. And recycled the cup."

ALEX

Personal Calendar ▾

O **NEW EVENT:** Head to Calle's

O **NEW TASK:** Do inventory of stuff that's left

O **NEW TASK:** List bed, sofa table and wine fridge for sale on Facebook Marketplace

Notice that the place has emptied since I was there last. It's a constant real-life game of *What is gone?* each time I visit. When Calle had just died, only his wallet was missing, safely in the police station waiting to be examined by the forensic-crime team. Next, his laptop that always sat on the breakfast bar or was left on the sofa went missing, back to his workplace to be emptied, its contents filed and handed over to Dan. Then Dan moved out. He was only ever here on the weekends anyway; two years ago, he had gotten a new job in Stockholm and had begun weekly commuting. A place like this is too beautiful to be enjoyed only on weekends by a single person, he says. And recently it had been much more Calle's place, since he was there full-time. I came over whenever I had nothing else on. Calle would joke that I saw him more than his husband did.

Dan wants to sell it now, and I get it, I do. Hate the constant sentimental thoughts that keep popping up. *If Dan sells his and Calle's place, then Calle no longer has any place…*

My parents and I came over and went through his belongings, helping Dan when he couldn't face throwing things away.

"Only Calle would wear this. It should go." (Mamma)

"I'll bring these frames to our place to keep safe." (Mamma)

Slowly his home was becoming a shell.

Pappa stood restlessly by the door, not knowing where to start or what to look at first, as if he'd gone to visit a neighbor and arrived at an inconvenient time. After fifteen minutes he quietly left. Found him later sitting in the lobby researching fitted-shelving designs on his phone.

Go through the sparse rooms now trying to figure out what has gone this time. It's the desk in the corner of the living space along with its chair.

Am alone today, checking mail and catching any subscriptions or bills that Dan has missed. He is in Stockholm this week, doing his best to move on, and maybe it's easier for him, away from all this. I have nothing more to do, the pile of envelopes torn open and tossed into the recycling bin and the worthy documents in my pocket, folded into neat squares.

Leave the apartment, stopping when the door closes smoothly to take in the name still on it, etched on a metal plate above the mailbox. I suddenly feel an impulse to remove it. I pick the Swiss Army knife from my trousers side pocket, where a screwdriver also lives, and start tugging at the sides of the sign. It is already pretty loose; it's never been attached completely but stuck on with some wood glue. I get away with only a small scratch on the door. I hold it in my hand and touch the empty surface where it used to sit.

Carl and Daniel Kristiansen it reads.

Carl and Daniel Kristiansen don't live here any longer. Carl Kristiansen—*Calle*—doesn't live *anywhere* any longer.

★ ★ ★

Talk to Klara later that day. She is obviously going some-where because, well, *whoa*. It's Klara but a different version, one I haven't seen yet. Her hair is long and shiny, hanging off her shoulders and bouncing when she moves. Her curves are hugged by a wrap dress in a hideous pattern, something my grandmother would have on a cushion in a guest bedroom, big '60s-style flowers and geometric shapes, but on her it's breath-taking, completely unique. I can't stop looking at her.

"You look…nice." Understatement of the year. I can hear myself swallowing.

"Thank you," she says. I wait for her to say something else; she looks like she's about to, eyes fixed on me. I smooth my sweater. I want to ask her if I can stay a little longer. She wrig-gles uncomfortably and glances at her phone on the table, as if expecting it to chip in on the conversation.

"I'm trying to find someone," I say, not sure why I'm sharing.

"Anyone?"

"No, a specific person. Sorry—that was odd. I'm trying to track down someone who can help me."

"I'm assuming you've googled?"

"*Woman with dog and red fleece* unfortunately doesn't return many results," I say gloomily. Let's pretend I haven't tried that exact search in a weak, desperate moment.

"No, but you have to ask the right question. Give details and Google gives answers. What type of dog was it?" I think. I did find out and put a poster up in the local service station.

"A schnauzer."

"Great. Write down everything you know, every detail you can remember. Then, send it to me. I can help." I look at her and realize she is the first person that's offered to do something. That hasn't just told me it's mission impossible and referred me for psychological help. I know nothing will come of it. How could it? But I'm seriously grateful. She didn't even ask why I'm trying to find her, just offered help.

"Right, I better get going. Tom will be waiting," she says, and I agree. She better go before I do something crazy like tell her how she's the most awesome human being there is and that her ears are the cutest things and—

"Have a good one," I say.

After she leaves, I pull out my phone and do what I can.

She should really be home on time. Because it's good for people to sleep. And we have a big workday tomorrow. Definitely not because I find myself suddenly unnerved at the thought of her being out with another man. That would be weird and possessive and pointless because she's none of my business.

○ NEW EVENT (ADDED TO SHARED CALENDAR):
7:30 staff meeting (there will be croissants)

That should hopefully get her home and in bed on time.

KLARA

Can I sleep with a guy on the 60th date?

Google Search   I'm Feeling Lucky

I remember reading a list of the world's most stressful life events. Like, death obviously tops it, then illness, having a baby, changing jobs. Well, a date in a fancy restaurant should be on that list. The silence, which makes me think my date can hear me swallowing, the upright posture I need to maintain throughout, and finding the balance between looking into my date's eyes and the food in equal parts, especially tricky if the food is more exciting than the date (*pizza, pasta, bread basket, fried calamari, tiramisu—I'm looking at you*). I'd much rather go for a walk, visit an exhibition or go horseback riding after finishing work.

But that's not where Tom has taken me.

"The wine is good," I say. It *is* good, better than the Waitrose Finest selection one I usually buy, feeling very grown-up when I do.

"Italian, from the Puglia region, which is less known for

their vineyards than other areas. You should try to visit some-time. The landscape is something else."

"Hmm, interesting."

"Did you notice my choice of water?" he asks. I hadn't. Other than that he asked for sparkling. I compliantly look at the green San Pellegrino bottle.

"Water is a lot like wine, actually. It has to be matched to the food. There is so much to learn—the level of sodium, the intensity of the fizz. San Pellegrino is made in Bergamo and has a salt content that should go well with both meat and fish. Anything like a pasta or risotto and I would opt for less salt—say, a Perrier." Gosh. I don't tell him that the only water tasting I do is of the chlorine levels of tap water. The sharper tang of Soho taps would go well with, well, *nothing*.

"How's life in London? What do you do in your spare time?" Tom asks next, as if he's following up on my CV.

"Sit. Sleep. Talk to Google a lot. Find comfort in '90s rap and in hot drinks of any sort. Cake. That about covers it," I say, and Tom laughs as if I've told a funny joke. I smile. I am going for a frequency of my earrings dangling every twenty seconds as this is a very *informal* setting. My cheeks are already slightly sore.

The menus arrive. I have already downloaded it as a pdf from the restaurant's website and made my choice but pretend to be eyeing my options as that is what people do in a restaurant with a menu in hand. I abstain from ordering spaghetti, because I'm a lady, and go for the creamy truffle penne. Tom chooses a steak, which he asks for well-done. The waiter must struggle with hearing as he says "Excuse me?" To which Tom has to repeat his preference. Food says a lot about us. I look at Tom. A well-done steak would equal comfortable character not prone to risk-taking or biting into a challenge. He wriggles on his chair under my gaze, and I take my eyes off him, sparing him my intensity.

"So what's new with you? Did you finish your law degree?" I say.

"Yes. Great fun that was. I did it here in Lund. It's one of the best schools in the country as I'm sure you know. It was crazy sometimes. The students are so close, and the partying insane. There was this one time—"

"At band camp." Tom looks at me sternly, '90s movie references clearly not his cup of tea. I want to be people's cup of tea desperately. I stay quiet and sip my wine.

"Well, uh… How about you? You moved to London to do that architecture degree. Did it work out?" he asks, expecting it to not have. He is right. I confirm his suspicions.

"No."

"I guess not everyone is cut out for higher education. Building work is so important. Always a demand. These are the jobs society can't do without. Builders, drivers, factory workers, cleaners. Money or prestige isn't everything. Well done to you."

I feel a sense of embarrassment now but am not able to identify the exact source of it. Rudeness masked as a compliment is the worst kind. I simply smile.

But there's a backstory here. I got accepted to UCL to study architecture, the highest-ranking course in the UK, probably Europe, possibly the world? Saga was already in London, a year into studying history. Now I had a reason to move too.

"God, I wished someone had told me that in England the first year doesn't even count! All this studying for nothing when I could have partied like the rest of the students. That'll teach me to always read the small print," Saga had moaned. She had found the perfect flat for us, a studio on Dalston Road, East London. We had a queen-size bed, and that was enough.

"You're here another three weeks. I'm sure you will have plenty of time to pack, darling," Mum told me as rows of neatly folded clothing piles were laid out across my bedroom floor after the space on drawers and chairs had run out.

Then I had received an email which caused unidentifiable feelings in my tummy.

Dear Klara Nilsson, the result of your IELTS English-language pro-ficiency test, at which you must receive a total score of 7.00 or above as previously stated, is still outstanding. Please send it to us at your earliest convenience so that the offer you currently hold will not be withdrawn.

Kind regards,

The Admissions Team

This was still not a problem. I had attempted the test once and received a mean average of 5.6. "Your English is amazing, don't worry!" Saga had encouraged me. "You must have made some silly mistake, K," Dad had said. Mum had given me a hug and told me to rebook it.

After I failed my second test, UCL's emails requesting the IELTS 7.00 started to feel like those from an aggressive debt collector. When August came around, the tone was one of ur-gency, and a threat of removal from the course was made.

They all came through my inbox, and I never responded.

"There is always next year," Dad said. Mum hugged me a lot. Saga was determined that I still move to London. I could practice my English and apply the following year, and if I didn't turn up, she would be required to flat- and bed-share with a complete stranger off Gumtree. I wanted my spot in Saga's queen-size bed very badly, to be close to her, like when we were children before my diabetes.

At least I still had my boyfriend. I arranged to meet Tom for coffee after his summer job finished. He was sorting out the files at his dad's firm, and it seemed to take a considerable amount of his energy as he had bailed most nights we had arranged to meet, leading to a total of only two dates that month, August.

I wore a graphic T-shirt, jeans and fun sneakers following the advice of Google's top article choice, "15 Coffee Date Outfits to Try This Weekend." He brushed his lips against mine, but they didn't pause.

"Let's get drinks."

"Yes, let's," I said and we stood alongside each other in the queue. I reached for his hand. It was hard to find.

"You go get a table and I'll come over. Same as always, Klara?"

"A coffee, yes please."

"Cool. Be right there."

I sat and waited for six minutes, which was probably too long to sit and wait for a coffee order and a boyfriend collecting it, before I went to check on him. The rest is history, as they say. I came back with a hot beverage and no boyfriend.

The original plan was this: study architecture while in long-distance relationship with Tom. The newly devised one was: not study architecture and not have a boyfriend at all. I decided to do what those in gap years do—take a retail or hospitality job while continuing to attempt the English-language test.

To date I have sat for a total of thirty-one IELTS tests and my highest score is 6.9. I stopped three years ago and found employment with YourMove, accepting that this will be my all-time high score. Which, really, is my all-time low score, if you think about it.

We stay until the bottle of wine is finished, then head out onto the cobbled sidewalk with rosy cheeks. There are many reasons why I shouldn't sleep with Tom. If you want them, ask Alice, not me, as I've now pushed them as far back in my mind as I possibly can. There is really just one thought there, playing on Repeat like an especially fascinating YouTube video. *Please want me.* I can't mute it—it's not really a YouTube video, is it?

I've given up deciding. I leave the decision to Tom. Does he want me? It turns out that he does.

"Come to mine for a coffee, Klara?" he says as we stand next to the replacement car the mechanic has given me while they do up the van. It's the perfect opportunity for me to say good-night, hop in and drive off into the night. The problem with me is that I'm very good at missing perfect opportunities (references can be provided on request).

"We just had an espresso after dessert." I can still taste the bitterness of the coffee on my tongue. My memory hasn't totally failed me.

"So have something else. At my place."

"Do you live close by?" What is wrong with me? As if it mattered how close he lives. *Oh no, that's too far to walk for my little legs. I will call it a night.*

"Very close." He is now standing *very close.* My heart beats faster. Tom takes my hand, and I follow him quietly, being led away, like a child.

"Okay then, let's go." *Before I change my mind*, I think.

His apartment is beautiful, on the top floor of an early nineteenth-century building. Spacious and extravagantly furnished. I would have been incredibly impressed, but I know that his apartment would cost less than a central London bedsit. I still tell him it's amazing.

"Are you making coffee, then?" I ask as he walks around the living room turning light switches on, dimming them to perfection. The duskier the room, the clearer his intentions become.

"We just had coffee after dessert, remember?" He walks over to me and puts his hands around my face. He is slightly taller than me, and I lift my face up to him. The only thing I'm thinking is that I hope I look beautiful; I hope he regrets what he did to me all those years ago.

I don't mind kisses or anything intimate, really, because it's predictable. Every guy has the same script. Lips meet, tongue tries to sneak in, pulling them apart like curtains, hand on hip/ breast/face (insert one), pull away and look into eyes. Repeat. Tom has read the script well. We are now on the third repeat.

In that moment I've decided to sleep with Tom. Google says not to sleep with a man on the first date, but I've dated Tom before and this would be date number sixty, or so I conclude after quick calculations. I can definitely sleep with a man on date sixty.

"Oh, Klara, I missed you." It's exactly what I want to hear. I take my dress off, looking at him for a reaction.

"God, you're beautiful. So much better than I remember. How stupid was I? Come here."

Mm-hmm yes, very stupid, keep going.

He undresses fast and pauses as if he's waiting for a reaction. He's fit, his pecs bulge, but all I can think of is how they are shaped exactly like the slobbery chicken breasts you slice up for a midweek stir-fry.

He places his hand around my wrist pulling me toward him, and I follow him into the bedroom where I sit down awkwardly on the bed, unsure what I should do next. It's been months since I was last naked in front of a man. I'm painfully aware of the fact that my twenty-six-year-old body is very different to the slim, almost skinny girl that Tom undressed all those years ago.

"God, Klara. So damn hot. God, look at you." I hadn't anticipated quite so much God in the room.

Tom kisses me again and pushes me gently onto the bed. He massages my breast as if the glands in them are particularly stubborn knots in a tense back that he is determined to release. I touch his body and remember how I used to feel about it. Now it's just a body, and not a particularly special one.

"Does it come off?" Tom traces the outline of the small round device that is my CGM, with his index finger. He has stopped stroking me.

"Uh, only every two weeks when I change it."

"It's just I find it a bit uncomfortable. Makes me think I have to be gentle with you."

"The equipment that keeps me alive disturbs you?"

"You didn't used to have it."

"Because I injected myself four times a day and pricked my finger with a little needle twice as many. There's been break-through technology since then."

"I guess when you put it like that…"

He's not the first one. In fact, men seem terrified of my robot parts. I have found it takes a warning before clothes come off, or else everything halts and an awkward *What's that?* or, worse, a stare followed by nothing and an attempt to continue even though the moment has been lost. Talk about a mood killer. Talk about *me* being a mood killer.

I pull away from him briefly.

"I'm sorry, Klara, forget I said it. Let's get back to where we were," he says as if we have briefly drifted from a meet-ing agenda.

ALEX

Personal Calendar ▾

O **NEW TASK:** Compose email to schnauzer society

O **NEW TASK:** Update Mamma/Pappa/Dan on new developments

O **EDITED TASK:** Hold off. No need to get their hopes up

Don't believe it. Unfuckingbelievable. Four days since I told Klara about trying to find the red jacket, and she hands over a printed-out email. It says *Swedish Schnauzer Club* at the top, and it's a list of its members in alphabetical order.

"It's worth a shot," she says. "Even if it's a long one." It's more progress than I've made in eight months. My hand shakes as I take it from her. There are seventy-nine female names on the list. I decide to include the male first names as well in my search. No stone unturned, no schnauzer-owning human unsearched.

"Feel free to leave early and get started." I look at the time, confused. It's almost 5:00 p.m. Which is when I always finish work.

"You want me to leave now?"

"Yes. Why don't you call it a day at 4:51 today?" I have no

urge to laugh because a gift of nine minutes is actually not laughable. Time is precious; the trial is only a few weeks away.

"Thank you," I say. "Appreciate it."

Wish I would have said what I meant: *I appreciate you, the only person who's offered any practical help in the last painful eight months.* But keep this to myself.

KLARA

> 🔍 What have I done to upset my sister?

Google Search　　　**I'm Feeling Lucky**

Somehow it's Thursday again, but it doesn't feel like it. Hanna and I are giving Dad a work briefing, but it's very different from the usual grilling we get. Dad tries his best to pretend he is keeping up with the work, but he keeps referring to a job we completed weeks ago and doesn't even ask to see the summary of the mileage-tracker data or the expenses spreadsheet.

Hanna is now showing him multiple videos and photos from our projects on her iPad. A quick task, considering we still don't have enough work to fill the weeks. I push the thought away. I still have more than a month until I need to hand things over. Things can turn around, there's time. There's no need to worry Dad just yet.

Halfway through he lifts up his hand.

"I trust you. Put it in an email, and I'll review later."

"You hate emails. You like chats and phone calls," I object.

Hanna gives me a look that says *It's okay, Klara. Let it go. Let him go.*

"You're right. There's nothing more to say, anyway. I was just about to wrap up, Dad!" I add a tad too brightly.

"Are you okay, Klara?" Hanna asks me when Dad has left the room.

"Yes. It's my dad who's not okay. My mum says it's normal to feel ill, and that it may mean the treatment is working." I have marked the day of Dad's end-of-treatment checkup with my strongest black marker as well as entered it into the Outlook calendar.

"I'm here if you need anything. Say, a cookie or for me to play a dedicated R and B song for you."

A warm, soft feeling takes over, and I think that the number of friends I have now is two. Alice and Hanna. Hanna, who is like a human Labrador: soft and friendly, sheds long brown hairs in my car (she insists on brushing it every time she's worn a helmet or a hat) and who thinks about the next meal of the day before she's finished the one she's eating. I've always loved Labradors.

The second reason it doesn't feel like Thursday is that I have my wine but no one to whine to today. I try Saga three times without any response. I wait ten minutes, then send a shot of my wineglass. Then fifteen minutes later I send another one with half the wine gone. Finally, I send her a picture of my empty glass. Then I decide to heed Alice's excellent advice on ghosting, shared by her during my brief period of app dating: the best plan is to treat your ghost as if they are invisible. So instead of texting Saga my thoughts, I just think them, as I pop my glass in the dishwasher: *Thanks for showing up.*

ALEX

Shared Calendar ▾

○ **NEW EVENT:** IELTS practice? (Your dad told me on drinks night...)

Reply (Klara): Dad should learn to keep family secrets to himself, like how Saga sucked her thumb until age seven, that he takes three sugars in his coffee even though the doctor has said he should only have one, and that his youngest daughter is unable to sit exams successfully if her life depended on it. Also, you do know it's an English-language test and you're not English?

Reply (Alex): I bit my fingernails until about two years ago. Seriously, you talk and I listen?

Reply (Klara): Could use math help. *If* I actually did want to pass this test one day and *if* I were to go back to school, I need math practice. And I'm not saying I am going, just that I could use the practice. Six years since I last studied. Let's do that instead?

Reply (Alex): Consider teacher hired.

Reply (Klara): Do you have the time?

Reply (Alex): You helped me find my witness. I want to give something back.

Have a reply. The group email appealing for witnesses was sent
out to the list of dog owners on Monday, and one day later I
have an email from someone called Berit. I could cry. Literally. May have already done it. Dan also can't fucking believe
it. We are staring at the screen together, and his knuckles are
white and fists clenched.

"Fucking douche won't be getting away so easily after all,"
he says, and it's probably the first time I've ever heard him
swear, apart from once when he stubbed his pinkie toe on a
boxed white wine.

"Wow, that felt good. I can see why you like swearing so
much," he says, then continues to move his eyes from left to
right as he takes in the contents of the email.

Berit, aka Mysterious Red Fleece Lady, was staying in an
Airbnb visiting her aunt that night last year, and she would love
to help. She promises to get in touch with the case officer whose
number I've given her. She may not remember everything, she
says, but in the next sentence she says this: *I do remember a lot of
noise and screams. My dog was barking and I reckoned I wouldn't be
of much use so I headed off once I saw help was there. The white van
stopped at the side, and the guy driving it looked over his shoulder. He
had dark blond hair and looked stressed, I thought, then about a minute later he sped off. The tire went over the curb when he drove off.*

Later that night she interrupts my ramen-slurping with a text:

Hello, Alex. I just remembered something that had slipped my mind
before. I'm very sure I heard him shout some rudeness about a cyclist.

I feel some glimmer of hope for the first time since… I don't
even know when. I haven't driven as often since I started work,

and now I can stop altogether. There is no need to be anywhere other than my bed at 2:00 a.m. on any given night.

Buzzing and can't wait to tell Klara. I enter it into the calendar we share.

O **NEW EVENT:** Hear Alex's good news; Location: The friendship zone

When I get to the office, I make two coffees, milk in hers, mine black, and wait like an eager child. I've known how she takes her coffee since the first day I met her. Watched her make it and memorized her every move as if it would one day be information that saved my life.

Realize suddenly that Klara seems less stern lately, and less annoyed with me. She's become the person I want to share news with.

It's 9:10 a.m. and she still isn't there, which is unusual. When she finally bursts in, I notice that she is wearing the same clothes as yesterday.

"Hi." Her hair is not straight like yesterday but has soft curls. *Why is she wearing the same clothes? And—why do you fucking care, Alex?*

"Sorry I'm late. I had a date last night," she says in a neutral tone. "Why did you want to see me?"

"I have some news. All thanks to you." It doesn't feel as sweet telling her this any longer. I'm deflated, and the coffee cup feels cold in my hand. I hand her hers. It's still amazing news and one of the best days I've had in a long time, so I tell myself to cheer up.

"I found the woman." Realize I haven't told Klara much about the trial—or anything for that matter—but now seems not the time.

"Schnauzer Woman? Okay, now I will probably always imagine her with a big snout." She laughs. *Is she happier than usual?*

"Yes. She fucking exists, after all this time. She will do a witness statement for us. It's all being taken care of." I pause. "I wanted to say thank-you."

"It was nothing."

"No, it was something. For me. It's everything, actually." If I could, I would tell her that I can stop driving at night, stop having an anxiety attack every time I spot a red jacket in a crowd of people, running after them like a mad person. But no words come out.

"Going to have a shower and start the day. Thanks for the coffee!" She walks into her dad's house, leaving me in the office with the dishes.

I write to Paul. At least I don't have to worry about my boss any longer. Turns out she is seeing someone. Relieved.

Not feeling relieved. But this is a good day, I remind myself. I pull up an old entry I wrote against my better judgment and that I can't quite believe I'm actually completing.

O **NEW TASK:** Find Red Fleece Lady; Mark as: DONE

KLARA

🔍 How do I avoid hurting people's feelings?

Google Search   I'm Feeling Lucky

Tom has messaged me: **Thanks for the other day, Clara. I would love to do it again. How about I cook for you on Saturday night? P.S. How is Miss Van Renault recovering? X Tom**

It's Klara with a *K*. I'm insulted. I used to write his name down in my teenage notepads, circling it with hearts and trying out my own name next to it, in case we ended up getting married. And he can't spell mine? Maybe I'm overreacting, but my name is *me*, and it's a mark of respect to spell it correctly. But then, sometimes when I'm insulted, I am told *it's a joke*. And *no offense*. I can't trust my instincts, as what I get upset over is not what others get upset over. I decide to put my feelings aside and use an objective lens. I come up with this: Tom enjoyed our night together. He wants to see me again. He makes an internal joke, which signals that we have a connection. Tom is single and within my three attempts.

I decide to accept his invitation.

I reply back to Tom as follows: I think you cooking for me on Saturday would be a good idea, considering all factors. I also have no plans and so I will see you then. X Clara. I decide to write my name to match his spelling of it to avoid hurting him. He may feel very embarrassed at having gotten it wrong if I write it with *K*.

"I got booked for a foot job!" Alice sings the news to me. Her limbs have graced the pages of numerous magazine pages showcasing jewelry, nail polishes and verruca plasters.

"My only body parts that are model-like," she says. "I'll get £75 and a free pedicure." She quickly turns her attention to me.

"So was there any sexy time?" she asks me through the car speakers.

"What are you, a '50s housewife?"

"I'm not the one looking for a man to open jar lids."

"If you must know, it was what I would describe as sex-in-no-time. I'm surprised he messaged me again saying how great it was. It's like he was in a different room than me. Like are we talking about the same sex?" I often have this happen to me. I seem to understand everything differently. I keep thinking I must be very bad at sex, if I don't feel what others do.

I don't mention that the fast turnaround had something to do with my mechanical pieces putting him off. When you know someone's reply (in this case it will most certainly be *he's an immature ass*) there is no point in sharing information.

"That's the difference between men and women. Women have great or bad sex. For men, great sex is great and bad sex is still pretty good." Alice continues with authority and a told-you-so voice. "At least you can give up the idea that he was your meet-cute rekindling with childhood sweetheart. Since there is nothing sweet about it."

I don't tell her that he is my only option, unless you consider the man of fifty-plus who winked at me in the screw section of the warehouse this morning. She seems to have moved on, anyway.

"There's always Tinder."

"A dating app is going nowhere near my phone."

Dating apps should work for me. Technically. If someone swipes, they like you. The rules are easy enough to grasp, much easier than reading body language and facial expression while not losing eye contact. *But remember not to stare as if you're giving them an X-ray, Klara!*

Number of times I have tried Tinder: seven. Number of second dates: zero. Somehow my humor gets lost whenever I ask my mouth to take care of the delivery rather than my fingers. Seven times I've been convinced that I've found the one, our banter so good I chuckled a whole night and neglected the eight hours of sleep I need to function optimally and keep a swift response time in the YourMove chat. There were times when, high on chatting, I have rushed off to meet a man, practically undressed already, just to find that we had no connection. *I was not what he had expected.*

In hindsight, I don't know what I was thinking even trying. To think that I voluntarily met up with strangers, oblivious to whether they were serial killers, had nail fungus or watched soap operas is incomprehensible. All three would be reasons not to pursue a romantic relationship, and the first one is a reason I would not allow a friendship to develop either.

I've spent a way-too-large chunk of the evening making hot cross buns.

"Why not just buy an Easter cake?" Dad says as I start my second attempt. I blame the first one on the Swedish instant yeast. "The bakery makes delicious ones."

"Sweden doesn't have a designated Easter cake, does it? It's the same chocolate cake and sweet treats smorgasbord setup as Christmas."

"I just figure, with everything you have going on, baking is a bit ambitious."

Yeah, well he doesn't get this problem of being stuck between cultures. I feel like if I give up the UK traditions, I'm not worthy of my passport any longer. I can almost imagine the border control when I arrive back at Gatwick presenting a form on my return. If I behave as if I belong on *The Great British Bake Off*, surely I will be welcomed back. When I finally got my British passport last year, I felt proud, like I was home. Despite a long and painful process costing me one month's salary and almost failing the multiple-choice test on British culture. *Which flower is associated with Britain?* Why intricate botanical knowledge is a must for us EU-migrants is beyond me. You'd think a preference for salt-and-vinegar crisps and knowing who won *Love Island* would be better measures of Britishness.

"Who are you trying to prove your Britishness to? Mary Berry?" Alice says when I call her for troubleshooting.

"You're definitely not Swedish anymore," Dad says over my shoulder.

"How come?" Surprisingly, I feel mixed feelings at hearing this. One part wants to smile proudly, the smile you do when someone compliments your pet or outfit, but another part comes out all defensive and wants to go *Why am I not Swedish?*

"You do the dishes with a sponge and not a brush any longer. And you apologize every time we cross ways in the house, even if we are just passing each other."

I present my third and successful attempt at our 10:30 a.m. break the next day.

"They look delicious, Klara, but I don't celebrate Easter," Gunnar says.

"Not for Easter." I remember that his religion doesn't permit him to celebrate and do my best improvisation. "It's my cat's birthday! Happy birthday, Björn!"

"Well, if you say so," he laughs. "Don't tell me you have another cat to celebrate on Christmas?"

I pull up the calendar now that I have his attention and scan it over twice quickly. "May and June are looking painfully empty," I say, wishing Gunnar would tell me there's been a mistake and he's forgotten to tell me about the ten new projects he just landed. I still haven't told Dad the extent of it. Soon he will look at the schedule, or the revenue, or the accounts and realize what I have done with this company. I blink a couple of times.

"They are. Listen, Klara, with the change of management and a new company operating so aggressively to take our jobs, it was never going to be easy. We've been around for years, though. Things will pick up eventually."

But will they? *I've* been around for years and *my life* hasn't magically picked up.

"Hanna has done a great job with the website and our Facebook page, but no one seems to be finding them," I say.

"What about running some ads on local radio?" Alex says. He is dipping a hot cross bun into a coffee, not how they are meant to be eaten. I feel offended on behalf of my baked goods.

"Too desperate. Customers will see through it. We've always operated on word of mouth," Gunnar replies.

"I'll have another chat with Lennart before I head off for the day," I promise. Not that he can do more than recommend us to every person that walks in his door.

Alex doesn't leave when Gunnar does.

"So what's the deal with your date? I see two Tom entries next week. This dude likes his Mediterranean cuisine. Italian on Friday and French on Tuesday." The downside of sharing my calendar with Alex is that he also gets to take part in my private life. His side is weird notes about bin collections and Saturday treats, and I'm thinking that's code for other, juicier stuff that he doesn't want me to know. Like *Saturday treats* would mean intimacy with the wife. Maybe they are the type of couple that have been together for so long and have such a deep connection, sex is secondary and needs to be scheduled. Difficult to imagine reaching that level of relationship with anyone, let alone Tom. *Oh right, Tom, the man you're dating, that Alex just asked you about.*

"Tom and I went out on Monday for a bite to eat, then I joined him for a legal presentation he was holding for a cohort of undergrads, dinner at his place on Thursday, and yes, now he seems to have made it a regular thing."

"Sounds like a fucking Craig David song to me."

"Whoa, there." But I do laugh. Because it's funny. Alex is low-key funny. He cracks the best jokes without looking smug, as if he hadn't planned for it to be a joke until it leaves his mouth, or perhaps he just enjoys giving out jokes for free, as opposed to the rest of the population who only entertain to receive admiration. This is why I laugh at his jokes and only move my mouth to dangle my earring at other people's.

I am holding a plank of polished birch wood for Alex while he focuses all his attention on it, marking it carefully. He slips slightly with his hand. My thumb gets caught on a sharp edge of the work top, a trickle of red emerging.

"Shit kebab," he lets out.

"Pardon?"

"Yeah. That needs explanation. Mum never allowed us to say *shit* so we covered up by adding *kebab*. Shish kebab," he says.

"Your mum sounds amazing." He hands me a tissue for my thumb, which I kindly reject.

"Nah. You don't waste blood." I reach into my bag for my emergency kit. If technology fails (which it does from time to time, nothing man-made is completely reliable, and unfortunately I rely on a man-made pancreas) I have the old-fashioned kit. I catch it on the test strip, giving it extra volume by squeezing the thumb sides until the drop is round and plump. It flows onto the paper strip beautifully. I wipe the thumb against my work trousers. Sterilized tissues are for first-year diabetics, then you get hardened.

"I have a new swear word, thanks. I can't believe you also avoid *shit* like the plague."

As I put my kit back in my bum bag, something falls on the floor.

"Don't tell me that was your lunch." Alex picks up a protein-bar wrapper with the same disgust as if it were a used condom.

"They are healthy. Easy to carb-count, 18.1 grams, no crazy blood sugar because I got it wrong."

"Do you do this often?"

"I kind of go off food. It becomes a way to stay alive and nothing else. I count the carbohydrates, enter them into my pump remote and then I eat them. When I have a busy after-noon, I don't want to take the risk of having high blood sugar." High sugars equal headache, nausea and excessive peeing. Not ideal for van driving.

"It sounds like I need to start taking you out for lunch."

"No!" That came out way too fast. The thought of having to socialize every single lunch hour is…exhausting.

"Okay," he says. Any disappointment, he hides it well. I con-clude that he asked out of politeness, that type of question you want the other person to decline. Such as *Shall we split the bill?*

"Then, I'll at least bring back an extra sandwich. Just in case."

"That would be fine. Thank you." I relax a little. Talking about sandwiches—that I can do.

ALEX

Personal Calendar ▾

○ **NEW TASK:** Cancel plans with Paul (in fact drop everything every time she suggests she needs me)

○ **NEW TASK:** Pick up math book after work (ditto: pick up everything she needs every time she needs it)

○ **NEW EVENT:** Klara study club 7pm (*not* at all overly excited—simply helping a *friend*)

Saved to Drafts

Calle,

Was thinking today not necessarily about you but about death. I had a friend from school, you knew him—he was a year above me at school. He died from cancer two years ago. I was shocked, although not enough perhaps; his funeral was the first one I ever went to. Remember I borrowed a jacket from you? Anyway, he left Sweden when he was eighteen. For months he talked about it, had gotten a scholarship to a New York university, couldn't stop talking about what a shithole Malmö was and how the big city waiting for him was, made it sound like the red carpet was rolled out and all he had to do was attend and things would fall into place.

He went to South Africa afterward, Cape Town, which from the pictures of it looked like Miami, all white beaches and trendy restaurants. Then back to America, Los Angeles this time, I could see him fitting in there. He only came back to Sweden for Christmas and Midsummer. Christmas Eve is our family celebration and Christmas Day is for friendships, for going to the clubs of nostalgia and catching up with school friends. And Midsummer is midnight sun, schnapps and dancing with flower scents in one's nose. He came back for that.

Then he got sick. He held on to the big, big world, got his treatment in a city where there was no one to bring him or his family quiches. Then he died—and finally came home.

What I understand from life is this: you live and travel and can build yourself up to be anyone you want, but in the end, you are returned to and buried in the soil you worked so hard to escape.

Graves don't mean anything to me. I haven't visited in months: yours could have a garden gnome on it by now for all I know. I go to the space where you lived. And loved.

I'm helping Klara study. Now I feel like I hear you inside my head going *There is an awful lot of Klara in these emails lately, bro!* and yes, there is because there is an awful lot of Klara in my life recently.

Lately I am not sure where I belong, which is a surprise, and not a pleasant one. I had thought this was a place on earth as good as any, and it is: it is not its lack of appeal or inferiority which unsettles me now but that there is a point I must follow, and if that moves, then I could too. I am not rooted here and would happily go other places to be returned to the soil one day, that's enough for me. Haven't spoken about it, but in a few weeks Klara is heading back to London, or *home*, as she calls it. After her dad's last checkup. London! Went for a weekend there once. Beer is overpriced or foul and the queue for Tussauds took longer than the walk around the museum. Also, what actually is the point of looking at wax dolls? London is now this big threat looming over my head, like I'm waiting for it to rain. I have to be supportive of her plans, I owe her that. She deserves it all, even if that's London and not me. Besides, we're friends as she has made abundantly clear, and she's seeing someone else. Not even available. But hard not to think about her when her name pops up in my calendar every morning. Today, tomorrow, the day after. And I can't really imagine a day when it won't.

Don't take Klara Nilsson away from me, London. You have enough fucking people already.

A

Already dark outside. Sometimes I think it's so dark it feels like it will never be light again. Wonder if other people have thoughts like that?

Klara's dad has an open-door policy, and after two knocks I'm welcome to proceed, so I do, taking my shoes off and placing them by the door. I walk to the back of the house and into a spacious living room.

"Peter." I nod to him.

"Hi, Alex. Klara is upstairs."

She's in her bedroom? Surely I shouldn't be going up there? Is it still a girl's room, or has she given it a makeover? Does she have childhood posters on the wall (horses? Eminem?) and a lava lamp? Can't help feeling like I'm a kid again and heading into a girl's home to ostensibly help her with schoolwork. Feel an urge to tell her dad my intentions are innocent and we will be focused solely on mathematics. University prep. Confidence-boosting. Except there's no need for that at all—I *am* simply helping her with math. Still, it feels polite not to rush upstairs into her space. I lean against the door frame and start updating Peter on our work.

"The nursery kitchen project is going well. We're waiting

for one pallet of tiles to arrive, but by next week that should be finished. I've fitted the shelving in the pantry."

"Good, good. You're doing well. Been a great addition to the team." Peter stands up slowly, hands gripping the coffee table. I resist the urge to help him get up. Wonder how I'd feel if I didn't have the strength to do ordinary things.

My phone beeps. I hold up the phone as an apology to Peter who walks off slowly. A message from Paul: Our catch-up canceled so you can help a girl with math?? Dude, if that isn't the oldest trick in the book...

About to answer, but the main distraction in my life enters the room and does what she does best: distracts me.

"What are we working on today?"

There she is. Hair wet and braided, and for a second I get a strange desire to grab the single, thick braid, feel the weight of it as I close my hand tightly. She looks comfy in a beige tracksuit and feet bare on the floorboards. It's the first time I've seen her feet. Small and square with toes spread out, gaps of air in between them. I wonder what they would feel like in my hands.

She just said something, didn't she? Physically shake my head to gather myself.

"Basics. Fractions and decimals."

"Sounds good."

Follow her to the kitchen. Have looked up the compulsory modules of an architecture degree. Algebra, geometry and trigonometry. Reckon we're not there yet. If I can up her confidence with the foundations, she'll be better off heading into it. What she needs isn't English-language practice, it's confidence and study skills.

Pull out the book I spent 199 kronor on, plus next-day speedy delivery, as we settle at the table.

"I found this lying around at home." It smells suspiciously of newly printed ink, but she doesn't question me.

"Fractions. I really don't like them because they are just different versions of decimals. For instance, ¼ is 0.25, but one is odd and the other even," she says.

"Fractions are not even or odd numbers. They're not whole numbers, only parts. You can't say that the fraction ⅓ is odd because the three is odd. I mean, there are ways to generalize parity to sets larger than the integers, but you'll likely have to give up some desirable property along the way—"

"Which means what exactly in Swedish? Or English if you wish."

"It means you don't have to worry about them being even or odd."

She lights up at this, as if I've taken a huge weight off her shoulders. Feel like I have more purpose than I've had in a long time. She twirls the end of her wet hair around her hand then lets it fall heavily against her shoulder.

"Did you ever think about the fact that maybe nothing is really odd? It's just one version of it? Anything can fit? You can rewrite any number and make it even," she says with delight.

It's not mathematically correct, but if it helps her, who am I to question? She pulls her legs up underneath her on the chair and grabs hold of her foot with her hand, rubbing her hand against the side of it. *So she likes them rubbed.* I watch her as she tackles the first problem in the book. She drops her pencil and looks as if she's just gotten the million-pound question wrong on live TV. Despair.

"God, I really *am* stupid."

Don't like that statement. Not the words and not the way she said it, as if she's repeating what other people have told her. Whoever said that could, well, fuck off.

"Who said that to you?"

"It doesn't matter. But if you must know, enough people to make it statistically correct."

"Listen to me. *Stupid* is a word that just doesn't go with you. Like…like wood doesn't belong in a wet room and pineapple has no business being on pizza. Got it?"

She attempts a nod.

"If you don't understand something, it's because no one's bothered to explain it correctly. Their problem—not yours."

"Thank you." It takes all my willpower not scoop her into my arms then and there.

"Right. Let's work through it together. There's no rush." I swallow hard.

She stares at the page and sits quietly for what feels like an eternity, then emerges from her bubble to grin at me.

"Show me."

"Look." She writes down her workings. "That's right, isn't it? I got it."

"Knew you would. You'll kick ass on the prep this time around."

"Sometimes I feel like even my own family have given up hope. Although they'd never admit it. You're the one person telling me I can do it. That shouldn't cancel out all the negativity from my past failures. Not technically. But then, what you think means a lot."

"It does?" Haven't heard her say that *Tom* means a lot.

"Of course!"

She looks straight at me. How can a cold kitchen light make a person look so good? It's not a fucking sunset, just an LED light bulb, but there she is all shiny and wide-eyed in front of me. My knee has been resting against the outside of her thigh for a good few minutes now, and she hasn't moved away.

She leans closer to the book, and her breaths are quick and so loud in the silent kitchen. Then she closes it, places the pencil neatly on top and leans in toward me, and her face breaks out into a huge smile as she pulls away from me.

"Alex! I just realized that I can make *seven* an even number. I just remove the *s!*"

What almost felt like a moment is gone. Lesson over. Class dismissed.

KLARA

🔍 What makes a good boyfriend?

Google Search   I'm Feeling Lucky

I've brought Hanna to an address in Lund. Her apprenticeship is going from strength to strength, and I enjoy the company of another girl.

"Are you okay?" I ask my second friend. She is walking a good few yards behind me.

"I've noticed that you prefer…um…space?"

"Only when it comes to some people." *People I might like too much.*

The door is opened by a pretty young girl with Down syndrome. Her blond hair is curled into soft locks, and she is wearing a glittery purple bomber jacket over a body-con dress. Even if I had completed a fashion degree, I wouldn't be able to achieve this level of sass.

"Maja? I'm here to check how the work on your bathroom is progressing."

"Hi, come in!" She beams at me. It's nice seeing a friendly smile after having spent most of the morning with loud Copperplate Gothic and his home spa.

"I want purple tiles. I already went to have a look with my mum on the weekend."

"Great. There's still time to choose. If you have something in mind already that will help and will make the quote more exact. Did you make note of the tile's serial number in the shop? Was it by any chance Lennart that helped you?" She collects a paper from the table and puts it in my hand. It's got notes of tiles and shower curtains as well as some sketches of lush-looking bathroom goals.

"These are great. Are you an artist?"

"Drama student!" I should have known. Her personality jumped at me the moment I came inside.

"I wish I could act. It would make my life so much easier."

"I just love it. We are doing monologues from the classics right now. I'm preparing one from *Romeo and Juliet*. It's my favorite love story. I adore love stories."

I wait in the kitchen for Hanna to finish the measurements.

"It's my first apartment. Mum comes every weekend to cook batches of food, and my boyfriend visits every Friday. Do you have a boyfriend?" Maja looks at me hopefully.

"Not at the moment. They seem quite hard to secure. But I'm seeing someone, I guess."

"Oooh. Do you have a picture? Does he bring you flowers? Mine brings me flowers and chocolates every time he comes over. Like a gentleman."

I stop to think on this for a moment. Tom's made me dinner, yes, but no, he's never brought me flowers. "Does he make you laugh? It's important to have fun in a relationship. My boyfriend is sooo funny. He does the best impressions of artists. We love One Direction and Billie Eilish. But they're not so funny."

I've never looked for *fun*. It's one of the most misleading, two-faced words I know. It has connotations of parties where I stand in the corner, strained team-building exercises and holidays where the strongest memories are sunburn and food poisoning. I try to think about having fun with Tom. I laugh more at Tom than with him, I decide.

"And does he give you butterflies in your stomach?"

"I don't think he does." He may give me something, but if I try to visualize it, it's more of a single moth fluttering around in my gut than a butterfly. The type that only come out at night.

"I think you should have butterflies," she concludes.

ALEX

Personal Calendar ▾

○ **NEW EVENT:** Couple's therapy

○ **NEW TASK:** Ask Klara out for coffee

○ **EDITED TASK:** Not quite ready yet

It's been a while since I was here last and two weeks since scheduling this questionable event. Too late to back out now.

Dr. Hadid's office has been decorated for Easter, even though it's weeks away. Small yellow chickens and colorful eggs sit on the windowsill. Paul is already there, filling out a questionnaire.

When we're called into the consultation room, I let him take the chair already in place and pull up another one to sit next to him.

"Are you sleeping better?" Dr. Hadid asks me.

"Much," I say, and I surprise myself by realizing, that yes, apart from the occasional late night lying awake imagining Klara's face, I am getting the hours I need to function optimally. I am not only sleeping better but I feel better.

"Have you had any challenges at work?" she asks.

"I guess so. Just getting up for work in the mornings, meeting people again and being, you know, *normal*. Also, my boss's lack of structure is frustrating, but we're getting there. None of these would be challenges due to depression, though."

"I agree. These are normal life challenges that everyone faces. You seem to be responding to them in a healthy way. If your sleep and mood remain stable, that tells me you are overcoming the challenges well."

She moves her attention from me to Paul.

"Could you tell me a bit about the ring? If that's okay for us to discuss, Alex? I understand you were there when Alex found it."

"Sure. This was back in August last year. I had come with Alex to collect Carl's things from the hospital, and at some point—I think it was in the waiting room when Dan was filling out all the forms and putting down signatures—Alex was going through the contents of the plastic bag. Then I guess he just put the ring on."

"I wanted to take it off again. Just couldn't." A childhood memory of having stolen a candy, Mamma asking me to spit it out and me refusing pops up. Once on, the ring was like that, impossible to return.

"Dan said to keep it. Alex was a mess. As in, we'd give him anything he'd ask for."

Watching Paul talk about it so casually, something I haven't been able to do, feels...liberating.

"This was really helpful. Thank you, Paul. And, Alex, you still find that the ring is helpful? Wearing it brings you some comfort still?"

"I honestly don't think about it much anymore. It's on and has just sort of remained on, since that day in the hospital."

"That's not a problem. But since you're not actively thinking about it, not actively relying on it for comfort as much, maybe you should give some thought to what it would be like without the ring, how you would feel if you were to look down and not have this reminder of Calle."

She goes through the questionnaire, ticking off points about friendship, my support system and whether it's changed since therapy started, and lastly she asks if Paul feels I'm able to give him what he needs in our friendship too. He says *yes*, and I'm proud as fuck.

"Do you—either of you—have any questions for me?" Dr. Hadid begins to wrap up the session.

I prepare for Paul's eyes to roll, and I say, "There is something that worries me. Is it possible that I'm transforming my grief into another emotion? Say, uh, being attracted to someone?"

Fighting it hard. Told Hanna I wasn't on the market when she asked if there was something going on between me and Klara. The market is not for men with depression, a therapist and a dead person's ring on their finger. Should probably listen to Dr. Hadid and actually give some thought to taking the ring off.

"You mean that you like someone and want to know if it's the grief talking?"

"That's it."

"It would be a highly unusual response to trauma this many months later. Have you considered that your feelings for this someone may be genuine?"

Shish. I have considered a lot of things when it comes to Klara. Remember the conversation with Hanna a couple of days ago.

"I don't care what you say, Alex. I've seen the looks. You two are couple goals."

"Yeah, right. Have no idea what you mean. Klara's long-term goal is London. And her short-term one is Tom."

But I had to ask, "Has she said something about me?"

"When does she not say something about you…?"

Shift on the chair now and address Dr Hadid.

"Thanks. That's…reassuring to hear."

Thirty minutes later I'm waiting for Paul to reappear from the bathroom when Dr. Hadid brushes past me in the waiting room.

"Alex," she says, "strictly off-the-record, maybe you should ask the girl out?"

KLARA

> 🔍 What are the next steps in a relationship?

Google Search   **I'm Feeling Lucky**

It's my fifth date with Tom since we met in the parking lot. I am back in his company for no better reason than he called, I answered, he asked, I said yes. Also, Alex canceled our math evening, and I have been on edge ever since. Doesn't he believe in me any longer?

I may have realized he is not my jar-opener, as I seem to think about Tom more like I do a bag of Smarties or tub of ice cream long after dinner. I know I should go to bed but I still want *something*. A message to Tom satisfies the craving.

We are halfway through our olive, nachos and roasted pimento pepper selection (which is paired with a sparkling Ramlösa, a locally sourced water with a low-mineral content and sharp fizz, Tom informs me) when my phone pings. It always appears more aggressive when I'm in a bar. *Ping!* instead of *ping*, as if it's been having some cheeky tequilas when I wasn't looking. A new event. Why do we need an extra staff meeting at 8:00 a.m.? I had planned on sleeping in. If 8:00 a.m. can be considered a sleep-in, but I take what I can get, and my first appointment happens to be at nine thirty. I curse myself for letting Alex be in charge.

"Early meeting tomorrow. I need to be going in about twenty-three minutes," I say and sip my water.

"You're not coming back to mine? It's a good forty minutes for you to drive home."

"You're right. It *is* very far. I should leave in eighteen minutes, really. Thank you." Staying over would delay me significantly and force me to skip breakfast. I hadn't even planned to go home with Tom. I have a busy day tomorrow, followed by my second math practice with Alex: no way am I being tired for that.

"You could have told me before." He is sulking like a child, his whole mouth turning down at the sides. These extreme facial expressions are helpful, as I don't have to spend minutes interpreting them or sorting through how they make me feel. In this instance, I don't sympathize with him. He could have made his expectations clearer and in that way received an advance response that I wouldn't be going back to his place.

"You didn't ask me to stay over, you asked me to a tapas bar." He is starting to get on my nerves. Tom has been a pleasant distraction, sure, but distractions should stay mellow and not stir things up. Emotional status quo. Distractions should be a slow-paced Netflix show, nothing too exciting, a mediocre background song, and, if a person, they should be enjoyable but not overwhelming or annoying. Tom is more and more failing to be a good distraction.

"Klara? I wanted to suggest something…"

"Yes?"

"I thought we could, you know, put on some *porn* tonight."

Seriously? I start to gather my things.

"I feel like we are ready to take this to the next level."

"Tom, that would be holding hands in public or me leaving a toothbrush at your place. Watching porn together is not a relationship stage."

"Really?"

"Really. I'm going home."

"Are you sure? Maybe you come over for a quick one? You would still have time to head home if we go back to mine now."

"Absolutely a hundred percent sure. Thanks for the offer, but no thanks."

"Suit yourself. We may as well get going, then." I don't like saying *no*, and I enjoy making other people happy, but like Alice keeps reminding me, *Start to make yourself happy, Klara. You are also a person and therefore you count.* And last time I slept with Tom, I didn't feel happiness.

"Tom, can I ask you something?" He is paying the bill, and I finally pluck up the courage to ask what I should have years ago.

"Why did you dump me?" Tom takes his card back from the waiter with a silent thank-you and looks at me, eyes blue and sharp.

"I was eighteen and immature. I didn't have finesse ending relationships yet, and you were so in love with me. I mean, everyone knew it. You were the type of girlfriend that just clung to me, you texted a hundred times a day, you wanted to meet every afternoon. I wasn't sure how you would take it, if you were going to make a scene or start crying. I'm not good with girls crying. I know it wasn't a nice thing to do, leaving you alone with a note on a cup. I had planned to sit down and tell you, I really had, but nerves got the better of me." He smiles. "Let's be honest, Klara. You're not exactly the easiest person to have a conversation with, are you?"

I want to ask why he didn't call me afterward, but he continues, giving me the answer that could have helped me years ago. That tells me he will always be one of three failed attempts with no future, not even as a distraction. The one answer that there is no point to argue with.

Tom says, "I guess I just wasn't that into you."

ALEX

Shared Calendar ▾

○ **NEW EVENT (ALEX):** Pastries in staff room

Reply (Alex): They are still hot

Reply (Alex): Okay, now they're probably cold...

Reply (Klara): Running late. See you soon. Don't eat them all

It's 8:14 a.m., and I watch my hopes of Klara having had an early, Tom-free night crumble like the pastries I have prepared on the meeting table. When she finally bursts through the door, I sense that something is different. Her dark hair is still straight from last night's styling, but she is makeup-free. The small birthmark on her chin is more visible without the cream and nonsense. I like it.

"Good night?" I ask.

"I guess." She grabs a croissant, wrapping it in a paper tissue, and bites off the crisp end standing up. She reaches for her pump remote with the other. She has an angry look, the same one she had when I first met her, and she wasn't Klara yet, just a weird Interview Lady. I'm guessing she is upset about something, and as much as I would like to ask, I refrain and instead try to be as helpful as I can.

"They are 26 grams of carbohydrates." I've already made a habit of checking packaging before throwing it away to know how much she needs to take insulin for.

"Thanks."

"No problem."

"I broke up with Tom."

"Thank fuck for that." Totally did not intend for that to be said out loud.

"Can you not swear?"

"Not sure it's possible. Mamma has tried for years. Apparently, Jesus didn't swear, although he was a simple man."

"Want me to find out?" She pulls out her phone and types at record speed.

"*You brood of vipers*, he's been quoted saying. Pretty sure that's the modern-day equivalent of swearing. So yes, you're in good company, tell your mum."

I laugh, then go on to ask, "Are you okay?" She seems okay. I very much *want* her to be okay without Tom.

"I am. Thank you. It's the first time I have ended a relationship. Kind of. Unless you count one where I had terms laid out for the continuation of the relationship, and I opted not to comply, leading to the two of us going our separate ways."

"I'd say you're right, that doesn't count. But he does sound like a moron." I nod, then ask, "Why did you break up with Tom?"

"Let's just say that it was a learning experience. I've now learned. And also because I don't want a loafer when I'm a sneaker," she says. Her Klara logic intrigues me, as always.

"Okay. Not following. You are a sneaker—as in plastic fantastic and tied up to something, strings attached? Should I be worried?"

"It's a metaphor, Alex."

"Not a universally acknowledged one."

"The common ones don't make sense, anyway—I tend to create my own. You know how people ask *What animal would you be?* Well, apply it to footwear. I feel like I'd be an old sneaker, and they're not always appreciated by the heels and leather brogues of the world."

"Sneakers sell for hundreds of pounds on eBay. They're very valuable, Klara." She blinks as if she's got an eyelash in her eye.

"Plus, he didn't like my pump. It embarrassed him," she adds.

"Fuck him."

"Yes, I feel sorry for whoever will be doing that now," she says, but I'm too angry to even smile.

Shake it off and start clearing the breakfast.

"See you at lunchtime for math?"

KLARA

🔍 How do I know if I'm a bad person?

Google Search   I'm Feeling Lucky

Lunchtime math went well. We sat side by side in the van, sandwiches and drinks in the middle, and I worked my way through two pages. I managed to stay friendly and professional by pretending that he was my old secondary-school teacher who had a mustache and smelled like a composting prawn. Alex gave me homework, which I've managed to complete already while waiting for him to arrive at our next appointment. I have been sitting on the curb long enough for my lower body to feel sore when his van finally makes a stop next to me and he hops out, efficiency and agility like a firefighter leaving his vehicle. I hop up and brush the back of my jeans where they have touched the ground, as if checking I haven't accidentally brought the pavement with me.

"There you are," he says, and I stare at him. There I am?

I've been here the past twenty minutes waiting for him. He knew my location—hence he's just arrived here with his van.

"Yes," I say. "Here I am, Alex."

"Sorry I'm late. Apparently the customer had asked for a quote from the competition and kept insisting it wasn't right that it was so much cheaper. I walked him through every single thing that we offer and they don't, but he may still give you a call to try his luck."

When will this stop? Who can keep working while an enemy is constantly trying to sabotage you? I don't have long left here now and will need to own up to Dad. Soon. Just not yet.

"I will just go and pay the parking. You go ahead and open up," Alex says. "The code for the door is zero-eight-six-five."

The building is yellow and four floors high and has a bicycle rack outside. I try the code Alex gave me. I repeat it again and again but force myself to stop. What happened to the code I tried to hold in my memory is this: 08 is August, 65 is the year my mother was born. The date was 03. My dad was also born on a 03, and also the month 03 and the year 1963. I remember his date of birth best because it's all 3s. *What was the code for the door again?* I have nothing, because the only number I can think of at this point is my dad's birth date, and I'm pretty sure that's not it.

"You okay? Is it not working?" Alex says as he comes up behind me.

"Sorry, Alex. It's slipped my mind." I do a laugh to pretend it's funny and I don't care, like you do when someone bullies you as a kid. *Ha! If I laugh with you, no one can laugh at me.*

"Here." He leans over and quickly enters the numbers, and the door opens. He holds it open with his body weight, waiting for me to go in first. "You're a brilliant, intelligent woman. I can't understand how you can't remember four digits for five minutes," he says, laughing along with me. I don't have an answer to that, so this is what I tell him.

"Memory of a goldfish."

★ ★ ★

Twenty minutes later we're in the van. Silences in cars are very loud. I turn up the heating to seventy-nine degrees because the noise the fan makes when it blows with all its might is lovely.

"I'm worried about Hanna. She's been working alone lately and is only just qualified. Do you think it's too much pressure?" I ask.

"I'd say she's perfectly okay. And you are a slightly overconcerned but very good boss."

"Isn't this how everyone is?"

"I wouldn't know. I've never had a woman boss before."

"So I'm your first. I like that." It just slips out of me, as if it's wild and unruly and meant to be said.

Alex's breathing goes shallow, and he looks me in the eye. I can hold it a total of six seconds, which is a near record of the week. The record is still held by Alex, but it was nine seconds on Tuesday when he showed me an amendment for an architectural plan I found highly fascinating.

"I'm just playing with you," I clarify. Remind myself that Alex is not even my type. Too tall, too blond, too confident. Too married.

I also tell myself to remember the statistics I face. Relationships attempted: eleven. Successful outcomes: zero. This means the likelihood for future success is a solid zero.

I put on some music, and '90s rap blurts out in wonderful, soothing waves.

"Thank Christ we usually have separate vehicles," Alex looks at me bemused.

"Yep," I say, but I realize that I don't mind Alex in my car, next to me, my ponytail sometimes swishing past and brushing his shoulder lightly when I turn to look around.

His hand is distracting me. I look at the traffic lights ahead to see if they have switched to green but end up glancing down at it again. The hand—winter pale and soft—just lies there rest-ing on his thigh, and I feel the strongest urge to reach out and put my hand over it, or perhaps inside it.

"Alex, it's green. Go."

Is this what flirting is? Each person taking a turn to say something funny and intimate which makes you want to move closer? I'm not sure. Because I've never been really sure. My flirting is usually limited to applying techniques learned in girly magazines and later Google. Touching your foot to his under-neath a table, for example. This is trickier than it seems when you have short legs. It requires me to slide down on the chair and reach with my toes, an action that is difficult to do while keeping a seductive face. It often results in a *You okay?* which startles me so much I kick the man's leg with my heel. I usu-ally just settle for smiling.

"So my van will be ready tomorrow, all the repairs done, if you can give me a lift and then I'll drive it back," I share when we arrive at my dad's at 6:19 p.m. No more sharing a van with Alex. *Phew.*

I wait for him to say something else; he looks like he's about to, eyes fixed at me. I smooth my shirt. I want to ask him to stay a little longer. To come inside Dad's house and sit on one of our kitchen chairs as I prep dinner. Maybe pet one of the ABBAs and talk about his eccentric parents or carpentry. I have no access to Google, no Phone a Friend option lifeline. Just me. *Think, Klara.* Would it be so wrong to have a glass of wine with a married man?

"If I were to open a bottle of wine and offer you a glass, to drink with me. Inside the house. There would be no harm in that, would there?"

"Harm in a glass of wine?" Alex says.

I laugh but nerves block it, and it comes out more like a snort.

"*Glass of wine*, as in singular—not the plural form—is gen-erally harmless, yes?" I clarify.

"Right. So one glass of wine it is, then. The harmless type."

When we get inside, we take our work boots off by the door, and I retrieve the bottle of red wine I opened a day ago from the shelf. We don't even talk. I always talk to people. Babble. Making every effort to kill the silence and have those earrings dangle if at all possible. We just sit there, close together, and sip on our glasses, occasionally looking at each other. Then, way too soon, Alex has finished his drink.

"I was looking at your ears. Admiring them," he says. Which is something I've never heard said before and therefore have no idea how to handle.

"I better start making dinner and check on Dad upstairs."

"Right, I better get going. Thank you for the harmless wine," he says, and I walk him to the door but keep the two-yard distance, which I seem to have forgotten lately.

Admiring your ears, he had said. I want to ask what he meant, but even to me, Queen of Overthinking Everything, there is only one possible answer now that I think about it, and that is not that Alex has a fetish for ears and goes around rating them in strangers and colleagues alike. No, it means that he likes *my* ears, he likes one of my *body parts*. I'm hardly an expert at reading people, but this is where it leaves me: Alex admires *me*. Likes me. But the ring on his hand means he shouldn't, and I shouldn't like him in return.

I notice that I'm on my tiptoes, a peculiar habit I have. People assume I walk around like that because I'm short and have a wish to be taller. I have noticed that it happens when I am experiencing confusion or stress, and so I don't think people are entirely wrong—in those situations I do wish I were taller, a bigger person. I'm not, though. Because at the door I say, "Alex, what if there was something different about the grapes?" This makes him stop, turn around and come back toward me. I try to remember all the reasons why I decided on a personal-space requirement, but I can't think of a single one.

"What do you mean?"

"In the harmless wine. You know, let's say there was an unintended addition—of a mischievous grape, perhaps—that made its way into the harmless wine as it was being treaded. The wine might not be so harmless after all."

"Okay. Let's say that could totally happen. Let's say the wine wasn't harmless. What does that mean?"

"I'm not exactly sure yet."

"Klara, when you figure out if you want it to be just a harmless glass of wine…or one that's not so harmless, and you want to talk about it, then…let me know."

And at that, he leaves.

ALEX

Personal Calendar ▾

○ **NEW TASK:** Not drink wine with Klara again. Ever

○ **EDITED TASK:** Not drink wine with Klara unless there are people around

Fuck it. Dr. Hadid said the tasks need to be realistic and achievable.

○ **EDITED TASK:** Not drink wine with Klara unless there's at least one cat around

Saved to Drafts

Calle,

Do you remember the first time you kissed a boy? Writing this, I wonder if memory dies with us. I never thought about death: I prefer science, and there is no science in death. Only in the first stage of it. In what happens to the body and the cause of death. I have thought about that enough. If I begin to accept the concept that something remains after we die, then what parts of us? Rationality, memory, emotions? Are we then a blur of feelings and fuzzy love? Or a rational, thinking being perhaps sharpened from life, even?

Anyway, memory. If you don't remember, in case you are simply love-unspecified or on a path to a new body (I hope you get to be a dog; you loved dogs and would make the cutest golden retriever puppy), I will remind you.

I think we were eleven and fourteen. When adults asked (it's always adults, kids don't ask these questions) what we liked most in school, I said *math* and you said *lunchtime*. Neither of us said *recess*. Because recess went like this:

"We catch the girls and keep them inside the den. You guard it, Calle," you were instructed. The group of boys was large, and the game was to catch the girls and not let them go (yes, primary school was a breeding ground for sexual harassment). Girls ran around excited and scared, depending on what rank they had in the class. The ones that got no boyish attention ran slower than the others, secretly hoping to be caught, to be wanted in the game.

"Game's dull," I said.

"Come on, Alex, if we don't play, we are done for," you said. This was true: whatever mad craze the class had gotten into was a join-or-be-shunned situation. If it was marbles that were in, you better bring some, or Pogs, round circular plastic things that our parents deemed a waste of money.

We hovered in the background, guarding the den or repairing it rather than chasing and dragging girls into it.

"It's your turn to kiss someone," a slender, freckled boy with teeth that sprouted rather than sat in his gums said to Calle.

"Nah, leave it. Dream on. Girl germs."

"You gotta kiss her! Kiss her, kiss her!" The chants were there now, and I looked around hoping to see a teacher approach and raise their voice, adjourning the meeting. But coffee breaks are long, and there was no teacher in sight. You wiggled loose from the boy's grip.

"Okay, I'll kiss someone." *Wooo* chants of excitement. Girls wondering who would be picked. Again, some with excitement, some with fear. I looked at my shoes. My hand flapped against my leg like a drum.

"Who's it gonna be?" the freckled one asked as if presenting a stock of animals at market, or options in a TV game show.

"You," you said, eyes straight at our enemy.

"Eww. No way. Pick a girl, weirdo."

"You said I had to kiss someone, not that it had to be a girl." Suddenly boys and girls cheer, everyone except for the chosen one. Brave from your triumph, you walk up and plant a kiss on the toothy mouth. I don't think it was how you imagined your first kiss, but I think first kisses are often bad, often embarrassing, often tinted with regret. Yours was a triumph and a power statement.

Chasing girls and keeping them in a den died out as quickly as Pogs and Tamagotchis did. And no fucking douche ever gave you a hard time about kissing boys when you got old enough to find the good ones and do it because you wanted to.

Seeing you kiss your Dan in the church that sunny May day was one of the proudest moments of my life.

Love you.

A

KLARA

Q How do I make the most of my viral moment?

Google Search   **I'm Feeling Lucky**

My head feels heavy the next morning. I've never had a friendship with a man, and Google results for *platonic intentions* are confusing. My gut feeling is not one to be trusted, and when I look at the facts I could be wrong. Moving closer and maintaining long periods of eye contact would mean something, surely. Maybe. But Alex wants me back in London. That truth is difficult to ignore. In fact, he wants me to go back so much he's helping me study toward that goal. Alice suggested perhaps he *is* into me but is more into his wife and therefore needs me gone. *Wife*.

I'm caffeinated and as alert as I will ever be as I start up the van. Having it back and in working order feels like being reunited with a long-lost friend.

"Hi, Klara. This is Maja's mum." It takes me a moment to register who I'm talking to. Putting faces to voices and vice versa was never my strong point. Although I can remember every wrinkle of a face I looked briefly at on the Tube eight years ago, I can't name acquaintances.

She helps me out.

"The apartment in Lund? I know you were going in today, but Maja has landed herself in hospital with a broken arm. She is having surgery this afternoon and will need to stay there to be monitored. Feel free to go in and work in the meantime."

"I'm so sorry to hear this. I hope she is staying positive."

"She was practicing twirling and doing some sort of dance move that involved a jump that finishes off into a break-dance move. Don't ask."

"That's exactly what I would have imagined. It sounds very Maja."

Her mum smiles, I can hear it.

"We will continue the work while she is away," I promise. "It will be a nice surprise for her to come home to, and at least it means she won't be there the day water is switched off."

The next day I'm back at Maja's to inspect the work. It feels empty without her there. I've brought Hanna with me. I figure the company won't hurt even if Alex is convinced she is ready to spend the day working alone on her own projects. Gunnar and Hanna have done a good job. The bathroom looks perfect, I snap some shots of the skirtings and send them to my dad for approval. The cleanup is nicely done as well, not a speck of dust left, but just as I'm about to close the door, it hits me how bare it is. This girl has paid a substantial sum to have her bathroom decorated, and like any company worth its reputation we should add some extras. You wouldn't want a hotel room without the free soaps and the bed made, would you? Or an espresso at a nice restaurant without the small chocolate or biscuit on the side?

I call Hanna over.

"Can you pop out and get some flowers, bathroom soap and towels? The big supermarket should have some. It doesn't have to be too fancy. If you find some bath salt or a candle, throw that in as well."

Half an hour later we are finished and inspect our makeover. From bare to homey.

"It's gorgeous," Hanna says. "Makes such a difference, doesn't it?" A soft white towel set is hung over the towel rail, soap and toiletries sit on the shelf above the sink, and lavender salt and a bath bomb decorate the white tub. We have placed toilet rolls on the holder and finished the current one off with those fancy folded ends you get in nice hotels. Hanna even found a bath towel with Maja's favorite artist on it, to match the posters in her bedroom. Job well done.

"I think you should make this a regular thing, the Bygg-Nilsson touch," Hanna suggests. It's not a bad idea. My mind starts to buzz with ideas, with excitement.

"I could get special toiletries with our logo. I could find a list of suppliers or even check if Lush are able to do a discount for us and we add our own stickers."

If I wasn't convinced there and then, Maja's evening call did the trick.

"What a nice surprise! It looks wonderful, and I just love the thought of new towels for a new bathroom. I never would have gotten around to buying them myself. The Billie Eilish towels are just amazing. I'm putting it all on my Instagram. I took about a hundred pictures of me in the bathroom, and Mum is helping me with the captions. Can I tag you?" I smile to myself, happy to have done something positive finally.

"Sure, why not? I will message you the company's handle." My colleague made an Instagram for us, but so far it has only about twenty posts and ninety followers, one of which slid into our DMs asking if he could request our female tiler from the staff group shot for a wet-room job, *a very wet room*, he clarified.

Maja goes on. "I'm really popular. I post my acting and dancing and about following your dream and not letting a silly extra
little chromosome stop you. My followers are so excited about
my new apartment. They will love my new space." She does
what sounds like jumping that I'm not sure her doctor would
approve of. Then she adds, "There are 200,000 of them. Followers, I mean!"

The buzzing underneath my pillow wakes me up. I laugh
when people talk about radiation and not having their phones
on when they sleep. Bluetooth saves my life daily. I'm glad to
see it's Nonstop Notifications rather than a diabetic emergency.

Mum: I'm proud of you.

I assume it's for Saga until I read the messages that follow it.

Saga: Have you checked Instagram and Facebook?

Saga: The number is going up by the minute. It's amazing.

**Saga: I'm thinking about contacting some interior magazines or the
local paper, get that photogenic carpenter in the shots with you and
your creations as backdrop.**

**Saga: Ok, on to the media now. Sent out a couple of emails, wrote an
essay on you. Think it may really hit home with the family company,
helping Dad and a woman in construction.**

Saga: Well done, K! xxxxx

Saga is giving me praise, actual praise, not with a hidden
message of some sort but no-strings-attached praise.

I log on to social media and see what she means. Bygg-
Nilsson's following has grown from three to three thousand

overnight. We have four messages asking for a quote, and none of them mention *female* or *wet*.

I call Alex.

"Boss Lady," he says. I grin like a silly person.

"I never expected this. Boss Ladies have perfect nail polish, hair and their shit together all the time."

"Your hair looks perfect to me, and I'd say a boss lady is one that actually is a good boss, cares about her employees, listens to them and wants to deliver the best possible product to the customer. If anyone is a boss lady, it's you."

It's Wine and Whine time. Although today we are having champagne, still high on our (*my*, since I'm not sharing the credit) success. And there is no whining.

"Who runs the world!" I sing (if you ask me) or shout (if you ask anyone else).

"Girls!" Saga shoulder-dances on my phone.

"Who runs the world!"

"Bygg-Nilsson!" We bend over with laughter, each on our own side of the screen.

"God, we're uncool."

"Actually, we're pretty cool. Ask our new followers. And the local paper who wanted a piece of us this morning." We catch our breaths and sip our champagne. I have celebrated met-customer-satisfaction targets at my previous job, but this is different. Now I'm celebrating my own achievement, basically I'm celebrating *myself. Us. My family.*

"Do you think this will really mean more projects? That I can hand Dad back a busy company?"

"Klara, I'm certain of it."

"I wish you were here."

"I need to tell you something," Saga says, and my stomach clenches in the midst of all my joy as if I'm attempting a crunch. Not another medical disaster or family drama. *Please.*

"I'm listening."

"I'm coming to Sweden. I've taken a few days of leave and I'll be joining you."

"But I'm okay, everything is under control." I refrain from saying it's a little late now that business is booming, and Dad only has a week left of his treatment. Saga continues, her eyes staring into thin air, not searching for mine in the screen any longer.

"I'm coming for *me*. The truth is I need to get away. I can't take any more right now. I just told Heinrich I had to take a weekend off. He got it, obviously, had seen it coming." I'm stunned. For a minute I don't say anything. Then Saga's eyes finish the dance around the living room that they had been doing and meet mine. You know you love someone when you see their pain.

I see Saga's pain.

"I didn't know things were so bad. Are you guys on the rocks?" I ask. Alice told me that the origin of the phrase refers to boats that run aground, but I imagine Saga and Heinrich now barefoot on a rocky beach. Foot soles aching, tiny and annoying pebbles stuck between their toes and torsos swaying for balance.

"Maybe? Probably? If nothing changes. I feel so stupid. I have one child—one! There are women who have four and manage fine. I'm not strong enough. But I just feel pulled in all directions, like when I'm a good mum I'm a bad teacher, and when I'm a good teacher I'm a bad mum. I can't do it all. Why? What is wrong with me?"

I love her more in this moment, vulnerable Saga. Her name means *fairy tale*, and she may look like one but that doesn't mean her life is one. I haven't seen her properly, her needs. I've been too busy bulldozing my way through my own problematic life to stop and be an actual sister. I don't care that she didn't finish the website, now I just want her here.

ALEX

Personal Calendar ▾

O **NEW TASK:** Don't bother Klara when there's an alarm. She's got this without your help

O **NEW TASK:** Don't obsess as if she's your business. She's got four other people on her app, not to mention she's been doing this without you most of her life

O **NEW TASK:** Seriously, find something else to focus on

Got the new witness statement. Was asked if I wanted to read the full file, but I'm in way too good a place to get dragged down. I'll be there on the day, and that's enough. I did my job: I found the witness.

Don't write to Calle that often any longer, but I reckon he'd want this news.

Saved to Drafts

Dear Calle,

Pushing for the most severe sentence after all. All thanks to the witness and the killer's apparent display of road rage. Looking through the pile the prosecutor couriered over this morning, and I think you'd be proud. In that little-brother sort of way. When you tell your friends and colleagues about me and take me for dinner to celebrate. You loved celebrating! I felt such anger that you didn't get to have your last birthday party—it was even planned. Dan rented out the beach club three months in advance because that's how well you always planned things. Seafood canapés, champagne and apple cider. It wasn't even a big birthday, not forty for many years yet, but you didn't get to have it. "Do the wake there," someone said. But Dan took the deposit when they offered it back. Told everyone to wear black for your funeral and served quiches and a buffet.

We haven't celebrated anything in a long time. This pile gives me some sort of hope, though, that there is at least that one bit of chance that it will go our way, and sure, that won't be anything to really celebrate: you're still gone. But I think if this goes through, if we do this, I imagine there will be that feeling of achievement as well, and I may just want to take Dan, Mamma and Pappa out for a meal. Which would be some sort of celebrating.

A

Put my phone away, open the car door and grab my backpack. Those minutes in the car before getting out into the world are stillness. My escape. Sometimes, like today, they extend beyond a couple of minutes into half an hour.

Paul is outside my building with what looks like a farmersmarket haul.

"I thought you said you finish at five?"

"Did I know you were coming?" I glance at my phone for a reminder or text.

"You've canceled on me twice. That means I need to check up on you to prevent it happening a third time. Okay?"

I've only just taken my boots off when there's someone new at the door. Dan appears, and it does feel good to see his face. It has been ages.

"Dan? Did I know—"

"No, you didn't. We were worried, okay?"

"Great. I'm alive and functioning, as you can see."

"Functioning? You're not a toaster. Anyway, I've ordered food. Hope you're in the mood for Thai. Didn't trust Paul to pick up the right ingredients to create something edible."

Paul looks highly offended as he digs into his paper bag and waves a parsnip at us. Thai was a good call.

"So why are you being so quiet?" Dan says. "Is it because of Calle? In which case, don't cancel us—we're in this together. Always. You know that. And you know how I've struggled, we've all grieved, but you were the one who got unlucky and ended up with depression." Know this, and know it makes no sense and isn't fair. Why couldn't I grieve like Dan? Healthy tears and a week in bed rather than six months of darkness. But that's depression for you; it clamps down on you, disregarding who you are and whether your grief is proportionate. Besides, Dan wasn't the one who prioritized his sleep over getting his brother home safely. He can tell me it wasn't my fault all he wants to, but that doesn't make it true.

Dan continues talking.

"Or—is it because you've found other ways to occupy your thoughts? In which case, we support you. Keep canceling our plans."

"Is there a *neither* option?" I reply, not sure I can quite admit to either right now. I feel ambushed.

"Alexa, play 'Brown Eyed Girl' by Van Morrison," Paul teases. It gets a laugh from Dan.

"Sure, I care about her." Actually, I've started to care about a lot of things recently. Seeing my parents happy again, eating vegetables, the state of the public health-care system, global warming, smiling at strangers.

"And what's with the language skills? No more two-word texts. Have you noticed how elaborately you've been writing?"

No. Hadn't noticed.

"As long as you don't start writing in poetry form, it's all good."

I go get them some beers to keep them quiet.

"So when is your boss leaving?" they ask in unison when I reappear.

"After her dad's last appointment."

"That gives you limited time to change her mind. You'd better get to work."

"It's not that simple. Even if I did want her to stay—which I'm not saying I do—it's not really about me, is it? She has reasons to go back, her own life to live. This was always going to be temporary." And what claim do I have to her? None whatsoever. Although, I can't help but feel some sort of satisfaction at her trusting me with her blood-sugar data, with some math help, letting me into her personal life.

"Surely you saw this coming. Come on, man." Apparently Paul is not giving up so easily.

"What? Appreciating a coworker's excellent job performance and general decentness is not the same as talking about her for weeks." I like my job, like working hard and feeling useful. I like *me* more lately too. Not willing to fuck all that up because of what is probably a tiny, little, insignificant crush on my boss I'm not even saying I have.

My phone pings with an alarm. As they go to find snacks in the kitchen, I take their absence to pull up Klara's stats on my screen but am met with nothing. *Alarm: no notifications.* Maybe she moved out of range briefly? Push the thought from my mind as best I'm able.

Hard to focus on the Thai food or the conversation, though it's good to have them both here. Find it even more difficult to focus when her readings are not back two hours later, the alarm still sounding at thirty-minute intervals.

"Something could have happened to Klara," I say.

"Why would anything have happened?" Paul asks, kindly.

"The data is always there. Never gone for more than an hour max. The last reading was low. Then nothing."

"You're checking up on her?"

"She's okay with it. It's a work thing." It does sound odd, but then none of this is conventional, is it?

"Maybe I should go over there? Just to check."

"Alex to the rescue," Paul teases. Dan stops him with a look.

"Remember, she's got her dad. It's not like she's all alone. You don't have to put this kind of pressure on yourself, man. You don't have to carry all this weight all by yourself." Dan is right, of course. Spent months looking for someone to blame an accident on. Why do I want more responsibility?

"You genuinely worried? Ring her, then. No harm in that, right?" Paul says, looking worried now.

He's right: I'll just call her, no reason I can't dial a friend out of the blue. Pick up the phone and hit Call, listen to the endless ringing in my ear. No answer. Now I'm even more worried, with reason to be. "I can't explain. I just have a feeling…" Shouldn't drive with alcohol in my system. Would never drive with alcohol in my system. I've only had a quarter of a beer, though. Still, grab a glass of water and down it before I pick up my keys and phone. "Thanks for being here. If you leave before I'm back, just close the door behind you." And with that, I'm out the door.

Even if it's silly, even if it's all for nothing, even if she's not for me to worry about, if there is the smallest chance that I can be there for someone when they need me, I will. Just realize how late it is, and I have a 7:00 a.m. start tomorrow, but this time I don't fucking care.

KLARA

A week after her call Saga is here, and I couldn't be happier. She gives me a big hug. I haven't seen her in person in so long, and I notice that her hips have widened and she has a new vertical line where her eyebrows meet. A worry line, I think. Her smile is infectious and warms me up. I don't know if it's just me or if all people feel the same, but I think she is the most beautiful woman I've ever seen.

She has been in the house for two hours, but already the windows are cleaned and a pink flower is planted in a pot on the front stairs.

"Therapy," Saga says. "I don't even get to clean alone at home anymore, since apparently the vacuum scares my toddler and the toilet brush is more fun than his train set." She is now washing her hands, scrubbing away at them with lavender soap (she cleans without gloves) and progresses to preparing dinner with the ingredients I bought earlier in the day. A white lasagna with spinach and ricotta. She chops onion like a professional.

"Can you believe that Heinrich gave me a French-cooking course for Christmas. Like, really? You think now is the right time? That I'm going to learn to make béarnaise sauce and pastry. This is the era of plain pasta, only butter allowed, and if you dare add pepper the toddler will frown as if he's an Italian being served it overcooked. Fish fingers, boiled peas and tinned corn is how we currently roll."

"I do have respect for you because, like, you get home from work and—whoa, there's a kid in your house! And you have to feed him and bathe him and get him to sleep for the night and make sure he, you know, doesn't die."

"Yes, that's how parenting works, Klara…"

Dad comes in the room holding an iPad where his grandson, Harry, is currently putting his mouth to the screen and doing something which is supposed to be a kiss, leaving a wet mark where Dad's chin is on his side of the connection.

"See you later, elevator!" he calls before turning around, looking for his next distraction.

"Elevator?" I ask Saga with a laugh.

"What? It's cute! I'm not correcting him," she replies. "Right, food is ready."

"Call your mum. She asked if she could join the family dinner," Dad says as he deposits the iPad on the table next to my place.

"So she can see that you're eating healthily?" I ask, placing the lasagna and the salad I made next to it on the table.

"I think she's given up hope on me. She now just sends me a daily text, which I try to remember to reply to but often forget. It always has the same content—Am I eating well? Is Klara managing? Should she send more vitamins?—like one of those mass emails. I wish there was an unsubscribe button."

I laugh and sit down.

"Okay, let me get her, then," Saga says, adding to no one in particular, "Wash your hands!"

"My hands are clean," Dad says, holding his palms up.

"Sorry—habit."

She props the iPad up against the kitchen paper-towel holder, and Mum appears on-screen, wearing a loose linen shirt and her glasses.

"Spinach lasagna," I say.

"Chicken salad," she replies.

"Cheesecake," Saga contributes.

"Yogurt," Mum says.

"Oh gosh. The crushing feeling of asking what's for dessert and being told there's a bloody *yogurt* in the fridge," Saga moans.

"Precious childhood memories," I add. Then I turn to Mum. "Where is your husband?" It still feels wrong to call him that. Maybe if I'd seen them exchange vows it would make more sense to me, but they simply booked an appointment at the town hall in order to get the Spanish-residency papers processed faster. The only proof that it had even happened was my mum's new surname.

"Dinner with his golf club." She looks at us with pride, eyes bouncing from one to the other. "It's nice seeing you together. I'm so happy you went to help her, Saga."

I glance at my sister. She hasn't told Mum why she's really here? Mum thinks she's swooped in to help her hopeless sister? Indeed, Saga avoids looking at me.

Dad has stayed quiet, chewing on his food slowly at the end of the table, but talks now.

"Klara is doing very well. No need to help her after that viral video. Or before that. They have a busy schedule over the next few days, but I'm sure Saga will be able to keep up."

I repress the urge to ask him to speak up, one more time, louder for the people in the back, please. It's recognition, and I'll take it.

Five minutes later everyone is chatting over each other, and I raise my hand high above my head, as if I'm in school sitting on the correct answer.

"Klara?" my mum says.

"We're not in a classroom," my sister says.

"Well, how else am I supposed to be heard in this crowd?"

They all burst out laughing, and I join in too, forgetting why I raised my hand in the first place.

After dinner Saga sneaks off to call Heinrich, and I clear the table with Dad.

"That was intense," I say. "Far from our quiet eggs-on-toast mealtimes."

"She often calls, you know."

"Oh, I know that."

"To have dinner, I mean."

"You have Zoom dinner dates?" This is new and peculiar information.

"She's not good at being alone, your mum. And he has a lot of commitments and friends that she shares him with."

I place the remaining lasagna into four plastic containers for tomorrow's lunch—one for me, one for Saga, one for Dad and one for Alex. He was nice enough to bring me a sandwich, after all.

"Why do you put up with it, though? She left you." I never understood why Dad never had the same bitterness that Saga and I felt and sometimes still feel. Initially there was sadness: he was like a child who had a treat taken away and doesn't quite know what to do with themself.

"Let me try to explain." Dad smiles warmly at me. "I used to play soccer semi-professionally for Malmö MFF."

I nod. We have an album full of him looking fit in a football shirt, and apparently he spotted Mum across the street as he alighted from the team bus. She was looking at a Levi's shop window with her best friend, and the rest is history, as they say. Well, now it's *really* history.

"Then I got injured. The other player got a red card, but my knee was still shattered. I broke up with the game and accepted that the sport didn't agree with me any longer. But here's the thing, Klara. You don't stop loving something because it doesn't agree with you anymore. I still watch the matches on TV and will always love soccer."

"So having Mum next to you on the screen when you eat dinner is like watching a match?"

"Something like that."

He ruffles my hair in that way which is set to ruin any hairstyle. This time the only place I'm going is bed, so I let him do it without ducking away.

"Saga is not doing so well," I say.

"I figured. Keep her busy, let her work and just be near you. She'll be fine."

As I take my glass of water and am about to leave the kitchen, I stop and look at him.

"Dad, can I ask you something?"

He nods.

"Do you ever miss…soccer? Wish you could still play? That the injury didn't happen?"

"No. Soccer is demanding and all-consuming. It controls you. I quite like how things have turned out and the freedom I have. I wouldn't go back."

The next morning, I show Saga around our current projects. I glance at her suspiciously in the seat next to me. She has put on her Girls Aloud playlist, but I still love her.

"Why haven't you told Mum why you are really here?" Again, it looks like hopeless Klara needs support, and accountable Saga sweeps in. Some part of me is desperate for that narrative to change, but more than anything for *her* to be the one to change it.

"There's no need, is there? If this all goes away and I feel better again, then there is no need to worry our parents. Not at this point."

"So they should only worry about me? That's unavoidable, is it?"

I see my sister thinking *Well, yes*. But not saying it out loud. Instead she says, "I told *you*. That makes you my person."

I ponder this. I quite like being Saga's person, and I'm not sure I've ever really been that before. I suppose I could keep something secret and even look like *I* need help if it means I'm someone's person.

"Okay, then," I say.

"Thank you."

"Why are you bouncing up and down?" I ask her.

"Oh. I keep grinding my teeth when I'm stressed, so I'm trying this thing where I redirect the urge. Thought it might work. I refocus my energy on something more useful. I do a pelvic-floor squeeze every time I want to grind my teeth." That's Saga for you. She could be sitting in a lecture room full of students talking about old bearded historians all the while casually squeezing her pelvic floor.

"How are you and Heinrich really doing?" I ask her over "Something Kinda Ooooh." It turns out this was a good question, because the answer is long.

"I *think* we are okay. It's a lot having a child. *He* doesn't mind that we end up sleeping in different bedrooms because Harry needs me, or that I have to leave Harry and him playing on the weekend while I head out to a coffee shop just to finish up work I'm behind on. He says it's a phase and things will get easier. He's a good man and dad. Really. But I feel sad. I'm not at the point where I have a family life, if that makes sense? I want the dinner together, the park on the weekend kicking a ball around, and a weekly date night. But it's not physically possible. I get why women start working part-time, but I promised I wouldn't give up on myself."

"You shouldn't, but your promise to yourself means nothing if you burn out." I am aware I may be repeating self-help advice I have read, but Saga doesn't seem to mind.

She looks sad.

"I don't want to choose. I want to be an example to my female students. I'd hate for them to see their professor go part-time because of a child."

"What if it's not because of the child but because of your mental health? Isn't that something they should admire?"

"Sometimes I feel that you are the smart one, Klara."

"Thanks, so do I. But not sometimes, all the time," I say jokingly. She sticks her tongue out at me.

"There is something else, Klara."

"Yes?"

"The nursery called me to a meeting about Harry." My pride starts to well up. I knew my nephew was a genius. Do they move kids up classes in Germany? Are they suggesting advanced homework or an IQ test?

"There are some concerns."

"Concerns?" Over brilliance? They really want everyone in a mold, don't they?

"Well, what she—the teacher—told me is that he has had some trouble *bonding* with the other kids. He mainly just plays with his train track, and unless another child comes over and joins in, he is alone." She pauses, and my hands squeeze the steering wheel tighter.

"Then, there is something about eye contact. Every morning when he comes in, sits on the bench and changes from his boots to his woolly, wholesome, Montessori made-from-all-organically-dyed-wool-or-something slippers, he doesn't say good morning to Miss Trudie, he just looks down at his slippers."

"Ah, focus. A great characteristic," I say. "If you were busy putting slippers on, surely the best place to look are the slippers? If you chop an onion, you look at the onion, correct? And if you are on a road driving, you look at the road? Shall I go on?"

"Missing the point. It's possible, actually standard, to glance up and then continue the activity."

"The demand they put on toddlers—multitasking skills, age two! Did you complain?"

"No. I didn't. No offense, Klara, but can you just listen for a second? Let me get to the point?" Every time Saga says *no offense*, it makes me wonder what her offense voice would sound like.

"There have been some flags at home as well. His eating is pickier, you know how he prefers the beige scale—pasta, chicken nuggets and corn—and the sleep is restless. I'm telling you because the more I read, well, I think you should know." She pauses as if waiting for me to say something. I don't. So she does. "I'm having him tested for autism."

My mother's sadness is one I always absorb like an uneasy feeling, a hovering stress ball at the base of my stomach. How the smell of smoke would penetrate your hair after a night out. That's Mum's sadness. In addition to her sadness, she has brought a prop to Zoom today, a cup of tea. As if its presence helps her. I decide I don't want to do what my sister did and keep things to myself. I want to talk about them even if they make Mum bring her sadness.

"What have you been up to, my sweet cabbage?" *Cabbage* is not the weirdest thing my mum has ever called me. Apparently calling children *cabbages* is a thing in a foreign language, but I can't remember which one. I do think there are other more sophisticated linguistic habits to keep up, but I don't tell her this.

"You know why I need to speak to you," I say, wishing she didn't look so sad. Happy people are much easier to talk to. I pause, not knowing where to begin. This phone call came about because of what she withheld about my childhood, yet it still appears the responsibility to start the conversation is mine. "Did you ever consider that I might be autistic?" The word feels strange. I have only said it one time before, to Google.

"You were booked in for testing, actually," Mum tells me. "The school had flagged some behavior. You never seemed to want to play with any friends. Only Saga." I remember this. I preferred to play with Saga, which makes sense. She is brilliant and superior to anyone I know. *What are you doing? Can I join? What is this for?* Her friends answered my questions and gave me a role in the game: the baby, the pet, the chaser (I was a rather slow runner).

"I'm an introvert," I tell my mum as if that explains and sums me up in a sentence and kills any suspicion of a diagnosis.

"Introverts also find friends. And love."

"I have two friends. And I've found love; however, it has always been withdrawn from me. The till closes just as I'm arriving ready to buy into the relationship."

"Yes, darling. I'm aware."

"If you were worried, why didn't you have me assessed? At least Saga is doing everything for Harry. She is being a good mother. *Parenting.*"

"You were booked in but then…you got sick." I swallow. The thought of needles, hospital lights flickering and *too much noise*!

"The last thing on our minds was your behavior. The assessment got canceled, and then it was never a priority. You always managed school, despite your diabetes you got such good grades and tried so hard. God, we were proud of you." I did do well in school. *Benefit of no friends: time to study.*

Mum continues, her hands seeking a new prop on the desk around her laptop. She finds a pen, which she proceeds to fiddle with.

"Even the school wasn't concerned any longer. Distraction is common with diabetes, so you got the extra time you needed as we had a medical note saying that low or high blood sugar could affect your academic performance. They didn't need anything more formal. And we thought, *How much can this girl handle?* How would you manage being both diabetic and… something else?"

"Autistic."

I feel so tired suddenly.

"You have always been special. Darling, it's a good thing. It quite surprised me, considering how ordinary your father is." If Dad is ordinary, then I wish everyone else were too. There for every school performance, pickup, and shoelace-tying. I don't bother to say that because I know my mum's response will be eye-rolling and a familiar *Sure, an exciting personality is not the only positive character trait one can have* remark.

"You're this brilliant girl who knows so much but can't remember simple things."

As I listen to what she just said, it hits me.

Can't remember simple things.

You're a brilliant, intelligent woman. I can't understand how you can't remember four digits for five minutes? Alex had told me. And what did Saga say, again? *Harry is a brilliant little boy, but he just won't follow simple instructions.* The similarity of the comments is suddenly obvious to me.

"I have to go, Mum."

"We only just started talking, honey."

"I know it's only been—" I glance at the time "—eight minutes. But I can't talk anymore."

"Klara, we thought we did the right thing. Not adding another diagnosis. I'm sorry if it wasn't the right choice."

Mum desperately wants a response from me, but I need some time. I block Nonstop Notifications. I remove them all from my Dexcom app. I feel alone. I turned off the data. *They can't even see my blood sugar now.* I'm hot suddenly, like I've sat in a sauna for too long, and the only way to return to normal is to jump in a pile of snow.

I walk over to the kitchen and open the freezer. I put my whole head inside, breathe it in. Then I place a bag of frozen peas against my chest. It burns and stings.

And I think, if someone asked me who I am, I wouldn't have an answer.

Sometimes, when I can't sleep, I lie awake and think of all the things Google doesn't know. Like the sound of my grandfather's voice. My feelings when Saga's height surpassed mine. The smell of my childhood car. They are all the things I have in my soul. Google has no answers for questions about effort, worth, desire or character, all things we have inside us. Who I am and who I want to be, that's one of those questions, and one I need to answer myself, apparently.

Me: Who am I?

Google: A better question to ask yourself is How would I like to experience my life?

Me: Please go ahead and explain.

Google: There is no plausible answer. Because our being is not a fixed thing. The emphasis shouldn't be on discovering who you are but on facilitating what you'd like to experience. Identity should be seen as an ongoing process, a flowing sense of self. How different would life be, Klara, if rather than asking who you are, you contemplated how you'd like to engage life.

Okay, I added my name in there, but I feel like Google and I are on a first-name basis now, considering we have been going strong since, well, the creation of Google or me coming of age to use it. Whichever came first.

★ ★ ★

Saga has driven to Ystad to spend the night with an old school friend. Dad is not hungry, doesn't have any appetite. I don't have any either, but I eat out of habit and need rather than want more often than not. I can't justify using up the ingredients for the meal I had planned—baked salmon—for just one person, so I proceed to take a single-serving broccoli quiche from the freezer. I bolus my insulin while the food is in the oven and have a quick shower. It's not until it's in front of me on a plate, some leaves of arugula balancing on top, that I realize I won't be able to eat it. It's physically impossible. I wrap it in cling wrap, place it in the fridge, and go to bed.

I should be an expert at this by now, but the truth is, all these years and I have never actually passed out. Alex is sitting next to me, and there is a second man, who I immediately recognize as a paramedic. Okay, how bad is it? I think. I mean to say it out loud, but it turns out I have just thought it. I try again. Alex leans down.

"Wait. There is no need to talk. Five more minutes won't hurt." Then he looks me in the eyes and sees that they are two big question marks and starts to tell me.

"You had a bad hypo. I didn't want to interfere, but the alarm kept going off, and after a while I just said fuck it and drove over. I hope that's okay?" Oh, it's more than okay, I want to tell him. "Did the app lose its Bluetooth?" I close my eyes. Guilty.

"It's okay, Klara. I'm here." My dad's voice comes from the corner of the room.

"Let's get you sitting up, shall we," the man with the green medical uniform says, gently placing a hand behind my neck to guide me. I sit up and feel as if I have been run over by a train. I'm handed an orange-flavor juice box with a straw.

"Here. Let me." Alex feeds me the juice, and it's about the nicest thing I've ever drunk. I feel like myself more with each sip. I'm noticing that Alex is rubbing my lower back. I don't mind it. There is a sucking noise as the carton empties, as if it's breathing in rapidly. I continue sucking at the straw even though I'm positive I've finished every last drop. *Don't move away.*

Ambulance Man speaks.

"Right. If you are well enough to be walking, we don't have to bring you into hospital for a check."

Alex looks as if he's just been told he's won a million pounds.

"I left the alarm for about two hours, then I couldn't stand it. Your dad hadn't locked the door, luckily, as he didn't wake up when I knocked."

"He never does. *Nothing to steal and no one worthy to kidnap,* he always says." *My voice, that was my voice. It's back!*

I am alert enough to check my own blood sugar and take a sigh of relief when it's no longer low. I am ready for all the attention to go away.

"We can bring you with us for a general checkup if you would like," Ambulance Man says. "But since you are diabetic, we know why you collapsed, and now that you are better there's no real need to have you taken in. You must make an appointment with your doctor, though. There may need to be some adjustments in your doses to prevent this from happening again." I don't tell him that I know why it happened, that it was because I made supper and gave myself insulin for a meal I never ate. That I cut my family off my app like a grumpy child, risking my life in the process.

"I'm okay, thanks. I'm going home in two weeks and will be under the surveillance of my regular endocrinologist," I say. "Who is very good," I add to Alex, as he has a strange look on his face, which I interpret as suspicion toward English medical professionals.

Ambulance Man notes this down and packs his bag.

Dad has gone back up to bed, after I repeatedly assured him I was fine. As soon as Alex and I are alone, something changes in his face. He places a hand on my lower back as I get off the floor, his eyes wide as if trying to transfer his thoughts by telepathy. I think of his finger touching my lips as I was sucking on the straw and am overwhelmed with uncertainty. Staring at various points on the wall straight ahead has been my coping strategy, but Alex turns me toward him now.

I hold on to him as I stand up.

I tell myself to let go of him, but my arms refuse to listen. From the outside it may look like him checking to see if I'm okay, that I can stand up, but in that moment I know that his arms don't want to let go of me either.

"We have an early start tomorrow," I manage finally.

"Who cares if we've got a 7:00 a.m. start?"

"Eight a.m.," I say. "We start at eight o'clock. Not seven."

Later that evening I find a new entry in our shared calendar, which Alex seems to think is some sort of private chat room lately.

O **NEW EVENT:** Tell Klara how I felt when she was unconscious on the floor; Location: Outside the friend zone.

I read it three times and then decide I'm clear on what it means. Then I think about the fact that this man has a wedding ring and secondly, that I'm leaving very soon. Thirdly, realizing I even *want* to leave the friend zone is overwhelming and I want that feeling gone. I add a note to the entry.

Reply: Alex to keep this to himself. Best, Klara

A few minutes later there's a new reply.

Reply: Got it. Won't mention it again. Alex

PART THREE

April in Malmö is a fresh spring month, with a speed of wind that varies from 8.6 mph to 10.5 mph. This means that you can expect that the wind rustles visibly. Average temperatures fluctuate between 37.8°F and 54.7°F. The last week is the month's hottest.

ALEX

Personal Calendar ▾

O **NEW TASK:** Continue moving on—from the accident

O **NEW TASK:** Find a way to move on—from Klara

O **NEW TASK:** Why is my life is all about moving on?

Saved to Drafts

Calle,

Yesterday I was there for someone. Didn't bail out, even though I tried to talk myself out of it, and although I knew deep down she'd be fine without me, it feels like I stopped something awful from happening. I played a part, did what I could. Of course, it helped that I could see this emergency building up before me. I had an alarm. That other time, I had no warning.

Confidence probably a result of this because I did something, finally, same feeling as when I jumped off the highest branch of the tree on our road to save your ass. There was no way I was ever going to do it if you hadn't bet half your Pokémon cards on it, but family honor and twenty-eight precious cards had me do it. Broke my arm, but you got your cards.

This time I didn't break my arm but may have broken my fucking spirit.

Don't mention it again, I promised. How can I not fucking mention it again? So now I know she wants me like I want her. Doesn't mean she'll do anything about it, though. She's made sure she's intending to do nothing about it, couldn't be clearer. Which means I can't do anything either. Because I'm not that guy. Not with her. You don't chase Klara; you wait for her like the fucking queen she is. To give me a nod, a sign, anything. Was it better not knowing? Yup. Now I find myself trying to dissect her every move and get into her thoughts. Now I know she is thinking about me, I need to know what those thoughts are.

All I do is think about her. Reasons I know Klara has a strong influence over me: I swear less and I've started googling random shit like *is mosaic Italian* and *what's the life span of a carrot*.

Keep telling myself that she will soon be gone. I have more important things to concentrate on, like work and a trial, and Berit aka Mysterious Red Fleece Lady offered to meet me for a coffee, which was such an amazing gesture. Closure is coming, I can feel it. But then suddenly I have my ludicrous brain going *the most important thing in the world is knowing what earrings Klara is wearing today.* And confirming that Tom hasn't messaged her again.

Urge is strong to call up Dr. Hadid and tell her I have all these new worrying symptoms. Let's see what she says at our next appointment. Will probably dismiss them as feelings. God, I fucking hate feelings when they feel like symptoms.

Will let you know how the chat with Berit goes: feels like I'm about to catch up with an old friend when all she did was see you for about a minute. But that was the minute that ended your life. Hence it's important to me. If the moment we die isn't a life-defining moment, then what is?

Love you. Didn't tell you enough, but I do.

Look at yesterday's failed calendar entries, a rare sight, and call it a day. One of those days when all I've achieved is writing an email that will never be read.

KLARA

Q **What actually is autism?**

Google Search   I'm Feeling Lucky

I have booked an appointment with a psychiatrist who'll be able to start the assessment process. Once I made my mind up, I couldn't bring myself to hold off until I was back in London, and anyway, there are waiting times on the NHS.

"I can't have both diabetes and autism." I say this to Saga as she is, inspired by the surge in followers, finally taking over work on the website and social-media account so that Hanna can focus on tackling the surge in customers we now have. I offered to help following her revelation of an on-the-blink home life, but her response was that my Instagram handle name immediately disqualified me from any social-media role. I've also been inundated with emails and calls asking for quotes. I've added something to the company, which Mateusz and his gang can never compete with.

"You are not being very scientific, now, are you? You think

one condition protects you from another? Plus, autism is not an illness, it's just how you are, a difference in how you see the world."

"If Harry gets diagnosed that will hand him extra challenges," I say, suddenly feeling very protective and emotional. I love Harry. We have common interests such as Lego-building (my preference is the blue pieces) and literature (*The Gruffalo* is very suspenseful with the ultimate twist). I don't want my nephew to feel as strange and different as I have. I say this to Saga.

"Knowing will help him. He won't have those challenges to the same extent, don't you see that? Diagnosis is a good thing." I'm still not convinced.

"People may treat him differently. I don't want people to feel sorry for him—or *me*. Or telling him—or *me*—their random neighbor's niece has autism. It's enough with the constant *my aunt has diabetes*," I say.

"So don't tell people. Make a judgment. Do I benefit from this person having this information about me? If yes, then you tell them. If no, you don't."

A thought that brings light into my soul appears.

"I've always felt like something was different about me. If it's just autism, that would mean there is nothing wrong."

"There is nothing wrong with you. Never has been and never will be. I would be proud if my son is like you, Klara," Saga says, and my chest swells like dough rising.

I walk fast as if I can't wait to get there. Three steps and a door with a brass sign that says *Dr. Svensson, Dr. Hultgren* and *Dr. Hadid* and their various areas of practice. There is no receptionist, so I walk past the desk to the waiting room. Then I stop in the doorway, half about to turn around and— *Alex. Why is he here?* Alex looks at me and smiles. I look at him too, but I don't smile. This is a matter of wrong person in the wrong place, and I am awfully aware that I will not handle this encounter well.

"Hi," he says.

"Do you come here often?" I reply.

"It's not exactly a bar, is it?" This is true. It's not a bar. But my experience of waiting-room small talk is nonexistent, and I struggle to find something else to say.

"Yes, I do come here often. Less so, recently."

I wonder what's happened recently. If it were a bar, I'd probably ask, but the receptionist returns to her desk and gives me a nod. I walk over to her.

"I'm Klara Nilsson, and I don't come here often, but I have an appointment at three thirty."

She hands me a bundle of documents on a clipboard. I would like to sit next to Alex, but there are nine seats and two of them are occupied. If I choose the one two chairs from him, it will be an even pattern, and I find this difficult to ignore. I sit two chairs away and place my bag on the floor, balancing the clipboard on my thighs, on my tiptoes to bring it up higher. It's only later that it hits me he may think I'm avoiding him because of the disastrous calendar entry last night. And partly I may be, but not fully. I like him too much to ever manage to fully avoid him.

She is wearing a pink sweater and a big smile when I step in through her open door. She has no name tag, but I assume that she is Dr. Svensson.

"Hi, Klara. Do come in. It is good to meet you."

"Thank you, you too." I sit down in a chair with red faded dots, and I wonder if this has been furnished by the same team that did the public hospital. I move the chair slightly as it's angled strangely. The room is hot and stuffy: no Swedish properties are prepared for spring heat waves, very few even have air-conditioning. If you have waited all year for eight weeks of summer, then you grin and bear it, sweat it out, as they say. We are also collectively too frugal to spend money on a system that would only be operated a sixth of the year.

"Is the temperature okay for you, Klara? I know it's quite warm, but if I open the window it may get noisy." I smile. I don't want the noise. I notice that there are no posters on the wall behind her; in fact, it is soothingly bare, and I feel welcome. *Understood.*

"I'm here for your professional opinion," I say. I have now had two full days to consider the fact that I may be Autistic and have collected enough supporting evidence. The issue is that it is all contradictory. For example, the online description states that someone with autism likes repetition and may choose the same parking spot every time, becoming annoyed if it is not available. I, on the other hand, have no problem parking on the even side of the road. I figure if all the spaces on the odd side are taken, it means the odd ones have made friends and have a busy life and don't need me. And even though I prefer to make a turn to the left, I absolutely *can* drive to the right. Which is a totally different thing and shows my flexibility, if anything.

Another example: an autistic adult may become obsessed with their love interest and show clingy behavior with and adoration of their partner. This does not fit me at all. If it had, I would not have broken up with Tom that easily. The only obsession I seem to have lately is Alex, and he is not my boyfriend.

"Of course. I know that you wanted to explore the possibility of an autism diagnosis. Am I correct that a close relative has recently been diagnosed?" I had hoped for a *yes* or *no* answer—those are my favorites—but I realize that I won't be getting one and that this will be a long conversation.

"He is currently being assessed. I would like to find out about myself as well. My nephew resembles me a lot."

"To get to that point, I'd like to know what makes you wonder about yourself." Her expression is the same. When talking to Dr. Svensson, it's very clear when it's my turn to speak, the opposite from social interactions where I hesitate not knowing when to cut in and when its someone else's turn to talk and I should just earring-dangle. Here the questions prelude my monologues and are always marked by a long pause and an attentive and focused expression.

"First there was my nephew. Then I did an online quiz, and it got me thinking. I'm different in a lot of ways, although in many I'm totally regular. I dress like everyone else and am really quite ordinary. But the way I think and feel seems to clash with other people's views often. Other people don't see fonts and sneakers instead of faces, they don't care about odd and even, and they somehow know how often to smile without cues. I've put it down to just being, you know, *strange*. My mum always says men are from Mars and women from Venus but what if there is another planet where some of us are from? Where I would *belong* if only I could find it."

"Thank you for sharing this, Klara. An assessment is a process, but I'd be happy to start it. It involves interviews with family members, conversations with you and IQ testing. Think about what you would like to get out of an assessment. For some people, it brings answers to events in their life, for some it can help find strategies to manage their life more appropriately so that they're on top of things and don't burn out. Others have no problems and don't see the benefit of going through the diagnostic process. I suggest you read some more online and think about whether it's something you'd like to do. Once you're sure, we will refer you to the right psychologist. Diagnosis can be a very positive thing."

I feel like talking to her has relaxed me. Even though her font is small and her voice soft, I feel like all the words she used are easy to understand. I repeat what she has said in my head on the way home and conclude that I very much want a diagnosis. And somewhere to belong.

★ ★ ★

"You could have told me."

I have just come clean to Dad about how much Bygg-Nilsson has struggled. My guilt was eased by the fact that the company is now fully booked until September. We have a four-month waiting time.

"I would have dismissed fancy soaps and towels as silly and unnecessary, to be fair. It's for the best you didn't consult me beforehand. Sometimes we need a fresh set of eyes."

"Is that you admitting giving up control was a good thing?" I tease him. "Be ready at 3:00 p.m. Saga is shooting new pictures for the website, and they can't happen without you."

Dad sighs but knows modeling for the website is nonnegotiable.

"Have you booked your flight back yet?" he asks. It comes as a jolt. Despite my moaning to anyone and everyone that will listen and initial resistance, the thought of returning home fills me with dread, a sort of deflating feeling. The idea of going back, picking up the job search and generally being back in my old life in the basement apartment of 243A Munster Road seems impossible. I want to shout this out loud. *Objection! The crowd has an objection*, I want to say. Klara returning would be an utter mistake. But Dad is calmly spreading butter on a piece of bread, in no rush, in fact stopping to sip coffee in between, the knife resting against the plate until he is ready to continue. He does not seem to have any idea that going home now would be a very bad idea. It's over, I think. No more of this job that I've come to enjoy, no more sense of being on top of the world after parallel parking, customer interaction or tile selection, no more coffee breaks with the team. No more Alex.

Good things about going home: my own bed, my own space and seeing Alice. But it also means that nothing will change. I feel shivery all of a sudden, quite aware that I must have lost my mind. Since when do I welcome change? In fact, I don't just welcome it, I feel terrified at the prospect of *nothing* changing. Of being in transit forever to an unknown destination. I want to say *Perhaps we could hold off on those flight bookings. After all, there is no rush for me to return, is there?* Then I remember that in addition to Dad's casual suggestion of me returning home, the other day Alex used speech indicating my departure, *when you're back in London.* All the study help. They want me to go. This is not my place. So I say, "I will get on that this evening. Thank you for reminding me, Dad."

There is a Volvo parked outside the office when I leave Dad in the house and walk across the courtyard to do an afternoon of accounting (apparently Dad's accountants mean to tell me that *supply receipts* does not mean *shove every receipt found in trouser pockets and cars into a large envelope and post it to them.* That incurs an extra fee).

"Hello," I say as the driver exits. I'm face-to-face with a man with a ginger beard, not much taller than me. He is wearing office attire, the stylish type that tells me he has a high-enough position to get away with it.

"Hi, there. I found you through recommendations. A neighbor used the company some time back. In July last year?" he says.

"Right. Wouldn't have been me but my—um—another gentleman." Trying not to sound unprofessional here, and I've learned that it's better not to disclose that the owner is off ill, and his daughter is in charge. I'm assuming whatever made this guy stop by is some sort of job. And I still want jobs. Even though our viral moment has more than made up for Mateusz and Ram's damage campaign, I want to hand back the company absolutely fully booked. If I can squeeze in one more job despite the waiting time, I'll do it.

"Would you like to come with me to the office and we can have a chat?"

"My brother-in-law works in construction," the man says as we walk side by side on the damp gravel to the home office. "I didn't want to give him the job. To be honest, I thought it may be too much for him. The place holds sentimental value to both of us, if that makes sense. Wouldn't want him tearing down walls and spending his whole day there."

"I see. That's very considerate."

He continues even though he hardly got a prompt from me.

"He's been doing much better, coming over less often. I just don't want a situation where he is back there every day of the week because he has to be. I want us both to keep moving forward."

I'm getting curious now, what is this place? I'm half expecting him to tell me it's a family castle full of treasures and riches or some other significant property. When he gives me the details, I'm slightly disappointed to hear it's a one-bedroom apartment in Malmö. I perk up when I hear that it's in Turning Torso. *They even organize tourist tours there!*

"I would need to visit to prepare a quote. I could potentially do it tomorrow. We have a window. In case you wanted to move forward quickly."

"Sounds good. I've got the keys on me. The place is empty at the moment, so you don't need to notify anyone. I'll text you the address."

"Perfect. I will try to go in sometime in the next few days and then be in touch with a quote and action plan."

"Thank you so much. I appreciate you squeezing me in. I didn't catch your name?"

"Klara. Klara Nilsson. Nice to meet you." I have started adding my surname. A month ago I didn't, for fear that they would think it's my company, that I own a construction company.

But recently I do it for the exact same reason: I feel a sense of pride knowing they put it together and see me as the owner. The man puts his jacket on and stretches out his hand to me.

"Thank you, Klara. I'm Dan."

ALEX

Personal Calendar ▾

O **NEW TASK:** Clean oven

O **NEW TASK:** Clean shower curtain

O **NEW TASK:** Repeat. Move on to any other unsexy task
I've ignored for the last six months. Bonus if it will help kill any
thoughts of Klara Nilsson...

Restless. Turns out, thoughts of Klara can coexist with cleaning tasks. Think of the way her body language changes and she becomes a fidgety mess when I'm near her. Can't help but smile at everything she says. "I don't come here often." Loudly in the waiting room. Part of me was desperate to tell her, to put all my cards on the table, the low and weak ones. But she's made clear she's not interested in that from me, and I promised to not mention it again. How fucking stupid is that?

Keep myself busy since I got home, but close to midnight I find myself doing something I haven't done since it happened—reliving the moment. Documenting it. Thinking maybe that's something. If I can share it with my Drafts folder, perhaps can share it with someone else too—say, Dr. Hadid.

Saved to Drafts

Dear you,

Keep coming back to the night it happened. We are standing outside the restaurant, I kick at a pointy piece of cobblestone sticking up in the pavement, wearing my Timberland boots since its bloody freezing. Calle is unlocking his new bicycle from the railing.

"You really can't leave it here until tomorrow and hop in the car with me?" Dan asks Calle.

"No way am I leaving this beauty on its own here. It's central Lund, and this is a brand-new bike." Calle is planning to commute by bicycle to work from now on, do his bit for the environment and get fit while he's at it. The bicycle is black and too sporty for him.

"It won't fit in the car."

"Alex has a van."

"And a 7:00 a.m. start," I remind them.

"Exactly. You don't have to take me. It's a five-minute ride to the train station. You take the car home, Dan, and I'll see you there." Calle leans in and meets Dan's lips, lingering there with closed eyes.

"Get a room, you guys. Preferably a teenage bedroom since that's where you seem to belong," I say, obviously equally thrilled and jealous as hell of my brother and the love of his life.

"Do you even have a helmet with you?" Dan says as he hovers. "Sure you can't give him a lift, Alex?"

"I'll be fine, Dan. It's evening and town's dead."

"He'll be fine. Just down to the train station is all." I echo my brother's sentiment.

"Exactly. Bye, Alex! Be good!" Calle sets off, shaky and unsteady first, then when speed picks up, he disappears around the corner, the bicycle only noticeable through its blinking light.

Two hours later, I get the call from Dan. The vehicle had crushed Calle with all its weight. If he had gone in Dan's car, he would have lived. If I'd driven him and his bicycle home, he would have lived.

Instead, he bled out in surgery, and Dan didn't even get to say goodbye. And I'm left with a clip I've seen on social media playing on Repeat day in and day out. The first few days I forced myself to watch it. Look what happened because of you and your fucking 7:00 a.m. start, I'd think. It's got a watermelon in a helmet; it gets dropped to the floor, and the fruit is intact. Then there comes another watermelon, without a helmet, and it also gets dropped to the floor. The fruit cracks. Pink juice seeps out of the crack onto the pavement, and the guy in the video makes a shocked face. The camera zooms in on the gaping crack, like a canyon. It's an educational video to show how important helmets are.

Except in my mind, it's a fucking horror movie where every second feels like an hour, and the gaping Grand Canyon melon is replaced with my baby brother's head.

KLARA

🔍 How could I miss that he liked me all this time?

Google Search   I'm Feeling Lucky

The building is fancy, about the fanciest thing I've seen during my trip. It reminds me of a riverfront luxury apartment complex in London. The Turning Torso is a landmark in Malmö. I did some research beforehand and found out that it was built in 2005 by the renowned Spanish architect Calatrava and that the finishing interior touches were designed by the famous Philippe Starck. This is no ordinary home address. For interested tourists and visitors, it's possible to book a guided tour to see it up close and enjoy the view from the top. It sits on the edge of the city with panoramic views of the sea. I make my way through the blue-lit foyer to a large elevator and look at the board, which shows fifty-four floors. I look down at the message from Dan, the man who came to see me a few days ago. It's apartment number ninety-eight on the thirty-second floor. There is no name at the door, but I find the number imprinted in small writing at the side of it.

The key slides in easily, the opposite of my family home's door where you need two attempts at least and simultaneous pushing on the door with your hip for it to be in the correct position to open. Old buildings protest and grumble when you want to go in them, like a relationship that's full of conflict but eventually gives way. New buildings always welcome you.

I'm met by a large space with uninterrupted views of the sea. The symmetry is striking, the type of thing I would find in my architecture books. I find the light switches by the door, but there is no need to use them, even at close to seven o'clock it is still light enough. I guess summer really is coming after all.

I remember the chat in the office. A dividing wall, positioned to keep as much of the spacious feel as possible. Two bedrooms instead of one to increase the sale potential. Something jumps inside me when I think of maybe, maybe being able to sketch it out. Dan may want an architect ultimately, but I could do the first drawing and email it. I see it all in front of me. I run my hands along the clean kitchen countertop. The oven clock has stopped at 2:13 p.m. I open the fridge, even though I have no reason for doing so. It's empty apart from a pack of butter, ketchup and a six-pack of beer.

I walk into the bedroom. It's empty apart from a bed made with ironed white sheets. Half the room opens up to the sea. This room will be untouched by the renovations, so I carefully close the door behind me and walk back to the living area. There is a lot of mess inside of me; like a tumble dryer, my insides churn with a mismatched load. Dad's illness, my sister's distance, Tom, Alex, tiling projects and autism. I stop in front of the large windows and look out over the calm water and the shores of Denmark in the far distance.

I'm not sure how long I've stood there when a noise startles me. I hear the familiar sound of a key in a keyhole. Strange.

Who would come here? *A robber? A murderer?! Please don't let me die today!* The door opens, although I can hardly hear it, and then I can make out footsteps. This is it. I'm about to be murdered by a crazy robber targeting empty penthouses. I can't even call for help because my bag is on the floor by the front door. I remember wildlife advice, information I've looked up in case I ever run into a bear or a wolf in the Swedish woods. *Walk away slowly. If it chases, play dead.* I can't play dead standing up. The steps come closer. *Closer.* I'm now convinced I will suffer a heart attack any second.

"Hello? Is there someone here?" The murderer must have seen my bag. I have no way out. Except...the murderer sounds an awful lot like—

Alex?

"Alex?"

I freeze.

He freezes.

"Klara?"

"That would be me," I say. My cheeks are burning hot, and I want to hug him for not being a murderer.

"What are you doing here?" He has come all the way up to me and is looking at me with eyes that make me blush even more. I look out at the ocean.

"I could ask you the same thing."

"Okay, but I asked first."

"I'm working."

"Working?" He looks at me. Our workday finished two hours ago.

"Well, not the looking-at-the-view part. That was me not working. Me taking a break. But before that. I'm here to give a quote. It's our newest project."

His eyes wander around the room as if he has no clue what to do and wants it to give him an idea.

"You never told me why *you* are here," I probe.

"This is—well, was my brother's place."

"Your brother?"

"He passed away last year." I didn't even know he had a brother. "His husband must have hired you—*us*—Bygg-Nilsson."

"Dan."

"Yes."

"Do you want to talk about it?" I say.

"Not really. Not now."

"Okay."

"I will leave you to it, then. Sorry for barging in and surprising you."

"No, no. I'm the one who should be going. I've got what I came here for."

I take a step to the right, but he's in my way and doesn't move.

"Klara, please stay. I said I wasn't ready to talk about my brother—not that I didn't want to talk. I do need to talk to you. I think we should have talked a long time ago."

I hesitate. Me and Alex, alone. It's definitely time to head off. To insert some physical distance between us.

"I should be going, though, shouldn't I? We'll have this job now to start on. I'll brief you on it tomorrow." He is standing still, waiting for me to leave. I take one small step toward the door, hoping my legs will do the work if I just set the motion rolling.

"Good night," I say, taking another three long, odd steps past him, not turning around, for some reason afraid to meet his gaze. I notice him in the reflection of the glass doors when I turn my head ever so slightly to the side. *Oh God.* Think, Klara. I'm frozen. Behind me he takes a step closer, and I am standing completely still, as if playing a childhood game of Red Light, Green Light.

"Klara," he whispers, his voice weak and hoarse. "You don't

have to rush off. I doubt you have an appointment after this, and Saga is at home with your dad, am I right?"

He is right. Those are not the reasons I'm drawn toward the door, the exit and the fresh air on the other side of it. I told him to drop it, to leave me—*us*—firmly in the friend zone. But deep down I know that's not what I want; it hasn't been for some time.

"I think you should know that I like you," I say finally. "Like I shouldn't, it's that sort of like, I mean. I haven't known the right thing to do. I've been googling. A lot."

"Of course you have." His voice is tender and amused, and I finally turn around. I am really close to him now. Inches away. Focusing on measuring the distance was a bad idea—only makes me more unsettled.

He lowers his head, and I raise my chin, our faces suddenly an inch apart.

"You have no idea how many times I've imagined telling you how I feel about you. I wanted to respect your wishes, though. And you told me never to mention it…"

"I had to." I take a deep inhale of breath, then say, "What about your wife?"

"What wife?"

"Your wife—the one you're married to. The one your ring matches. Or did you forget about her?"

He suddenly looks a mix of total insult and bemusement.

"I'm not married—this is my brother's ring. I've had it ever since the accident. I can't seem to take it off. I feel like he's with me when I wear it. You thought I had a wife? Three months of working together, and I didn't mention her once? You know my Social Security number and my shoe size but thought I was somehow hiding a wife?"

"What about the couple's therapy?"

"Inside joke. It was with my friend, Paul, who I'd love to introduce you to, by the way. My therapist wanted to meet someone I was close to, a friend, as part of my therapy. So I labeled it couple's therapy."

Did everyone except me know this? Gunnar? Hanna? Even *Dad*? Didn't he once mention that I should invite Alex over more? And I thought it was because *he* enjoyed his company. Am I the only one who's gotten it so incredibly wrong? Inside my mind, missing pieces click into place.

"I need a few moments to reset. Refresh the feed, so to speak," I say. *Alex is single. Alex is single. Alex is single.*

"You never thought to ask me? A simple question could have solved this," *single* Alex says.

"I don't tend to ask questions to which there are obvious answers," I say. "Rings are recognized devices for indicating marital status, just like headscarves can indicate a religion." I find tokens helpful. Name tags, bright orange vests that shout *Ask me for help.* My eyes flicker between the ocean and the door, and Alex's hand reaches out and touches the side of my face, guiding my eyes softly back toward him so he has my attention.

"You're right, of course, anyone might have assumed as much. But there is no wife. No one. Absolutely no one in my life. But I'd like to change that."

"You would?" I whisper. "Tell me more."

"Klara, you are strong and fearless, beautiful and smart, with a kind heart. And you have the best bum I have ever seen." He brushes the backs of his fingers across my cheek, and I find myself leaning in. His fingertips smooth over my bottom lip.

But he still doesn't kiss me. Instead he whispers against my mouth, the air from his breath tingling my lips.

"Do you really mean it, Klara?"

It dawns on me that Single Alex is insecure too, and that I perhaps misread his confidence like I misread his ring. I move my face closer to his, standing on the very tips of my toes and still not fully reaching him, nodding.

"Does that mean *yes*?"

"Yes, you twit."

He pulls me close. *Finally.* I feel like I'm losing my mind, a little, like the time I lost all inhibition and ordered chips *and* mash as sides. I press my mouth against his.

First the kiss is a slight brush over my lips, then hungrier. Alex kisses me with all the determination I know is part of his character, that he brings to everything he does. There's a whole swarm of what feels like very bright and very yellow spring butterflies in my abdomen.

When I come up for air, I need something to say, anything.

"I thought you were a girl, the first time we met," I say and he laughs in a way that makes it clear it's with me, not at me.

"Even my parents thought I was a girl the first time I met them. I'm named after Princess Alexandra. At least my parents had the decency to put only *Alex* on the birth certificate."

"So you're my princess—not my Viking font!" The stare Alex gives me is so stern I burst out laughing.

I burrow my face against the curve of his neck and take in his smell. I'm scared, but I think it's a good scared. Alex is worth a little fear, a step outside my comfort zone.

"God, Klara. Your eyes..."

"Oh?"

"They're piercing, absolutely on fire."

"People always tell me I'm too intense. I have to try to re-member to blink and look at various objects every now and again."

"Too intense? You don't even understand what you do to me, Klara Nilsson."

"To me it's incomprehensible that not everyone looks at you that way," I say. How could I not notice all this the first time I saw him? He was so distracting to me because I *liked* him.

My hands run down his back, from the shoulder blades, along the spine.

Alex gently stops me, taking my hands in his. The wave of

rejection washes over me. Memories of googling *how to kiss* pop up and the stress of always performing, running through each technical step in my mind as I do it, hoping I'm good enough, mutes me for a minute. Being too much but also never quite enough. It's about to happen again.

"I want to sit with you in this moment, just like this, for a bit longer." He drapes his arm around me and swivels us around to face the windows, ocean before us. "You've made this apartment a happy place for me again."

Things fall into place. His attitude when he first turned up, his shortness.

"There's an amazing sunset starting in about ten minutes. Dan cleared most of the furniture, but I think we can pull something together. We have a front-row view," he says. He goes away and comes back with some blankets and a heap of pillows.

"This will do."

We arrange them across the living room floor, and I stand there hesitating as the orange begins to take over the dusky sky. I think how this is very much like a fantasy, but also very different. I haven't rehearsed a version involving a sunset and a den floor.

"This is where you sit down, make yourself comfy and let me hold you. Okay?"

"Okay." I swallow, relieved to have instructions.

It's unknown territory, but I wriggle myself into sitting comfortably. I rest my head against his chest.

"I like it here. I've been coming almost every week since the accident. Sometimes my brother-in-law comes over, and we watch a movie and have a beer. Even now that the place is almost cleared out, I haven't been able to stay away."

"Dan. He seems nice."

"The nicest."

Alex doesn't say anything else, so I do. "People tend to define things as *before-and-after* something. A turning point. Was losing your brother the turning point in your life?"

"Yes. Calle, his death."

"So all this time, when I've been going on about my sister, all the moaning... I'm so sorry, Alex. I didn't know." All the times I had complained about Saga—my sister that I love, that I still have, can still talk to and hug and see—he'd been hurting. It must have been torture for him.

"It's okay, you couldn't have known. And I'm glad you still have your sister."

"Yes, I do." A great one, it turns out. That I haven't given enough credit. "I wish you had told me. Tell me about him."

And Alex tells me everything. From childhood to growing up, to being best man at the wedding where Calle married Dan. Holidays together and the type of sibling relationship most people dream of.

"If you sit with the pain, it gets easier. Nothing lasts forever," I offer when he's done. This is what I do when I can't run. Option one is escape, when the world gets too intense. But when I can't do that, I sit with the stress, the overwhelming feeling I'm drowning in, and wait for it to pass.

Alex is quiet for a while, then says, "I guess I've been running away from it. Driving—when I was moving and trying to do something, I could handle it, ignore the pain. It stopped me feeling."

I feel our hearts beating through our clothes, out of sync, one odd and one even, perhaps.

"I could stay here all night," I say.

"Why don't we? The sunset is nothing compared to the sunrise. I'll order us some dinner."

I stiffen and doubt creeps in. I don't like sleepovers. Never have. The houses always smell of other people and their laundry detergent. It's like being breathed on with their warm breath for the duration of the stay. I feel good now, *wonderful* even, but when you sleep with another person, there is sometimes less air to breathe, and cold feet touching you with sharp toenails, and indeterminable sounds that wake you. But then I wonder if staying here with Alex could be just like it is now, in this moment. The up and down of his chest and his scent, the only difference being that I close my eyes and sleep.

"Alex, I'd very much like to do a sleepover with you."

ALEX

Shared Calendar ▾

New Note (Klara): Last night was amazing

Reply (Alex): *You* are amazing

Reply (Klara): Please go ahead and schedule some dates if you want to. Various locations

○ **NEW EVENT (ALEX):** Next Tuesday, 7pm. Dinner at Alex's

Reply (Klara): It's a date

I could get used to this, Klara in my arms. In fact, *on* my arm, stopping the blood flow and leaving me with a tingling sensation. I should nudge her off, but I don't want to disturb her. The curtains are long gone, so I woke up when the sun did. I feel calm for the first time in God knows how long. I know it's okay: if anything, Calle would be happy. Brush dark hair away from her cheek and kiss the top of her head. She stirs, eyes with slight traces of black makeup open.

"I thought you'd run for the hills if I told you how I feel," I say when she wakes up.

"What hills? We're in the flattest part of Sweden." She smiles, and I can feel my heart swell.

"I have to get going soon. I promised to stop by my parents' and look at the case file properly ahead of the trial." Still haven't been able to read his defense or look at the images. Pushing the thought away for now.

"How are your parents? I mean, how have they been since the accident?"

"They're okay. My dad kept building things for months afterward. Mum kept baking. They just kept going to the extreme, never stayed still. I stopped, completely stopped in my tracks. My dad grieves with his hands, not his brain or heart. He can't relate to my experience at all. The garage is full of things he built. Birdhouses, chairs and sleds. You name it."

"That makes me feel sad. A museum of processing loss."

"When you put it like that… Maybe he should get rid of it."

"Well, we work in construction. We could make an inventory and offer the items to customers for free?"

"He'd grumble and protest, but I think you're right. It's time the garage emptied. I'll talk to him about it."

"As for your mum—is that why you always bring cinnamon rolls to work?"

"Let's just say we have enough for the staff meetings this year and next."

This year and next. Let the reference to the future slip, pass, like tiny annoying symptoms of a cold that you push through and go to work with, knowing they'll eventually floor you. Ignore them, and I know she does too because she just nods. Want to keep this a happy memory.

And in happy memories, one person doesn't head back to London.

KLARA

🔍 How many times are you allowed to sit IELTS?

Google Search   I'm Feeling Lucky

When I leave, I message my sister.

Me: The man I assumed to be married has turned out to be single.

Saga: Who? Alex?! This is good news, little sister.

Me: There is something I can't get my head around.

Saga: It's simple. You like Alex. Alex is single. Happy days.

Me: Yes, but if he were single all this time, and if he liked me, surely he should have made it known?

Saga: You were dating Tom… This would have stopped him from making any advances. Also, your attitude when thinking he was married may have factored in.

Me: So my relationship was a token like the ring? It had similar repellent action?

This makes a lot of sense. Saga can always explain so I understand. We both had tokens that prevented us from seeing the attraction. How was I supposed to know that the ring wasn't his, and how was he supposed to know that I wasn't enjoying my time with Tom? That is the problem with tokens: they don't tell the full story.

That evening, I remember Google's advice to think of how I want my life rather than who I want to be. I write the list that Google asked me to compile.

I want to experience both Swedish and English life.

I want to work with properties. But not with their font-speaking buyers, the actual properties. Drawing them, visualizing them, making them change.

I want to make a positive impact in my nephew's life. Both in terms of my presence and in terms of achievements that could make him proud of me.

I want my family and my friends in my life. Alice is dying to see me, and I decide to stay in touch with Hanna when I go.

I want to have Alex in my life but not in a WhatsApp group or as a friend. No, Alex I have no boundaries for. Even though we are taking things slowly, I know that I'll be wanting him next to me, in front of me, behind me, on top of me and under me.

The first two points stand there without a solution. I can't add *find similar job to YourMove* because replying to questions and dealing with technical glitches is not working with properties. It also wouldn't be the career that inspires my nephew—because it's not what I really want. I can't hide the fact that I would like to be an architect. The measurements, seeing a vision come to life. Learning about carpentry has only strengthened this. I would have less customer interaction and less driving, which would be a benefit to my mental health. And here I curse Google. It's all good to write lists and focus on what I want until who I am stops it all.

I am Klara Nilsson. I am diabetic and Autistic. I have dreams and aspirations. But I can't even pass an IELTS test to make them happen.

ALEX

Personal Calendar ▾

○ **NEW TASK:** Find a way to make this work

○ **NEW TASK:** See previous

○ **NEW TASK:** Because this could be fucking everything

A week passes in a strange blur of me and Klara together. Within seconds of us arriving for work everyone knows. Don't mind. She used to walk a yard away from me, and now her arm constantly brushes the side of my body. It's like I'm her center point, and I love it. When she moves away her eyes stay on me. Revel in the odd sense of constant well-being.

"You are like a werewolf that has imprinted," I tell her.

"I didn't realize you watch teenage vampire shows. Also, not sure werewolf is that flattering of a comparison." But I can tell that she is taking my comment in a good way.

Think of the past months. All the time we—I—wasted. And not just the time since I stepped into the home office on the farm and saw her for the first time, the time before that. The years before I knew that I've spent settling, floating, accepting life to be average.

★ ★ ★

Dump some fruit in a bowl I just bought. Went all out and got a scented candle as well. Vanilla, which makes me think of Calle. And place mats for the table. Oh, and a flower in a ceramic pot. Just in case she likes to see any of those things in someone's home. Most important buy is the kitchen scale, which I'm carefully putting portions of pasta onto now, making a mental note of carbs per hundred grams. Want to get cooking for Klara right. This is our first date, after all, unless you count sharing a sandwich in the van.

Mamma has left a voice note, and I listen as I wait.

"Alex, love, it's Mamma. But I guess you saw that on the screen already. Hi. Would you say to wear black tomorrow? Or would some color be acceptable? I know it's not a funeral, but I can't imagine color in a place like that, can you? Will you be wearing your suit? I've ironed Pappa's, which is charcoal, if you remember? Anyway. I'll probably call Dan and ask him if you don't get this message."

Write back to her, finishing with a red heart. Wear what feels comfortable. Not too tight, something you can breathe in and not suffocate. You'll be fine. Trying to be a support for my parents now, as they've been for me. Feels good to resume a role I can fill.

A reminder pops up. *Dinner at Alex's* has been edited from 7 to *7:20* with the note *Can't find parking*.

I reply: I'll be right down.

Her van creeps slowly along the street, and I wave at her to stop. There is a perfectly fine parking spot on the opposite side, but she doesn't seem keen on it. How many times has she tried and driven past?

"Hop out. I'll park it." I steer into the space with one hand on the wheel and hope that I haven't offended her by offering. Just want to be useful. When I walk toward her, her face lights up, which is a relief, and she waves enthusiastically as if I'm the best thing she's seen all day.

★ ★ ★

After dinner, which I can barely focus on, I decide to bring it up. What's been holding me back. It comes out fast, in one breath, voice slightly off.

"I know you saw me in the therapy office. And... I want to talk to you about it, I want to tell you why. I've had depression, may still have it as some innate part of me," I tell her.

"Okay," she says. She doesn't tell me that I seem so happy, or that I'll be fine, or that I'm stronger than it. The older I get, the more I appreciate when people say less: it often means more. You can trust fewer words, and especially the singular ones, which stand tall on their own legs. A forest of words you get lost in. Sounds like Klara logic. I'm just about to share it with her when she interrupts me.

"We all have our quirks. I am most definitely diabetic. I also hide in the van and listen to rap when I'm uncomfortable and care way too much about even and odd numbers." She pauses. "I hadn't planned to share this. Usually, I preview my sentences in my head three times before I let them out into the world for judgment. But... I may have autism. That is, I may be Autistic."

I look up at her and respond with an echo of her reply to me just then.

"Okay."

Because in this moment everything is fucking okay. Still, very aware it's just a moment.

"What do we do next?" I say.

"I don't know how this goes. My longest relationship as an adult was six weeks. And for two of those weeks, he was traveling."

Why do I take so much joy in knowing no one's been able to keep her for longer than a few weeks? What would it take? Not much. It wouldn't be difficult at all. Then I remember that all this is temporary.

"You're going back to London."

"In two weeks."

So soon. For months, time has been my enemy. I've cursed it and taken it personally how it's crept along too quickly. The trial will soon be over, but now I have a new date to dread.

"If everything is well with Dad. If he needs more treatment, I may have to stay."

Of course. We have all been on edge knowing Peter's checkup is coming. He *has* to be okay. Any other desire would be selfishness on my part.

"Let's hope he's okay. And that you can go back. Do your test. Get on with life."

"Let's not talk about it?"

I swallow hard. Does she maybe…not want to go?

"Just for now. Tomorrow is a big day for you. Once it's over, we can talk," she clarifies as if she could read my excitement, and I feel myself and my stupid hope wilt like spinach in a hot pan. *She won't be changing her plans for you, Alex.*

"Sure."

Will have enough to worry about tomorrow, and she's right: everything can wait until it's over.

I'm wearing my suit for the third time in a year. Hate this suit. After the funeral I shoved it into the back of my wardrobe, tempted to burn the thing as though it were moth-infested. Relieved I didn't. It seems fitting that the suit I bought to see Calle off should be the one I wear when I meet his killer.

"I could come with you," Klara offered at dinner. She could. The trial is open to everyone; the gallery will be open to the public. I imagine her sitting there. In a way it would be comforting to have a person specifically there for me when I listen to the details of how my person was taken away from me.

"I'd like that. I'm not sure I've told you, but you calm me down."

"Like an emotional-support animal."

"Something like that." I smile. I smile all the fucking time lately.

"Then, I'll be there."

The courthouse is a brown '80s building that looks like nothing good can come from it, like a school kitchen or telling yourself you'll have just one more drink. I hope its appearance is misleading. It's so mundane and not what I had expected. I had imagined vaulted ceilings and intricate woodwork à la American legal dramas, judges with expensive shoes and a crowd of people eager to cheer justice on. In reality there are two bored-looking law students with notepads, tired benches and equally tired-looking legal professionals with stacks of files covered in Post-its in front of them. I want to scream at it all. *This is important! Someone died!* But if I did that the bulky security guy by the door would doubtlessly escort me out.

When we reach the bag-check point, I start to fucking sweat.

"Alex?" Klara's hand is no longer in mine. Hadn't realized I shook it off.

"Sorry. I'm fine. This is *fine*." But it's not fine. Obviously. Should have known anxiety would hit right about now. Wish I had brought my meds. Feverish chills, and lungs filled with something sticky, making it impossible to breathe. At least Klara knows not to touch me. Or ask silly questions that would make everything worse. Instead she stands there next to me, arms hanging by her sides, like a strong and steady pillar. As if wanting to remind me that the world is *there*. Solid. Waiting for me once I come out of this anxiety attack. I feel my shoulders relax ever so slightly, and I bring myself to look at her.

"I'm not sure how to be supportive," she says.

"I like this version of it. Thank you."

"You always tell me I can do things. That I'm smart and strong enough. You have my back, so naturally I can't even object to you doing those things for me. Counting carbs, snacks in the car, those little things that just support me, you know?"

Clear my throat but don't move on to the next step, which would be to actually say something.

"Do you ever do those nice things to yourself? Tell yourself you can do stuff? That you're good enough? That you care about people around you to the point of it almost killing you?"

Well. No. I don't. Should I?

"I'll say them to you, if you'd like, then."

We stand next to each other, like trees in a forest, for a while. I handled it. *I had an anxiety attack in public, and I handled it. It passed.* So this is the worst that can happen. It feels freeing in a sense: I've imagined this moment as some major catastrophe that had to be avoided at all costs. The cost was me not living. But this—I can handle this. And if people look at me, then let them. Klara doesn't flinch when people look at her equipment, her robot parts: she wears them proudly. Anxiety may not be something I should be proud of, but I certainly shouldn't be ashamed. So I do what she's just suggested, and I tell myself that I can do this, that I'm capable, that I can be here for the people I care about—Mamma and Pappa and Dan. And I am.

KLARA

🔍 How could I have known?

Google Search   I'm Feeling Lucky

I'm not sure what just happened, but whatever it was, I felt it in my soul. I've made a mental note to ask Google about anxiety attacks. There must be more helpful strategies than to freeze as if a gun were pointed at me. I'm stuck to him now, won't leave his side. There are articles called "9 Signs Your Partner Is Too Clingy and What to Do about It," but walking right next to Alex feels better than the two-yard distance we used to have. *Clingy* can mean that you are too emotionally dependent, but it can also mean tight-fitting, like a garment. I'd like to be clingy to Alex like a comfy top would.

Alex's parents come toward me. I recognize Dan next to them.

"Hello. I'm Alex's mum." She wastes no time waiting for an introduction.

"Thrilled to meet you! I'm sorry that this is where we all

meet. I wish I could have known Alex's brother." Alex's mum is small and round, the opposite of her tall, majestic son. She looks like what she lives off is love and cuddles. If comfort food were a person, she would be it. His dad reaches out a hand and nods as I take it. Approvingly, I think.

"Come." Alex takes my hand and leads me. I don't mind it. His grip is firm, swallowing up my small hand, fingers and a part of my wrist. Like a seasickness band on a boat trip, he quenches any nausea. I hope he feels the same when my hand is in his.

There are only a few people there. A man wearing a suit sits with his back to us; he's not bothering, or daring, to turn around. Next to him a small legal team, the only ones chatting. I've never been to court before. Once I moved a discount sticker onto a full-price item in Waitrose, but no one noticed, and I escaped the eye of the law.

Alex pushes some papers into my hand.

"Take these. I'm just going to the bathroom one last time." He pushes his hand through his hair and kind of shakes his head, sending the motion all the way down his tall body.

"Sure."

I look down at the paper in front of me, which states the order of events and the people involved. I turn the page, and then I see it. My body reacts before my brain has even registered what I'm reading, my stomach turning itself inside out. I see it but I don't *understand it.*

Defendant: Mateusz Holm.

In a trance I flick the pages in the file until I get to the one with the details of the vehicle. It's a make, model and registration number I recognize. *Our company van.*

It's too late to leave, too late to grab Alex and say *Listen, shit is about to go down, but just hear me out.* In fact, it's too late for anything because Mateusz is suddenly next to me.

"Klara? What are you doing here?" He utters a tense laugh

and puts his hand on my shoulder, as if I'm a little child in an adult-only environment and he's about to escort me out. The touch makes me jump, then shudder.

"Get off me," I say, disgust in my voice. Mateusz looks at me with confusion.

"Why are you here? Is Peter here as well?" he says, looking around the room as if it would give a clue away. I look at the area between his eyebrows where a deep ridge has formed.

"Why are *you* here, Mateusz?" I ask. But I know why. He's here because he drove a van through Lund nine months ago. Because he didn't stop at the scene.

Alex is next to me now. Then Dan. Then other people who look serious. This is not personal to them, I understand. One of them speaks.

"You shouldn't be talking to each other. Please go and take your seats." A man gestures with a hand full of documents to an area on our left. No one moves. Except Mateusz, who takes an almost unnoticeable step back. He's never met Alex before but knows to be intimidated by him.

Dan pulls at Alex's jacket sleeve, worryingly.

"Come with me, Alex," Dan says. But Alex doesn't seem like he's going anywhere. Alex is like a giant statue, like the thunder god, Thor, towering over us all, his cloud of emotion building up with impending release. I imagine his head being filled with all the angry symbols of the Wingdings font.

"How do you know him?" His eyes don't leave Mateusz, but the question is directed at me.

"He…he used to work for my dad's company. I used to work with him." Alex's eyes grow wider. "But I fired him, right when I arrived. He was terrible. He said horribly inappropriate things."

"This is the guy I replaced at the company? You needed a new carpenter because you'd fired him for some inappropriate comments? Did you know he had run someone over too?

Forgot to share that detail, didn't you? Jesus, Klara, this is the fucking dude that ran over my brother! He had 40 mg of alcohol in his bloodstream, and he's here fighting like a sissy to get out of any blame!" I have never seen Alex like this.

"Security!" Mateusz pipes up. Alex is much taller, wider and angrier than Mateusz, who is quivering just at the sight of him. I instinctively take steps backward, ending up bumping into Alex's mum, who looks at me with pain on her face. Mateusz is ushered away. Dan puts his hand on Alex's shoulder.

"Alex. Breathe," Dan urges him.

"Fuck, Klara." He is wild, his eyes like some panicking horse that is cornered and has nowhere to flee. As if he's trapped in his worst nightmare. *I'm giving him that feeling.*

"What even is this mess?" He rubs his face. "How could I be so stupid? I've been driving one of those vans every day for weeks now—"

Then it hits him: the possibility.

"Was I driving the same van that hit my brother? Have I been driving the same fucking van?"

"I didn't know," I say quietly. I know that I should stand up for myself, but then when people start shouting I always want to sit down.

"You didn't know? And your dad, did he know he'd been employing a criminal?" The mileage tracker, I think. Yes, Dad must have known. Why hadn't he fired Mateusz? Why was he still there when I took over? Dad can't have known everything, I decide. No way.

"I know you're not the best at math, but even you should be able to put two and two together." *Even you.* Shame hits as I think that maybe I should have, maybe I got this fundamentally wrong, and it's yet again my fault.

"I didn't know, I promise. And I fired him because I knew he was a bad egg." I feel sick now. Realizing who I had been dealing with. Making my professional life difficult was nothing compared to what he has done to Alex's family. To his sweet mum who greeted me with open arms and his dad who is the spitting image of him but even taller.

"Alex, I'm so sorry. He doesn't exactly have *killer* written on his forehead. Dad can't have known the full extent of what happened. Mateusz probably played it down. And he wouldn't have known about the connection to you either. I'm sure of it."

"It's time to sit down. Please, Alex…" Dan tugs at his arm. I hand the pile of documents I'm still holding on to over to Dan.

"Just leave." Alex turns his back on me, and I have no choice but to walk out of the building, tears stinging in my eyes from both shame and sadness. I want to say something, *anything*, but the emotions are too strong. Then there is surprise, and these new warm feelings for Alex that don't stop, not even for a second. Even now that he *hates* me. It's overwhelming, and I need air. The van. My book on Scandinavian architecture. Rap. Anything that will calm me down. I hang my head so that all I see is the floor ahead of me and walk away to the sound of Alex's voice.

"And, Klara. In case you hadn't figured—I fucking quit."

ALEX

Personal Calendar ▼

○ **NEW TASK:** Appeal fine

○ **NEW TASK:** Fuck it—totally worth it. Pay fine

○ **NEW TASK:** Go back to Jobcenter

So this is Mateusz. Also known as *him* and *the killer.* All this time I've been wondering what the witness in the red fleece would say, then I couldn't wait to see *him.* Now I have, he is sitting just a couple of yards across the room from me. This is what I see when I stare at him: big teeth that he can't seem to hide away enough. A thin mouth that has dried spots at the edges (healing cold sore?). Mousy hair that is thin and may recede more as he ages. The ears—they are average. I stumble here, not knowing how to bear witness to the common. The nose is thin and slim. There is too much thinness in his face and not enough roundness: it is a noncompensated face. I focus again on his lips, moving but not yet saying anything. These are the lips that suggested a price on my brother's life and on his own freedom, and also the lips that chatted and maybe even laughed with Klara.

Never thought of myself as an angry person. Actually, the contrary: I'm mild to the point of being meek. Have been known to stop fights and apply diplomatic skills worthy of the Swedish state (no war in Sweden since 1814—a world record). Something is happening to me. I want to hurt him. I think of my brother's head smashed against the pavement, and then a second thought takes over. *Him in my job.* His fucking hands with blood on them touching the van I've been driving around. And then there's *Klara.* Did she like him? How could she have worked with a *fucking villain?*

I zoom out and wake up as if I'd nodded off when the hearing is over. When I walk past him on the way out, I swerve to the right, toward him, ignoring the voices behind me telling me to keep walking. To ignore. I only stop when I'm right in front of Mateusz.

Then I commit my first act of violence in my twenty-nine-year-long life.

KLARA

> 🔍 How do I even go on?

Google Search   **I'm Feeling Lucky**

It's been two days since Mateusz ruined my life. I have been in my bedroom for those two days, minus quick breaks for a pee and to rummage through the kitchen for a snack (thankfully discovered that Dad still hides chocolate in the house, despite the only other person living with him being me. Marabou milk chocolate found behind toaster). I wonder if Alex is counting the days too.

I haven't spoken to a soul apart from Dad, Saga and the lady I called yesterday to complain about breakup ice cream being overrated. The stomachache, blood-sugar spike and extra shot of insulin was not worth it.

I said this to the individual taking my call at the Ben & Jerry's helpline.

"My sister bought your ice cream, as it was recommended to me in my circumstances."

"Your circumstances?" The lady was doing that thing when you repeat what the other person has said. Most successfully applied when you want to avoid coming up with a solution and let the other person do it for you. *The audacity!*

"I used to work in customer support," I said hoping to instill some respect or, even better, fear in her. "The flavor, *Half-baked*, was suggested to me during a Google search which landed me on your company's website. It was said to be the recommended flavor for people having been *dumped*." I exhaled sharply at that word. *I said it.*

"I am disappointed to say the ice cream offered me no relief from my destructive-thought pattern. I followed all the instructions, ate it with a spoon straight from the tub, even though I'm a lady, and watched reality TV at the same time. When it was finished, I still had negative yet unidentifiable feelings."

The lady suddenly had her voice back.

"Unidentifiable feelings…?"

I let my annoyance over having to explain to her the simplest of things come through in my voice.

"Well. When you're in love—have you ever been in love?—you get those butterflies in your stomach. See, I used to have them. But when purchasing your ice cream, I had more of a swarm of moths in there. Dark and blind and especially active at night. I'd hoped they'd go away."

At this point, I decided that the person I am talking to is hopeless and that I would rather not have my 49.99 kronor refunded and ended the phone call.

I closed the blinds and went to sleep.

I find my blood-sugar readings soothing. I look at them when I can't sleep. The black little dots that form a graph, each one a number and live reading of my blood. The most common number on the display is 6. I sleep better when it's a 6. An 8 makes me wake restlessly and reach for my phone in the early hours of the morning. When it says *No data*, I feel like I have disappeared from the earth, like I have left my body. Everything is empty, and I hold my breath again and again until I am back there, in the shape of a line of black dots. Then I know I'm still alive. I've checked my followers, and there are still five. Alex still follows my blood sugar.

There is a knock at the door.

"Can you open up, please?" I reluctantly get off the bed, duvet scrunched in a mess and a chocolate wrapper somewhere on the floor. A glass of water sits in a dangerous position on the floor next to the bed, waiting for someone to knock it over. An outsider would find it hard to believe that I am the same Klara that styles bathroom projects and has gone viral for her interior finesse and attention to detail. This Klara can hardly brush her teeth.

"I'll come downstairs soon," I say, wishing he would leave me alone.

"Can I come in?" Dad could have left the question mark out because he's not waiting for an answer. Before I can reply the curtains are drawn aside, light flooding the room, and he is sitting on my bed, pushing the duvet to the side and collecting the chocolate wrapper and pocketing it.

"I understand things didn't go well between you and Alex." *Understatement of the century.* Every time I have to relive that morning in the courtroom feels like a punch to the gut.

"At least my time here is up, and my ticket home is booked. I won't have to see him again." *Home* sounds different when I say it now. The word sounds like home as in perhaps *home screen* rather than a cozy, safe place. A home screen would just hold content together. Not be an actual home.

"I'm sorry that it ended like this. I really thought you guys were a good match by the sounds of it." I get the feeling that Dad wants to say more but shies away from the words.

"You've done an amazing job, Klara. Don't you see that?" he says instead.

"Really? I crashed a van. Two employees left. Actually I've just caused a third to resign."

"But then you fixed everything. What you have done is not just picked up the pieces, you have managed to turn a successful but aging business up a notch and give it an edge. And as for those two, good riddance. There is no room for sexism in a workplace today, to say nothing of what Mateusz did. As for Alex, he's the one who should apologize, in my opinion." He glances at me at the mention of his name, regretting he said it.

"I kept thinking you would have wanted Saga here."

"I love your sister the same as you, but this was definitely a job for Klara."

"I don't think Mum agrees."

"Has she been texting you every day? Because that's what she does when she's worried about someone. She's texting me. Not you. Because she knows you're okay."

Well, no, she hasn't texted me very often at all, I realize.

"I always feel like I'm the immature one, still finding my way while Saga's got it all figured out."

I was waiting tables when she was writing her dissertation. My only academic achievement or mark on the world being that I wrote the names for the bar's cocktail list, the Sour Sister Sass being my favorite.

"That's not true. You were always so mature. I kept waiting for you to have a moment of fun and figuring yourself out. Your whole childhood you took care of your health, inspiring us all with your strength and determination. You injected yourself at age six, for goodness' sake! If anything, we were relieved to see you not being too serious, enjoying life a bit and not diving into commitments too soon."

I had never thought about it this way. I blink a few times to stop my eyes from producing tears.

"I've loved it here, actually." It's true, I realize as I say it. It wasn't only to do with Alex but running my dad's company gave me a purpose. It had been so long since I'd thought about Mark the Ex or any of the things my old life had to offer. Even seeing my surname on the side of the vans fills me with pride, and not the embarrassment I felt the first week. I was proud to drive that van and proud of what we as a team had achieved.

I've finally gone outside for fresh air, and I see the stars for the first time in days. London is too bright, so busy shining its own artificial light on its people that it drowns out the stars. Every capital has replaced the stars in the sky with human ones.

"Do you see *Karlavagnen*?" *The Big Dipper.* My built-in translation system repeats it in English. Dad has appeared next to me, his cloud of breath traveling north as he tilts his chin up to look.

"I do. We used to call it *Klaravagnen*." *Klara carriage.*

"It was your carriage. A princess carriage, as you pointed out. You would have painted it pink in the sky if you could." I smile. I had a good childhood: you don't have your own carriage of stars in the sky if you don't.

"Are you happy, Klara? I mean, Alex aside," Dad asks. I think about his question. I am not as happy as I thought I'd be, looking at age twenty-six as some faraway land as I did as a teenager. It was meant to be lined with success, romantic gestures, a house that would have *Elle* interior journalists queuing up outside it. I am not that type of happy. But I'm happy when I solve a challenging project, I'm happy when Dad and I eat together, and I was happy when my calendar pinged with an entry from Alex. It's a scale, happiness, and I've realized lately that the goal is to hover along the middle between euphoria and intense sadness. If I could only find that middle spot and stay there. I say this to Dad.

"I've been happier than I thought I'd be."

"It's not an easy place or age to be in, your midtwenties.

You're told that the world is your oyster, you've been fed it since youth, but then you arrive to find the shell shut and the oyster out of reach. It was different when I was your age. I was already married, owned a house and had a child. It was possible for a simple person to buy a house back then and to feed a family. We didn't have to spend our twenties just saving toward a deposit."

"I've somehow arrived at the middle of them, without permanent work or a relationship. I don't even have a degree." I doubt I'll ever get one. That dream seems further away than ever.

"You don't need a degree to run a company. I don't have one, didn't even finish secondary school. Your mum has a degree, and what has she done with it? She sells vitamins off a pyramid scheme," Dad says. I laugh.

"We do get free vitamins."

"They have an aftertaste of seaweed."

"It's called spirulina," I say by way of correction.

"Diluted in water, it works wonders on the flowers."

"She would go crazy if you told her that's what you use them for. They are meant to cure your cancer."

"I'm getting there without them. But let her think her pills have helped."

"A shooting star!" I point it out with childlike enthusiasm, almost looking over my shoulder to check if Saga has seen it before me. But of course, she's busy somewhere else doing God knows what.

"Make a wish, quick," Dad urges me.

And so I do.

The next morning, I wake up to a message from Saga and what is apparently an urgent matter.

Saga: There's a spider in the bathroom. Has made its way underneath the door to what I assume to be the outside of the door.

Saga: Please hurry because I'm going to cry.

Saga: Klaraaaa?

Saga: ?

I type back:

Me: Klara is dead. You're next. Best, Spider.

"Not funny," Saga says as she appears from the bathroom five minutes later, her hair in a navy blue towel turban that makes her eyes even bluer.

"Well, the spider would agree with you. He's now a squashed shadow of his former self inside a tissue in the kitchen garbage." Saga looks suspiciously at the kitchen cupboard that hides the bin but decides not to worry about spider ghosts and grabs a cup from the shelf.

"Can't tell you how nice this is. Coffee that's hot. The problem with cold coffee is not the taste but how it reminds you of the fact that you are not on top of things," Saga tells me as she cradles the Stuttgart University–logo mug with her whole hand. "If you don't have time to finish a beverage while it's hot then—pardon my language—you are screwed in terms of that famous work–life balance. This is the first time in months I've burned my tongue on coffee," she adds for clarity. Then she closes her laptop and eyes me up and down. I'm suddenly aware of the three-day-old joggers with holes on the thighs and the rest of my braless look.

"This is *bad*. It's time we got you out of the house properly. I've booked us horse riding tomorrow," Saga says. "And I have questions about bathrooms. We need you back at work to do a proper handover to Gunnar and Hanna."

"I have paperwork to catch up on. And we have Dad. And I was planning to bake something and to paint my toenails."

"Oh, because you've been so productive lately? I'm pretty sure you just made those plans up."

"I'm a bad liar. Doesn't mean I should be punished with team-building exercises," I mutter, longing for the upstairs.

"It will be fun. When was the last time you and I did something together that didn't involve analyzing an MRI scan or working out how to make tiles look appealing on Instagram? Please." She does have a point. When was the last time I did something just for me? My hobbies are confined to tidying the living room and stacking the dishwasher.

I think of the warm nuzzle of an Icelandic pony nibbling at my hand for a treat and putting my nose to its mane and breathing in the smell. Horses smell earthy and ground you. You can't breathe shallowly when you have the musky smell of horse around you.

"I'm certain scrolling on your phone has a negative impact on both balance and the nature experience," I say to Saga, who is holding her reins with one hand and her phone with the other. Her horse walks calmly along the path, with mine next to it. My horse is called Pontus and is brown; Saga's is called Vega and is white.

Saga keeps fiddling on her phone, and I think that it seems less about getting me out of the house than whatever she is doing on the phone. I'm just about to look through my mental library for a snarky remark when I realize her distance could mean many things, not just that she is ignoring me. I wonder if I should ask Saga something like *Are you okay?* It seems to be the helpful phrase when you get that nagging feeling of worry that I've just identified. But then I remember how she usually sneers and makes faces at questions like that. So I instead put down some ground rules for our afternoon together.

"No phones for an hour. I will even put mine on Silent too, which you know very well I dislike." It's not easy to talk when you ride a horse. She turns her torso back to me while bouncing along, and her speech comes out stuttered. I lean forward over my horse's mane to catch the words.

"Fine." She pops it in her pocket and puts her hood over her helmet. It's started to drizzle ever so slightly. I know this to be the start of something.

I'm right: water soon falls on us in a steady supply. Not the polite drizzle you have in England but a rude, heavy rainfall. The wind also seems to be picking up. My hair is escaping its elastic-band constraint hair by hair, and there is a wailing noise in my ear. *Great.*

"Why are you muttering? You have a raincoat on." Saga's voice is almost drowned out by gusts of wind.

"I'm not two, and this is not a muddy puddle. Most adults don't enjoy being soaked by freezing water," I say.

"There is no such thing as inclement weather—just inappropriate clothing." Gosh, she sounds like *Mum.* Or any other Swedish parent. This is an actual, established Swedish saying. One that kids are peppered with when they are told to take the bike to football training, go out at recess or clean the front yard in the middle of a snowstorm. *There is no bad weather…*

"Do you think we should turn back?" I shout to Saga, having to ask the horse to trot faster to even be heard.

"We've paid for two hours!"

"God help us if we would return even a minute before that, then." I would usually do the same. I like to keep end times—they are useful. Bookings and activities are great like that. Kids' parties have a start time and an end time. When you're an adult you enter one massive gray zone. Really, the only reason I dislike dinner parties is that I'm not sure when the guests will leave, and hence, I'm not sure when I can turn the music off, wash my face and teeth, and go to bed. I do like having Alice's family over because they live outside London and have to catch the last train home—the 10:14.

"Klara, just stop talking, will you?"

"I won't stop. Let's have a good time. You wanted team-building? Well, let's build this team of sisters!"

"No, seriously—just stop talking. Because I think we're lost. Give me the number for the riding center," Saga says, hand out-stretched as if collecting rent.

"You organized this, didn't you?"

"Thanks, you've been a huge help," she sighs, pouts and then straightens up reassuming her composure. We both rummage through pockets for a business card with a horse on it. Contents of mine: a measuring tape, dirt, blood-glucose kit, a lollipop and a few nails. Hers: a pack of tissues, lip gloss and a hair band, the plastic spiral one that doesn't ruin the hair. Nope. Nothing.

I don't point out that this was her idea. That she was in the lead or that it was a fight initiated by her that made me lose my sense of direction. I stamp angrily at a puddle on the ground and hold on to the reins of both our horses. As she shields her phone with one hand she tries to make out what Google Maps has to say. I know Google better than her.

"It won't work here. There are no roads drawn up."

"We still have a location," I say hopeful.

"Fine, so you figure out what direction we need to go with-out roads. Shall we just trudge through the forest, then? At least we'll be shielded from the rain if we stay here and wait it out."

"I thought there was no bad weather, only—" I'm inter-rupted by a loud explosion of thunder and instinctively move closer to my sister. I wish I could google the risk of lightning striking in a pine forest, but Google has its Out of Office on. Saga is visibly anxious. Ghosts, spiders, loud noises—come to think of it, there is lots that scares her.

"Let's move away from the trees and try to find a clearing," I say, pretty sure I can recall high school or a random science book telling me to do so.

"And get soaked? I'd say we shelter under the biggest tree we can find! I'm literally shaking from cold, K."

"Freezing, or hit by lightning? Choose your death, dear sister! I know my preference."

She mutters, sulks, looks around herself as if she would be able to see lightning coming after her, but she does follow me as I walk on in the hope of spotting an open area.

"A clear space," I hear her say. "When did you get so practical?"

"I'm not hopeless, you know." A thought hits me as I say the words, and I stop. "Wait, if you think I'm hopeless, why did you send me to Sweden? Do you realize how I could have messed things up?" I'm shouting. Not sure if it's because of the rain or because I really want to shout at my sister in this moment. How can the sky be so dark suddenly? I'd forgotten how scary Swedish rainstorms get.

"Mum and I had a conversation. It was enough with the customer chats and toxic men. You needed a challenge other than your own medical condition. You have so much *potential*, Klara. We just wanted you to realize it."

"So you pushed me into trouble knowingly? I can't bloody believe it."

"Listen, I really couldn't have gone. That part is true. But yes, and no, we didn't push you into trouble but a *challenging environment*."

"You knew how hard this would be for me!" I'm angry, but the presence of Pontus forces me to calm down. I'm never angry at animals or children: they often fail to understand things and respond appropriately. I know how they feel.

Saga looks guilty, so I know my reaction is appropriate.

"I'm going this way." I pull gently at my horse's reins. I know it's the right way, even though I don't have directions showing me exactly where to go, and every row of pine trees is identical to the last. "You can trust me, your hopeless sister, or go and get lost, literally." I walk off, rain falling off my shoulder and onto the ground with the force of an overflowing gutter. My eyelashes struggle to keep up with the drops of water, and my hands have turned pink and stiff from the wet cold. My socks are soaking, and the ground makes noises as I step on it.

Only once I get to the first bend of the road do I turn around. Saga and her horse are following after me, with a twenty-yard distance, walking slowly, two heads bent down. I stop and wait for her. For the first five minutes we seethe beside one another, horses in tow. Then she says, "Why do you think I always tried so hard? You had their love whatever you did. It was always *Klara is so strong and amazing.* The only way I could get praise was to achieve top marks, and even then, it didn't feel like much. I used to wish I would get ill too! So that I could have a week in hospital with Mum to myself and Dad arriving with presents and treats." For a moment I am stunned.

"You never told me any of this." I had thought she was angry with me. When people are angry at me, I understand the anger to be evoked by me—my person, my words or my body—I never consider that the anger could be coming from *them*. I think now that perhaps I haven't made as many people angry in my life as I thought I had. Perhaps the only person I've failed is myself.

"Telling you I was pushing myself beyond my limits to compete with you would have ruined the purpose."

"I'm sorry, Saga."

"All this talk about perfect Saga, the fairy tale…well, I'm not. I have a confession for you. That summer road trip when you were a baby and cried the whole trip? I pinched you the whole time. Literally every time you stopped crying, I reached for your thigh, silent and sneaky when Mum and Dad had their eyes on the road and the map."

"Oh my God. You brute."

"Yep."

"I guess you were four years old. You're forgiven."

"What about thirty-year-old me, am I forgiven now? For leaving you alone, for not doing enough?" I think of myself and what I do to qualify as a good sister and can't come up with much. I've found excuses not to come and visit Saga. I hated the flight there, and she was always busy, leaving me to wander the streets of Stuttgart alone and go to museums, the contents of which I never really cared about. I would be looking at the carpet of a stately home or a scarcely clad marble statue wondering what she was doing in her office that very moment and wishing I had her next to me so I could tell her that the statue looked like our secondary teacher with the large nose. My solution was to stop visiting altogether.

"I've also been a pretty shitty sister, haven't I?" I admit.

I can't remember a single time when I haven't succeeded in being short and difficult to my sister. Or just absent. In many ways, we're strangers, my sister and me. That's not what I want; I want to spend more time together. I want to know my sister Saga. If someone asks what my sister is like I want to have the answers. The words fall out of me.

"You told me I'm your person, but I feel inadequate. For what you need, I mean. I always need you there for me, but what do I offer in return? I never actually check how you are. I didn't even know how you struggled with motherhood."

Saga starts to open her mouth to, I assume, debate this statement and make me feel better again but then changes her mind and simply says, "Hmm."

"You are so amazing, Saga. You can set anyone at ease. You can talk to anyone, just instantly get on with them. I, on the other hand..." I swallow hard "...I can't even go to the hairdresser. I find the silence once we have discussed the usual—where we're going on holiday, where we work and what our weekend plans are—unbearable. I attempt to deliver *Mm-hmm*s and *Oh yes*es until the hair dryer comes out and finally drowns out all the chatting, but I just can't do it." This gets a laugh from her.

"Thought your hair looked a bit long," she says and adds, "I have signal back! And I think I recognize that log cabin we just passed. I'd say we are officially not lost anymore."

I'm just about to fall asleep when the sound of feet reaches me.

"Hey," Saga stands in the door opening. I've slept in the office on a mattress so that she could have her old room back.

"Can't sleep?" I ask her.

"I was wondering if you wanted to move the mattress into my room."

"Worried about the shadows?"

"Nonsense. It's not very often I have my sister under the same roof, and it feels silly to put a wall between us now that I do. It's my last night here."

I smile and hop up from the floor, starting to drag the mattress behind me on the floor while she collects the pillow and duvet for me.

"Maybe it's a little bit because of the shadows. There is one that looks like Piers Morgan."

"Wow, that *is* scary."

Inside the main house, with the mattress next to Saga's bed, I pull my duvet up over my chin, needing my whole body to be covered to be able to sleep. The sheets are worn, washed so many times that they are thin and light and soft from fabric softener. Mine have flowers on them, and Saga's set is covered in small princess crowns.

"Having a sick dad is hard," I whisper into the dark.

"Being a mother is hard," she replies in another whisper.

"Running a construction company is hard."

"Being married is hard."

"Being hopelessly in love is hard."

"Being thirty is hard."

"Being twenty-six is hard."

"Being a *human* is bloody hard."

"I always thought of us as shoes."

"Shoes?"

"You know, you the glossy heel and me the dirty sneaker." She breaks the whisper with a laugh now.

"Klara, I'm a bloody Birkenstock or a worn bathroom slipper stolen from a hotel and long past its heyday. The only thing that's glossy about me is my oily forehead."

"Saga, you were right about me being able to handle Sweden. I'm not saying you should have forced me to come, but I am saying that I was able to handle it, and that perhaps you seeing my potential wasn't an entirely bad thing."

"I love you, Klara."

"Love you too."

ALEX

Personal Calendar ▾

O **NEW TASK:** Give ring back to Dan. Wasn't even mine to start with. *Done*

O **NEW TASK:** Sell car—don't need it. Don't actually want a high-end car. *Done*

O **NEW TASK:** Get over Klara Nilsson. Not fucking done at all

It's been a week. Suit is thrown back into the wardrobe where I hope I will never see it again. This time I may actually burn it, maybe a ritual like that will send fate a message. *Stop messing with Alex. He's not prepared for it. Hasn't got the fucking suit!* It's over. Months of searching, pulling my fucking hair out and agonizing is over now. Feel relief. But do not feel like celebrating.

Five missed calls from Klara. She doesn't like phone calls so she must really need to talk to me. Can't talk to her. Don't want to hear her explain anything. Because there is nothing to explain, is there? If I talk to her I may blow up. I've sat on the couch for three hours straight and am having flashbacks to two months ago when I was in a very different place to now. Saw her calendar entry, she's going. Not sure what reaction she's hoping for and what the point of those five calls were when she's so clearly moving away. Moving on.

Know what it feels like to have your heart broken now. I have known for two days and five hours. If depression is the lack of feeling, this here is the presence of all negative feelings in one, squeezed together in an elevator, commuter train or other incredibly claustrophobic space. I reckon if you stay with them, you may end up fine: once they starve, they're shut off there in the elevator. I'm trying to sit with it. Fear, anger and *regret*?

KLARA

How do you throw a Beat Cancer party?

Google Search   **I'm Feeling Lucky**

We are sitting on metal chairs padded with tired blue patterned fabric, bright lights flickering above our heads. There is no reason to make consultation rooms cheerier, if it's good news they can look like a junkie's apartment for all the patient cares, and if it's bad news beauty will simply sting the eyes. The room is perfect.

We are ready. Mum is quiet on the iPad. We are quiet as well. I have stopped my mindless, nervous babbling after Saga pinched my thigh. My cue to shut the eff up since childhood and still as effective.

"So." Dr. Singh tenses his lips pursing them gently, getting ready to speak. His eyes move between Dad's face and his computer screen, stopping at the latter for extended periods of time to read and gather information about my father and his body, *his case*, which is what he is reduced to in the doctor's eyes. "I have your MRI back as well as your PET scan images, Peter. It looks as if there is no lymph-node involvement in the nearby regions." He abandons his screen, breaking into a smile, "Which means that you are cancer-free."

"Are you kidding?" I blurt out, my body leaving the chair to half stand up.

"I'm not joking. That would be quite a strange joke, wouldn't it?" Dr. Singh smiles at me.

Mum starts cheering as if we've won the lottery, which I guess you could say we have.

"We should totally throw one of those Beat Cancer parties," Saga says. "Where we make a tumor piñata and bash it to pieces."

We hug my dad, and as the relief washes over me I feel something else as well, a selfish unexpected feeling that tells me my work here is done, and this means I have to go home. I had come to accept, perhaps even like, that my trip had no end in sight, no return date set.

I wish I could tell Alex. We had been gearing up and hoping for good news together: his trial and my dad's health. And now we both have the good news that we wanted, but it doesn't feel quite as wonderful as I imagined.

It has been three months. I can't quite get my head around it. In a way it feels like I just arrived yesterday, but on the other it must have been years, because I arrived a different Klara than I am now. It was as if a piece of me was missing and, however cheesy it sounds, I found it here.

"You know you are always welcome to stay," my dad says it with hesitation, as if he worries I will bite his hand off at the suggestion. I would have, the Klara that landed a few months back to start the biggest chore I had ever been given by a parent.

"Maybe one day. I have to go home. I have my life in London." I have my flat share waiting for me, my belongings, my savings account with what is supposed to be a deposit on a first-buyer home in some London suburb and half of my two friends. *If Alex didn't now hate me, perhaps things would have been different...* I push the thought away. I've screwed up in every way possible, in every iteration of the verb. *I screw up, I screwed up, I've screwed up, I'm screwed.*

"Will you be okay when I go?" I ask him.

"I will miss you, but I'm ready to jump in again, and I've missed my eggs on toast. Stir-fry Tuesday just isn't the same."

"I've prepared some CVs for you. They're in a green folder in the office. This time I mentioned that we want to keep the ratio of fifty-percent women-held positions, and my ad wasn't removed." This train of thought obviously leads straight to Alex, to when he turned up with his messy hair and Scandi cheekbones. *Oh, Alex.* If only I were normal. I've never wished for it this much before. I would know what to do, what to say to avert the crisis. I could have explained how I felt about him— *feel* about him. What was once an unidentifiable feeling is clear to me now. I, Klara Nilsson, have now been in love. I could tell him all this, and perhaps my words would be enough. But they never are. Where poignant words should sit, I have *deficits*. That's what the first part of my assessment, emailed over by Dr. Svensson, called it. *Autism is an invisible disability.* It doesn't feel invisible, standing in front of me now, blocking my way to happiness. This is what I say in my head, of course. What I say out loud to Dad is "There are a total of six candidates that I feel would be suitable, and they are the ones in the folder. I am sure the company's future will be as bright as ever even after my departure."

"Thank you," Dad replies, smiling at me. "I've decided to try Hanna in your position when you leave. If anything, this has taught me that I'm not the only one that can run this company. It's time I take a back seat and let your changes work for us. I'm thinking two days off a week won't harm me."

I have a thought of my work here having a scent, like a perfume, and that scent will linger in the air after I've gone home. I like the thought of something of mine lingering here. Something I can perhaps come back for one day.

"Come, I have something to show you," Dad says now. "You have to leave this room and come outside, though."

Dad points toward the toolshed, which holds less tools than random crap, and I follow as he opens the door. A motorcycle, black, blue and shiny stands there, its cover taken off to reveal it in all its metal glory. It smells of *new*. Dad beams with joy.

"My new toy. I thought I deserved it after this ordeal."

"It's amazing, Dad! I never knew you liked bikes."

"A dream I had, but I was always too sensible to follow it. I'm thinking this will keep me busy all spring and summer, the flat endless roads of the south. I'm joining a group of bikers that drive once a week." I give him a hug. He is getting started on his bucket list, just like me. He will be fine.

"Good on you, Dad. You only live once. Unless you're a salamander or an amphibian. Then you live twice."

Later, I think of *you only live once* and go visit Google because I too do not have the life cycle of a reptile.

Google: Should I text the man who hates me?

I call Alex five times and listen to his voice mail saying *Hello, it's Alex*. Then I decide to send one last message to him, despite my better judgment and my search engine's advice.

I write as if he's dead: Thank you for everything. Gone but never forgotten.

The rumor of my once-again failed love life has spread— surprise, surprise—all the way from Sweden to Marbella.

"It's Mum." Why do parents do this? Your children have

your number and can see who is calling. You should know this since you also all have smartphones that show a name when said person calls. Oh, and hang on. This is an actual video call so your face is filling my screen as I press the accept button.

"I know it's you, Mum."

"How are you, my love?" No sunset or blessed hashtag to share today? That's a first for Mum. Maybe it's raining in Spain. Mum is wearing her glasses, and her hair is swept back. Her hands are still and not fiddling with anything.

"I want to say sorry to you. There has been a lot of pressure on you. Some of that pressure Saga and I put on you by coercing you into helping your dad. We always assumed that you could handle it. You are so strong and resourceful."

"What choice did I have?" I am trying my best to hold back tears now. Somehow technology makes me more vulnerable: I must keep my head in the square, but in real life I can look away, move my body and hide my emotions. Here I'm exposed. I hate video calls with a passion.

"I'm sorry. You're right."

"The man I love now hates me. When it comes down to it, no one wants me in the end. And yes, we only just met, and no, we're not married, and yes, I will probably get over him, say, sometime next year. But I don't want to get over him. And I shouldn't have to. This wasn't supposed to end." Words flood out of me as if my mum had opened an invisible dam.

"If he is the one for you, he will find his way to back to you. Don't give up yet, Klara. Don't start to hate him just yet. He is hurt, correct? Time gives people perspective. Anger doesn't last forever, no matter what someone has done to you."

"He doesn't want anything to do with me."

"*Now.* You may be right, but all you can do is wait."

The corner of my mouth moves into the smallest of smiles. I can't remember the last time she gave me relationship advice. I think it was in kindergarten when Oliver the Brute was biting me all the time. I get a sudden urge to hug her, or rather for her to hug me.

"Once I've got myself sorted with a new job, I could come and visit you. I need some sunshine," I say.

"I'd like that."

I realize that despite Mum's chatty, dizzy nature, she is also lonely, not in the traditional way but with the type of loneliness that only comes from having your children far away from you.

It seems I have a full day of FaceTime ahead of me. Saga is next. She is back in Germany and has revised a plan to improve her mental health. But today she's not talking about her challenges but mine.

"IELTS. You have to try, Klara." Her face fills the phone square.

"I have tried. There is a fine line between optimism and stupidity. Between hope and ignorance. What difference will a few math lessons make?" The confidence I had started to build up left when Alex did.

"Things will be different now. There is help. You can have extra time. A quiet space where you sit alone. It's not stupidity trying again when the circumstances have changed."

I ponder this. *Of course.* A seed may not grow in a dry, waterless soil, but if moved to the muddy soil of Skåne it may peek out ready to see the light for the first time. I love Saga for saying things I would never have thought about but that become obvious to me once she says them.

"Apply for your course. If you get an offer, you have the summer to book and prep for the test. You will have received your formal diagnosis by then, meaning extra help. You may make it this time, K. In fact, I *know* you will," Saga says.

That evening I fill out my application. It was four years since I last did it. When I'm finished on the UCAS website, I book

an IELTS test. I'm not going to wait until the summer. I hesitate at the disability box, then tick it and write *Autism* next to
it, feeling a strange and unexpected sense of *belonging* as I do.
I enter it in my calendar and on a whim decide to share it. I
want him to know that I'm trying, that *I've* made the decision
to still try. That I won't just give up.

Shared Calendar ▾

○ **NEW EVENT:** IELTS test

The day after I land, I will know if I can do this or not.

ALEX

Personal Calendar ▾

○ **NEW TASK:** Apologize to Peter for quitting on him

○ **NEW TASK:** Ditto Gunnar

○ **NEW TASK:** Ditto Hanna

Paul: You all right, man? I heard the good news. And the bad news. Want to talk about it? I'll do my best to be emotionally available and a good friend.

Dan: Alex, you know I never blamed you. Neither did your parents. Hope the sentence means you can stop blaming yourself once and for all. See you tonight for one last beer in the apartment?

Hanna: Alex, Klara is a wreck. You've ruined her. Hardly turns up for work. She only eats protein bars and doesn't wear earrings, nothing dangles on her face. Because she's not smiling. I get that you left, hurting and all. I don't care about you walking out on the company for no valid reason, but this is not how things end for you guys. I won't accept it. Mope around, do your depressed-guy thing, then pull yourself together and make things right. Have you forgotten that she's leaving today?

This image of Klara kills me. *No valid reason.* Klara didn't kill my brother. Asked her if she knew but didn't wait for an answer, didn't even give her a chance to respond. I blacked out. I wasn't myself. *And then I quit.* Am not a guy who quits on people. Who walks out on his team, his friends. Not really. That job saved me, *she* saved me, and I need it back. But first I need her. Would she still be at her dad's house getting ready to leave? Not sure. What would I even say if I call? Get a sudden sense of urgency, aware that I've wasted time. Enough of that. Dr. Hadid tells me I can stop creating tasks, but I reckon I need this last one.

○ **NEW TASK:** Go to airport

○ **NEW TASK:** Find Klara

○ **NEW TASK:** Tell her what I've learned

Shave, dress and put the aftershave on that she told me I could never change. Delayed by Mamma calling to tell me that Dan has given them a large chunk of the damages awarded. There will be a unicorn statue in Calle's name (thank fuck and Jesus Christ he will never know) and a donation to a charity promoting road safety and providing free bicycle helmets to kids. I hear Mamma's joy and feel peace I haven't felt in a long time. Tell her I love her.

Through the train window I can see Malmö becoming smaller as we ride above the sea toward the Danish coast. Turning Torso is the last visible landmark before the fog blurs the city. Inside it, the work will have started to make a space for someone else.

I find a seat, and then I go find my brother.

Saved to Drafts

Calle,

Man, I haven't written to you for four days now. The first day without an email came and went, and I didn't even notice it. There is a life for me without you. I didn't think it was possible, but your void doesn't have to be filled with anxiety: it can just be empty. I don't need to fill it. I thought I did and worried because I knew it was impossible. No one can take your place, but now I know they don't need to. There is endless space inside me.

I got the justice I needed. I saw the face. Actually, I punched the face. Totally worth the 2500-kronor fine for unruly behavior in a courtroom.

I know there is another void, besides yours, that I can fill, though, and I'm planning to make it right. Mistakes happen, and I can't let one small mistake push me back to where I was. Who I was before her. She is my before-and-after; you are what I will always carry with me, forever healing, but she is what makes me alive.

Guess that means this is goodbye or something. I'm not sure what to do with all these emails. They will stay in my Drafts folder, and let's just hope I don't ever accidentally send them to my lawyer, gym manager or a random person.

Some people wear rings, some hold on to empty apartments, some bake and some fill a garage with random shit they built. But we're okay. We can all stop now.

Love you, my brother. Always.

    As I'm getting off the train at the airport along with a whole carriage full of holidaymakers, it dawns on me that I don't know where Klara is and that finding her here won't be easy. Kastrup is a big airport. As in LEGO-flagship-store big. Then it hits me what I need to do.

She seems to prefer that way of communication anyway, be more at ease and able to absorb the words.

Our calendar.

KLARA

The airport bustle either pulls you in and sweeps you off your feet, embracing you with its excitement and childlike adventurous spirit, or it suffocates you, reminding you that you have lost your direction within a sea of moving people.

I've passed security, producing my Swedish passport. It has to be British for the British and Swedish for the Swedish. I like that I get both a *Have a nice holiday, miss* and a *Welcome home* and can confirm my belonging to both countries.

I have just finished a Danish, vanilla-cream middle, which serves as both my lunch and dinner today, sitting on a bench outside the lounge to which I don't have access. I watch suit-clad men and middle-aged couples flit in and out with their golden tickets to a cold buffet and free beer. My thoughts are mostly on the IELTS test. I had an urgency to get it done and booked the first available slot. I have to travel to Liverpool Street to sit it, but it's worth it. Or it may be. *Please let me pass this time.*

But some of my thoughts are on Alex.

A reminder pops up on my screen.

Reminder: New Event; Location: 7-Eleven, Terminal 2

That's peculiar. I can't remember seeing this before. And who would I meet? Then, I think. There is only one person I share a calendar with—Alex. *Alex says I need to be at 7-Eleven. Now.* I almost run back to the corner where I walked past the shop just half an hour earlier. Oh, for fuck's sake, Alex, couldn't you pick a closer location? I'm not a runner and even less so when I'm dragging my luggage with me.

When I get there, I look around frantically, at backs and unknown faces and shelves full of belly-filling food. No Alex. I fix my hair, sleeking the sides out, and stand up tall. Still no Alex. Seriously? I give it five more minutes, each one longer than the previous one.

I still don't see an Alex-shape form, and my hopes dwindle. He isn't there. Nothing. It must have been a mistake. Why did I get my hopes up? *It's over.* I feel so stupid. I've watched too many rom-coms.

Just as I start to walk back toward the gate, *it's there.*

○ **EDITED EVENT:** 7-Eleven; Location: Departure lounge, before security

What is this game? I don't know what to do. I've already gone through security, if I go back now I may miss my flight. There are too many people, they're too close to me, and I'm starting to get overwhelmed. If I miss this flight there may not be another, and I must be back in London by tomorrow. I know Google would tell me not to change my life plans because of a man. Part of me wants to yell at Google. *You don't know this man! You've never met Alex, Google! He's not even on Google! If he were, you'd understand.* I want to turn around more than anything, to run through the crowds and believe that it's really him. But it's a firm *no* from Google. If I spend more time following the entries, I will miss my flight, and I can't do that.

Because I need to sit the IELTS language test for the thirty-second time.

ALEX

Shared Calendar ▾

New Note (Klara): You think you can just edit my life?

Reply (Alex): So much I want to edit, to delete

Reply (Klara): This event has passed

Reply (Klara): You can't change it now

Reply (Alex): Try to stop me. I'll add as many new entries as it takes, until you believe me. Check back here tonight

Reply (Klara): It's just calendar entries, not an actual relationship. This doesn't mean anything

Romance is dead. At least if you ask the security guard at point 17, Terminal 2, Kastrup Airport.

"Please, man, I just need to get in for half an hour. Here's my passport, my car keys and my credit card. You basically have my life, and I have to come back for it."

"Sir, there is no entry without a boarding pass."

"She's the love of my life."

"I'm thrilled to hear that, but there is no boarding pass exemption for people in love." Told you, romance is dead. "You better make your way back to the ticket desk and buy one. Seeing she is the love of your life." He winks at me as if he had said something funny. It's encouragement enough, and I rush to where his hand had pointed at.

The girl looks up from her computer where she had been busy organizing itineraries. Or checking Twitter. Who knows? I look at her name tag.

"Hello, Tina. I was hoping you could help me with something. I need your cheapest ticket to get into Terminal 2."

"Did you forget something? It will be brought out to Lost Luggage by the end of the day." I sense whatever is on her screen is more important than my person.

"I kind of lost something, but it's a person. A girl." Tina looks at me now, assessing me for murderer potential, deciding whether to call the police, but she seems to give up suspicions of the lost person being a body inside a suitcase.

"If a child is missing, we need to make an announcement on the speakers." The thought of Klara's name being called out plays on my mind for a second. But that would be the lazy way out, letting someone else call for her. This was my task—*my* to-do. My final one. A public-address announcement may also send Klara into a rap-requiring meltdown.

"Please, just get me into Terminal 2. I love this girl. And she's about to board a flight to Gatwick."

"Oh. Cool. It's like Hugh Grant in that movie." I finally have her attention: it turns out Tina at the ticket desk is a hopeless romantic.

"We have a seat to Reykjavik for 2600 kronor, leaving in two hours. In case you don't get the girl and fancy going, it's a lovely place. You only have twenty minutes until your friend's flight closes," she announces, at which point I shove my credit card at her along with a thank-you and get ready to sprint.

I run toward gate 22, my pocket contents banging against my thighs and heat starting to creep up on my face. This was not how I would have imagined myself turning up to ask for Klara's affection. Like a schoolboy running for the bus. Also realize I should not come empty-handed—flowers, chocolates, anything.

It turns out I don't have to worry about that.

"Final boarding call for flight 342 to London Gatwick," a voice crushingly announces. If I were someone else, say Usain Bolt or a politician running away from responsibilities, I would have given it my all, spurted ahead and made it with a second to spare. But I have to admit my limitations. I'm Alex, and on the best of days I couldn't run a half mile in about two seconds. I stop and catch my breath.

I'm not winning Klara back today.

Give Dan a hug when I get there. Had told him I might not make it, but turns out I did.

"All good?" he asks me and hands me the obligatory beer.

"All good," I echo.

We look out over the wild sea. There's nowhere to sit. There's a ladder and some other equipment by the door and the lights in the ceiling flicker as if they know their days are numbered. My legs ache from being on my feet all day.

"The wine bar didn't look too busy when I passed it on my way here," I say.

"I wouldn't mind a sharing platter," Dan says.

"Shall we have the next one there, then?"

"Let's."

It doesn't feel sad when we leave, or not as much as I expected it to. Because I still have Dan, and that's something. I turn off the lights, and Dan locks up behind us. We bring the beer bottles with us and throw them in the recycling bin in the lobby.

★ ★ ★

That evening when I get home, I scroll back over the weeks, looking at each day to see where it—where *I*—went wrong. Realize, strangely, I wouldn't change the past, even if I could edit it like a calendar entry. Because I need to be right where I am now. So does Klara. Know she said it's not real and that I can't edit life, but the future is still open. I can create a digital future, show her what Klara and Alex's story could be like. I start to add entries.

Shared Calendar ▾

O **NEW TASK:** Apologize to Klara. Never should have lashed out at her when nothing was her fault

O **NEW TASK:** Tell Klara about the first day we met. How she blew me away

O **NEW TASK:** Tell Klara I've grown more and more crazy about her with each day

O **NEW TASK:** Figure the future out together (long-distance relationship?)

She may never read them, but at least it exists now—the future I'd like.

KLARA

Where would I be without you?

Google Search   I'm Feeling Lucky

The room is large and airy. The test invigilator has striped yellow socks that remind me of a bee. There are a lot of boxes on the paper in front of me, and I don't mind them: I like when they are ticked, and I try to make my ticks symmetrical. The spaces for writing, on the other hand, bother me: they are large and empty and very white, and I am supposed to fill them. So far, I have written two sentences. Everyone else in the room seems very busy. I don't understand how they cannot hear the buzzing of the bee socks that is so obvious to me.

The forty-five minutes are coming to an end, and more and more people get up and leave. I have to resist the urge to get up and push the chairs in after them. I feel sorry for them—the people, not the chairs—as I can't imagine someone who fails to leave the desk and chair neat would have nailed the test.

The question stares at me. *Many people think technological de-*

vices such as smartphones, tablets and mobile phones bring more disadvantages than advantages. To what extent do you agree or disagree?

My extra time has started, and something strange happens. The box-shaped space with its lines for writing transforms itself into a speech bubble and words start to form inside me. I write. In fact, I write so much that I have to add a line outside of the box to fit my last sentence in. I discuss how I might have died without diabetes technology, and how social media can give opportunities to people who desperately need them, say, young girls with Down syndrome or another young woman trying to run a business. Google can find schnauzer owners, and it can hold a whole family in one little square app. Then I argue how technology can aid mental health, say, by helping a young man beat depression by enabling him to keep track of small, but measurable, achievements. And how it may know that two particular people belong together and should sync their lives before they even know it themselves.

When I put the pen down the swarm of moths in my stomach have gone to sleep, or died perhaps—a moth's life span *is* very short—and I smile at the bee-sock man as I hand him my papers. I tell him, "Thank you. Have a nice afternoon. I'll just buzz off now."

ALEX

Shared Calendar ▾

O **NEW TASK:** Fly to London

O **NEW TASK:** Go to Klara's house

New Note: (Putting this all here in case you see it, Klara, and don't want the surprise. Hope you do. Think you do. But just in case)

I have arrived in London. Saga provided me with the details I needed to plan a smooth trip to Klara's home: address, Tube line and a telling-off. "It's about time, Alex. I hope it's not too bloody late, you moron." I deserved it so thanked her for the good-luck wishes.

Klara lives in a narrow, whitewashed house wedged in a row of almost identical houses on a quiet street. I walk up the small front garden to the door and can see someone peering out of a curtain on the second floor, like a nosy neighbor. I can't make out whether it's Klara or not; all I see are eyes gleaming against the dark like a cat's. I hope this someone will open the door for me.

She does.

"*Hola.*" She has pale freckles and a smile that seems permanent. I notice her well-manicured nails because they are profoundly different to Klara's bitten-down ones. I shift uncomfortably, even though I'm prepared.

"*Jo napot.*" She looks at me like one big question mark, her head even tilted sideways, just the dot on the bottom missing.

"Random *Hello* in Hungarian," I explain, and she laughs, then stops as if she remembers herself and clenches her mouth shut.

"You're the guy who messed things up with my roommate."

"I prefer the guy who fell in love with her, *then* messed it up," I say.

"Don't you get it? You don't mess it up with Klara. She may seem rock-solid, but she's fragile."

"Can I come in?"

"Did you come to apologize?" she asks.

There is no point in not being transparent.

"I did."

"Well, since you have pure intentions, come in."

I follow her inside a narrow hallway into an open kitchen and living room. Their house is full of stuff, colorful and warm. It's a bit like two grannies who can't bring themselves to throw anything away, love of knits and flower details strong, but who equally enjoy contemporary interior design.

"Here." Alice puts a plate of cinnamon rolls on the kitchen counter, which I've chosen as my spot to stand and wait.

"So she's baking again?" I say, remembering the national-identity crisis that inspired the hot cross buns last month. She has that in common with Mamma.

"Yep. Had only just arrived when she dug out the ingredients. All Swedish stuff."

I'm definitely not in the mood for something sweet, but it's Klara who made them, and it's like I have her next to me insisting, and I don't want to be rude. I'm eating the bun when the front door makes itself known through a loud keyhole clink. Alice disappears, and Klara is in front of me. *Finally.*

"Alex," she says, and I breathe deep as something inside me relaxes at the mere sight of her.

KLARA

Should you forgive the person who loves you the most?

Google Search   I'm Feeling Lucky

Alex. In my flat. In London. It doesn't make sense; it feels like he belongs to a different world. I would be lying if I said I hadn't hoped and wished for this moment, that he would come after me. As improbable as I thought it was—no one chases after Klara Nilsson of 243A Munster Road. She is someone you stumble into, at best. Keep for convenience rather than desire.

"I've missed you," he says.

"You missed my calls, as well."

"I needed space. When I got my act together, you were already about to leave. I'm sorry I wasn't ready earlier."

"You could have just called."

"You hate phone calls."

"Phone calls are acceptable in an emergency. This *was* an emergency, Alex." He smiles at me and reaches out a hand to touch my face. I don't stop him.

"You did nothing wrong, Klara. I said some things I should never have said to you. You saw me at my lowest point, my worst. I'm asking if you can give me a chance, having seen the worst I can be?"

The Klara I was months ago would have forgiven any man for anything, just for the promise that he wanted me for another week. That's not why I feel myself soften and decide to forgive Alex. It's because he is *good*, and even at his worst I know I won't doubt that.

"Why did you have me running all over terminals like a fricking plane spotter for nothing? Why weren't you where you said you'd be?" I'm still not satisfied with his explanation. But the entries I found this morning softened me. I like the events that he's mapped out so far.

"Sorry. I had every intention of making it to the gate, but it turned out the only ticket I could get was to Iceland and—"

"Iceland?"

"I wasn't allowed in without a flight."

"Well, duh."

"I was so close to making it. But I'm here now. I came. I want to tell you that I've been a douche. A real one. It was my emotions talking, and I had no right to act the way I did."

I have this vague idea that I should be upset despite the apology, out of principle. But somehow I'm not, somehow these small words have punched a hole in my anger and replaced it with happier feelings—much happier feelings.

"You were hurt. I get it. Listen, if I could take it back. All of it. That sleazy moron—"

"The murderer, you mean."

"Hanna told me. I'm glad he was caught. I'm guessing someone brought you up to speed on why he was fired—why *I fired him?*"

"Yes, I know all about him now. Which only sweetens the fact that we won—he's an asshole, a selfish prick. His alcohol level was through the roof, and the fact he fled the scene after made it an easy day for our team. His defense that he didn't see what happened was torn up when the witness was brought in and recalled how he shouted at the victim on the ground. Mamma can buy the whole fricking Pride unicorn if she wants to. Which is obviously exactly what she is trying to do." He laughs.

I stop for a moment and wonder how many sexist jokes Mateusz can get away with in prison. I decide that this is the last thought I will spend on him. Ever.

"It's okay. It's over."

"So, what now?"

"I've come to say that I'm the most stupid man in the world, and would you please forgive me? I'm happy to wait while you ask Google for advice. In fact, let's do it together—" He pulls up Google and types in *Should you forgive the person who loves you the most?* Warm feelings flood me, and I would like nothing more than to take a screenshot of his words. *Love* in writing.

"I thought you hated me," I say as we both read off the screen, and I draw a big sigh of relief that the search engine is on my side.

"Hated you? Klara, even when I was so angry I couldn't bring myself to see you or hear you out, I never hated you. I love you, and I want to do it all, to do life *with* you. The house, the morning coffee, the shared duvet, the hypo snack-stocking. I want to see what you look like at forty. And at eighty. If you think you can forgive me, that is."

"Alex, I've already forgiven you." I'm amazed at the ease with which it comes out.

We kiss like there is a film crew present, like our only instruction is to complete a scene titled The Love Kiss. It's glorious. And brief. Phones buzz with a *low soon* alert, mine and his.

"*Scheibe*," I say.

"Shit kebab."

"Talk about ruining the moment."

He digs in his jeans pockets, the ones that for months now have held sugary snacks just in case, and hands me a Kit Kat.

"We still have some things to talk about. I don't know where home is anymore—London or Sweden. Lately it feels like all roads lead to Skåne, but I want to stay in London. I did my IELTS today, and I'm sure I passed it. I had extra time and got to wear noise-reducing earplugs. I'm not stupid after all, Alex."

"Stupid?" He grabs me now, as if wanting to shake sense into me. "You are an incredible woman, Klara Nilsson. You could never be stupid. Your logic makes more sense to me than anything I've ever been told, and you notice things no one else does. And I'm going to make it my job to get you to see what I see. Every single day. In London—if that's where you'll be."

"Seriously? You would move here for me?" My face is dead straight.

"Seriously. I was planning to beg your dad for my old job back, but I think I could do with a fresh start. All you have to do is ask. You know I can never refuse your *please*."

"Then, *please*, please move to London with me."

"Consider the task added. The country doesn't matter to me. For me, all roads lead to Klara."

"My Viking font," I say.

"Klara Nilsson, I love you."

ALEX

Personal Calendar ▾

O **NEW TASK:** Cancel apartment lease

O **NEW TASK:** Arrange for the car to be delivered to new owner

O **NEW TASK:** Cancel all upcoming appointments with Dr. Hadid

Hanna couldn't be happier when I called to ask her to step up and take over my workload. I discussed it with Klara and then Peter, and we all agreed she was ready to do so permanently as well.

"Anything, as long as you guys are happy."

"Thanks, Hanna. I'm going to miss you," I say, not reflecting on the sentiment until later, and I realize I haven't just got Klara now, I've got this huge work family that I didn't have three months ago, and I know we will stay close no matter where I live.

Alice is already at a table in the far corner of La Bottega by the time we get there, and I push my way through the clusters of wooden tables and matching chairs, Klara following after.

"Sorry, I'm borderline late," Klara announces and plonks her backpack rather than herself onto the chair, taking her jacket off and fishing out her tech from the small side pocket.

"I ordered you a latte," Alice says, pushing a cup toward Klara. "Not sure yet what you drink, Alex, but I'm guessing I'll find out soon."

"No problem. I'll grab something myself."

After knowing me for four days, she's not fully won over yet. I get up and walk over to the counter. La Bottega is a swanky deli slash coffee shop with an equal focus on Italian pesticide-free wine and vegan cake, where a small cappuccino sets you back £4.80. You'd think with those prices, a hedge-fund manager runs it, but it's a bearded Essex boy named Steve.

"Black coffee," Alice remarks when I return. "Traditional, efficient and to the point."

"Pretty accurate."

"Black-coffee drinkers are also more likely to be psychopaths."

Klara shoots her a look and gets one in return.

"Alice, about the room," Klara starts, shifting forward on the chair. "I know the lease states single occupancy, but as of last week I am no longer single. I'd very much like to still occupy it. I'm not going to tell you that he won't take up much space since we both know how tall he is, but he has very few annoying habits and tends to bring home croissants regularly."

"Oh my gosh. I thought you were going to tell me you were moving out! I thought I'd have to start looking for a new roommate and only see you fortnightly for brunch."

"Not if you'll have us," Klara says.

"Thank you," I add, and Alice smiles back at me. Since I won't be stealing Klara from her presently, I'm that much closer to winning her over already.

Klara suddenly sits very quietly.

"Alex, I've just forwarded you an email," she says. "Just look at it. Follow the link because I can't."

Pull up my inbox and wait for it to load. She jiggles her leg next to me, and Alice leans over my shoulder to read.

I feel a huge fucking smile appear on my face.

"Guess what I'm doing this week?"

"What, Alex?"

"Getting some birch wood and tools and building you a new desk."

"A desk is where you sit and work."

"Exactly. You'll be working this September—studying, in fact. You passed!" Turn the phone around so she can read the email for herself. "And 8.1 is an awesome score."

Tears roll down her face and she lets them, declining the tissue Alice hands her.

"These are happy tears," she clarifies. "Have you seen the state of the world? You'd be crazy to wipe out anything happy."

ONE YEAR LATER

KLARA

Q Is it possible to be too happy?

Google Search　　　**I'm Feeling Lucky**

Love is, Google tells me, an intense, deep affection for another person. Love is a lot like muscle ache: it doesn't show up on X-rays, but we know it's there. I am happy to say I, Klara Nilsson, am in love.

There's a cup of coffee next to my—*our*—bed, and I can see that someone has plugged in my phone to charge. I know he checks my battery before he falls asleep, always on edge for another data failure and bad hypo like the one in Sweden.

"Morning." I turn my head in the direction of the greeting.

He's just stepped out of the shower but hasn't dried his hair properly, drops of water falling off his head and landing on his shoulders, arms, chest. Trickling all the way down to where a towel sits. I try to think about when I love Alex the most. Fresh from the shower is right up there. But then anytime Alex looks at me like this would be my favorite, when I can tell how happy he is to see me—*I make him happy.*

I reach for the coffee—the next best part of my morning routine.

"Your dad called," Alex tells me as he pulls a white T-shirt over his head. "Apparently another newspaper wants to profile the company. *Small, predominantly woman-led company rivaling big-city firms in Stockholm.* He's asking if you can join the call via Zoom with him and Hanna."

"He called already? Remind me what time it is, again?"

"To be fair, Sweden is an hour ahead. His 8:00 a.m. is a totally acceptable time to call."

"I'll call him back later." I've quite enjoyed the media appearances that have continued to roll in since last year. I don't mind talking about something I'm passionate about, and believe it or not, I *am* passionate about bathrooms, tiles and joints.

"I'm off to work, then. See you later tonight, Klara." Alex doesn't call me *baby* or *sweetheart* or, worse, *honeypot* (which I overheard on the Tube the other day and resulted in me spending a good fifteen minutes trying to peek into the young lady's large purse to look for said pot before I realized it was her, *she* was the pot of honey).

His finger strokes the inside of my wrist as he sits next to me on the bed for a minute and kisses me. He tastes like minty toothpaste, then leaves for work.

I don't have classes today, Monday. This typically means that I will meet up with Alex for lunch while he's on break. Sometimes I miss our lunches in the van, but he is keen on what goes under the vague term of *atmosphere.* Previously this entailed loud noise, overwhelming smells and the clink of glasses being put down too violently, but since Alex has entered my life, I can see the beauty. It's not about what goes on around you, it's about the small bubble that you create with the people you are with. I am not meant to focus on the group of guys grunting and discussing soccer at the table next to me, or the fact that the lady across the room sits in silence while her husband looks at his phone more than at her. This is just the backdrop that exists to strengthen the bubble I'm in. To surround me and Alex and make us connected. In the noise, we find each other.

I collect my study materials into a neat pile. There is more math than I would have wished for, and I am the second-oldest student in the architecture course, but *oh, it is exciting*. I send a snapshot of the start of my current project to Nonstop Notifications, and within seconds I have all sorts of encouragements. It turns out my family can be incredibly supportive, that it wasn't limited to my time at Dad's. I have been trying hard to make sure they feel supported by me too, Saga in particular—even when it looks like she has it all together, I know she still needs me. She's working from home two days a week. Fueled with energy and Scandinavian air in her lungs, she made her case to the board and managed to convince them that it was a hybrid work schedule or nothing, that they may risk losing a highly favored professor if they didn't agree.

I've become better at putting my energy where it's deserved: when meeting a stranger, I don't feel like I *have* to smile because, as Alice put it, I have no obligation to smile for anyone but myself. Being officially Autistic helps me with these little things. I'm allowed to have quirks that others don't, say, the need to walk around the room to score an odd number on my step counter or not smile at people who haven't earned it. Instead I now think about the people I love when my earrings brush against my cheeks, and *that* makes me smile. The ones who *do* deserve me. Remembering to send them a message. Or adding a calendar reminder to do it.

I browse our shared calendar as it pings with a reminder. Alex and I still use it to communicate.

○ **NEW EVENT:** Can't make lunch but meet you for *dinner at The Oak.*

I have to think about this: we don't eat out on Mondays. Then I frown and do a double take at the note that's been added. *We may need to celebrate.* Confused, I look for more and find something that strikes me as odd.

Reply: Once wished I could edit the past. Now I want to schedule the future.

Alice is there when I get in, casually holding out a shiny black dress for me.

"I know black means business, and today you may well seal the deal."

I think I must have missed something. Perhaps there is a Bygg-Nilsson Zoom before dinner later?

"Thanks. You're the *best*—no pro*test.*"

I try the dress on, and of course it's perfect, although I decide a scarf may be needed over my cleavage for the work-meeting part. My hair is loose and wavy and my ears bare.

Just as I finish the walk from the Tube and arrive at the restaurant, my phone pings, and another notification pops up. In fact, tens of them appear. I open up our shared calendar and freeze, not able to take another step.

○ **NEW EVENT:** Engagement-ring shopping; Location: London Wedding Ring Company

Oh.

As if the entries are time-limited and about to expire on me, I rush to scroll forward, they reach all the way until next year.

○ **NEW EVENT:** Engagement party; Location: A surprise (the good kind, don't worry)

○ **NEW TASK:** Try on wedding dress

○ **NEW EVENT:** Spa day with Saga and Alice; Location: To be determined

○ **NEW TASK:** Cake-tasting

Then I *feel* him. I tear myself away from the screen for a moment, and there he is, on the opposite side of the road, next to a bus stop. He's been there, waiting for me, the whole time.

Oh, Alex. I stare straight at him, and I swear I can feel from across the street how his heart is beating, as I pull up the last and final scheduled event, in February next year.

○ **NEW EVENT:** Klara and Alex's wedding; Location: Sweden

Who gets married in February? *Alex and Klara* is the answer. The month we met, dreary and muddy, an unusual date for an unusually perfect couple. I RSVP *yes, yes, yes* and watch Alex's smile break, his shoulders relaxing, his perfect person taking a sigh of relief. There is nothing to edit and nothing to delete, because he's mapped out a future the same way I would have. I run toward him, out of breath with my bum bag slapping against my hip. Then I'm next to him, in a large embrace, and the world order is restored. Background noise gone. Just like that.

And I think, couples are a bit like shoes in the lost and found. There is no point rummaging and looking, wasting time trying them all on and ending up with blisters. You have to wait until your match turns up, and you will know it when it does, then you brush the dust off and walk off into the sunset.

ALEX

Personal Calendar ▾

○ **NEW TASK:** No new task

○ **NEW TASK:** No new task

○ **NEW TASK:** No new task

Floating on a fucking cloud. Brain busy with love and Klara, the stuff of dreams. Nothing more to add here. Over and out.

★ ★ ★ ★ ★

ACKNOWLEDGMENTS

My writing journey started fairly recently, back in 2021. Or rather, it continued after having been dormant since my teenage years. Despite this whirlwind from first draft to publication, I have collected a lot of people to thank along the way.

Firstly, thank you to my brilliant editor, Meredith Clark, whose enthusiasm for this story was felt from our very first phone call and which hasn't wavered since. To the whole team at MIRA—thank you for giving this Sweden-set little novel its US break.

To my clever agent, Tanera Simons. You believed so wholeheartedly in this book and worked to convince others of its brilliance without pause. So far you have convinced a *lot* of people. Also thank you to Laura Heathfield, who has read every draft since my first submission and has been a part of this novel's journey from the very onset. To the rights team at Darley Anderson Literary, TV and Film Agency—Mary Darby, Georgia Fuller, Salma Zarugh and Francesca Edwards—getting your emails (the new deal ones, not the tax form ones) are my favorite part of the week, whatever the week has entailed. Thank you for your continuous efforts in bringing *The Happiness Blueprint* to readers all over the world.

A huge thank you to Curtis Brown Creative—Charlotte

Mendelson and everyone else involved in these life-changing courses. I've been met with nothing but support and it all started with you.

Thanks to my writer friends. This novel wouldn't be what it is without you, and this writer wouldn't be who she is without you. Emily Howes—sharp, funny, talented author who has been there from the very beginning. I'd be lost without our daily chats. Becky Alexander—wise, supportive and a tremendous writer. Thank you for the time you give to my novels and for your friendship. To Roisin O'Donnell, Fabian Foley, Abi Graham, Jenni Lieberman, Natasha Dandavati and the rest of my CBC-friends—thank you. Your advice and reading of my early drafts made this book better. I am lucky to have you. A thank you also to all the authors who have supported me over the past year, from my agency and beyond. Because of you all, I've never questioned my place in this industry.

To my brother and nonwriter friends who I've often neglected while working on a first draft—I'm sorry I haven't called you enough. Thank you for sticking with me and for being proud of me. Also a thank-you to Ragnar Von Beetzen for answering my legal queries.

To my parents, thank you for never pushing me in any direction but also for never being surprised at my life's achievements, but rather acting as if you'd expected nothing less of me. Dad—thank you for the fact-checking. *The Happiness Blueprint* just wouldn't be the same without the accurate drying time for tiling joints.

To my children, Alfred, Olivia and Ivy, who despite their initial disappointment over me not writing children's books, and even with their horror upon learning that the book contains *actual swear words—bad ones!*—still support me in their own ways. Hearing you say that Mummy is an author brings me such joy.

The biggest, most obvious thank-you to Alon for giving

me love, support and the space I need to write. Thank you for, well, *everything*.

Lastly, my heartfelt thanks to Google for answering all my questions on how to write a novel.